CW01629653

A N

COURAGE, CONFLICT, AND THE HIGH PRICE OF WAR

A WWII HISTORICAL NOVEL

EK-2 PUBLISHING

Your Satisfaction Is Our Goal!

Dear Readers,

First, we would like to thank you for purchasing this book. Our goal is to inspire readers from all over the world with our historical and military novels and biographies.

We are a family business, and our team thrives to offer you a unique reading experience and of course, we want to increase our quality with each book published.

We are grateful for your feedback as well as ideas about books you may want to read in the future. Your opinion matters to us. Do you have any comments or criticism? Please let us know. Your feedback is of great value to us and of course to our authors as well. Be part of our publishing journey and our EK-2 publishing family. Write to us at:

info@ek2-publishing.com

And now we wish you an entertaining reading experience with this book.

Your EK-2 Publishing Team
The publisher close to its readers

Sometimes all you have left is the future

Chapter one

Gestapo Offices – Cahagnes – Normandy – July 1944

With the pair of pliers gripped in his right hand the Gestapo officer approached the man seated in the chair strategically placed in the centre of the room. As he drew nearer a smile tugged at the corner of his thin mouth. It seemed he might not need the pliers after all, as judging by the dark stain between the man´s legs it seemed the wretched fellow had already lost control of his bladder.

Positioning himself in front of the chair the officer stared down at the face of his prisoner. His pale blue eyes fixed on the man´s pupils. Even though the room was quite chilly, droplets of perspiration had formed on the man´s forehead. Another indication of the feeling of terror the man was experiencing.

Placing his index finger under his chin the Gestapo officer tilted back the man´s head, bending forward as he did so until their faces were just inches apart.

"So, let us make things easy for each other, shall we?" Although infected by a slight Germanic accent Otto Brohl´s French was flawless.

Instinctively, the man´s head jerked up and down rapidly, his teeth clamped shut to stop them from chattering.

"Excellent!" said Brohl, pulling himself upright. "I congratulate you on the wisdom of your decision. Now, my colleague Herr Fengler," glancing towards the tall, stockily-built man standing beside the door, a black fedora perched on his bulbous head "will provide you with a pad and pencil and all you have to do is write down everything we need to know. Do you understand?"

"And then... and then you will let me go?" the man stammered.

"Of course, I am a man of my word. Isn´t that true Fengler?"

Fengler gave a sort of grunt. His thuggish features failing to disguise his disappointment at the prisoner´s speedy capitulation. He always enjoyed watching his superior at work. More used to inflicting pain with his huge fists himself, he was fascinated by the surgical precision with which he used simple everyday tools to loosen the most reluctant tongue.

Robbed of his moment of pleasure, Fengler walked across to the chair, and with his nicotine-stained fingers, he unbuckled the straps securing the man´s arms. Removing a small notebook and pencil from his jacket pocket, he pushed them into the man´s trembling hand. Watching disinterestedly as the Frenchman began writing down the first of the names.

With the act of betrayal completed the prisoner handed the pad back to Fengler, watching nervously as he in turn deposited the notepad into the outstretched hand of Otto Brohl.

"Just these five?" Brohl asked, scanning the page, a hint of disappointment in his voice.

"There were others, Monsieur but I was never told their names."

"I see. You´re quite sure now only I would hate to think that you were not keeping your side of the bargain."

"Quite sure Monsieur." His gaze instinctively drawn towards the pliers gripped in Brohl´s hand.

"You, you have my word."

Brohl didn´t answer right away. Silence was another tool in his armoury. Applied at the right time, he found it had much the same effect as pointing a loaded pistol at a person´s head.

"Very well, we will save them for another time. For now, we will deal with the ones we have."

Turning his back on the prisoner, Brohl slowly walked across to where a table had been pushed up against the end wall. Running his eyes over the array of implements, he returned the pliers to their allotted place amongst what he liked to call the tools of his trade. If you put things back where you found them, you will always know where they are when you need them again was one of his late father´s aphorisms. Sadly, in Brohl´s line of work, this wasn´t always possible, certainly not where the fingernails and amputated fingers of the people he interrogated were concerned. But then these were things his father probably wasn´t referring to anyway.

"On your feet!" ordered Fengler, his voice as menacing as his appearance.

Having replaced the pliers where he had found them alongside the secateurs, and perfectly in line with the claw-hammer and the dozen-or-so six-inch-nails, Otto Brohl turned his attention to the poor wretch who an hour earlier had entered the room filled with such youthful bravado. What was he, Sixteen? Seventeen? It seemed that the Maquis were having to scrape the barrel for their members these days.

Casting an eye over the list of names, the smile returned to Brohl´s pallid face. When these five had been rounded up, it seemed they were going to have to scrape a little harder.

"Take him out through the rear entrance," Brohl snapped, eager to get this judas out of his sight.

"But what if I am seen? What if someone recognises me?"

"Don't worry I have a scapegoat in mind," Brohl replied, staring into the teenager's face, "after all I wouldn't want you coming to any harm."

If the young man was reassured by what the man had said, it didn't show on his face. The fear was still there, evident in his eyes, and the involuntary trembling of his bottom lip.

Dismissing the grovelling creature with a movement of his head, Brohl watched as Fengler dragged the informant towards the door.

When the two men had gone, crossing to the window Brohl pulled back the heavy brocade curtains, flooding the interior with natural light. The room was not at all like those he was used to working in. They were usually more austere. Dungeon-like in many ways, with their stone floors and bare brick walls, which if they were painted at all, it was usually in a drab grey colour. Those fortunate enough to have an outside wall would sometimes have a narrow aperture set into the brickwork just below ceiling level. But in the main, most of them were windowless.

This room had previously been the kitchen. A place where the family would gather each morning to enjoy a typical breakfast of warm croissants and coffee. Surplus to requirements, Brohl had ordered three of the four chairs which had once stood around the table to be removed together with the cast iron range, and cupboards, including those fixed to the wall. The tell-tale patches left behind in the lilac paintwork revealing the room's original décor.

The sink, its glazed porcelain bowl crazed with age remained, a neatly folded towel and a block of carbolic soap placed on its well-scrubbed draining board. Attached to the cold-water tap by a wire clip was a coiled length of hosepipe, another of Herr Brohl's playthings. Hanging from the ceiling on a length of chain was a rustic light fitting in the shape of a cross. A solitary bulb covered by a faded lampshade attached to each of the four horizontal arms. Strips of patterned lino covered the tiled floor, worn away in places by the constant coming and going of people's feet.

Rescued from his reverie by Fengler's reappearance, Brohl turned his attention to the matter at hand.

"Take Metzinger with you and bring in the woman", said Brohl, handing the notebook to Fengler.

With a nod of the head, Fengler turned away.

"Keep her here overnight and then release her in the morning."

Responding with a slight shrug of his powerful shoulders, Fengler made his way towards the door. Sensing the man's disappointment, just as he was about to open it, Brohl tossed his henchman a bone.

"Perhaps before you let her go you might wish to inflict a little punishment?" His words bring a smile to Fengler´s face. Not something you see very often.

"Although don´t be too rough." said Brohl, waggling his index finger in the man´s direction. Well aware that on occasions Fengler could be a little over-enthusiastic in complying with his instructions, particularly where women were concerned.

Chapter Two

Abandoned hamlet near Bremoy – Early August

Spread out at intervals on both sides of the narrow dirt road, with their rifles at the ready Sergeant Albert Clemens and the six men of the seventh battalion of the Royal Hampshire regiment made their way towards the cluster of limestone houses. With their orange pantile roofs and shuttered windows like so many of the pretty villages they had come across, they were the very essence of pastoral tranquillity. But as they had discovered to their cost during the fighting around Cahagnes three days earlier, looks can be deceptive. So, tranquil, or not from now on they were not taking any chances.

Approaching what appeared to be the main street, no sooner had Privates Redman and McCormack rounded the corner when they were greeted by the unmistakable sound of an MG 42. Instinctively, both men took cover. Redman trying desperately to squeeze his body into a narrow doorway while on the opposite side of the road, McCormack found sanctuary behind a rectangular stone horse trough with a cast iron hand pump attached at one end The incoming rounds from the German machine gun gauging out furrows in the cobbled roadway.

"Where is he?" Sergeant Clemens yelled out, his voice cutting through the bursts of machine-gun fire.

Rolling onto his side, McCormack peered cautiously around the end of the trough his eyes scanning the buildings ahead of him for the machine gun´s position.

"Gotcha," McCormack muttered to himself, ducking back into cover.

"House at the end of the street Sarge, first-floor window on the right."

Signalling with his arm to the two soldiers on the other side of the track Sergeant Clemens gestured urgently towards the house on the corner of the main street.

With a nod of acknowledgement, accompanied by Private Yates the company Bren-gunner, Corporal Clark sprinted across to the building. Reaching their objective, with their backs pressed against the outside wall the two men inched their way towards what appeared to be a stable door. After searching in vain for a handle, with brute force the only option, slamming his shoulder against the weathered woodwork Yates forced open the door. Hampered by their backpacks, trying not to think too much about what might be waiting for them inside, the two soldiers squeezed through the narrow opening and entered the building.

Thankfully, the room they found themselves in was deserted. Relieved, the two soldiers took a minute to survey their surroundings. Like most rural properties in France, much of the ground floor was taken up by a single room. A combined kitchen and living space, each area defined by its furniture with the more comfortable chairs clustered around the open fireplace, and the remainder strategically placed around the long wooden table in the middle of the room. Judging by the remains of the half-eaten meal it was obvious that the occupants of the house had left in a hurry.

After a cursory look around the two soldiers made their way to the wooden staircase leading up to the floor above. Taking the narrow stairs two at a time they soon emerged onto a wide dog-legged landing, which judging by the single bed pushed up against the end wall, and the wardrobe tucked into the corner was being used as a bedroom. With the Bren gun resting against his hip, finger on the trigger Yates stood ready as Corporal Clark kicked open the door in front of them. Finding it unoccupied, skirting around the oversized bed the two soldiers crossed over to the picture window which overlooked the main street. A street which for Redman and McCormack had become like a shooting gallery at a fairground with them as the proverbial sitting ducks.

Drawing back a corner of the faded curtain Corporal Clark peered out at the house at the far end. Moments later, with a numbs up to Yates using the butt of his rifle, he smashed the lower pane of glass. Like a well-rehearsed double act, Private Yates dropped to his knees, and propping the Bren gun on the window ledge, he quickly lined up the sights on the German machine gun position. Satisfied, cuddling the butt of the Bren into his shoulder, he opened fire. A smile creased his unshaven face when the MG 42 instantly fell silent.

In the street below, taking advantage of the Bren´s covering fire Redman clambered to his feet, and hugging the side of the building, he scurried towards the recessed doorway of the adjoining building. He had barely covered half the distance when the MG 42 opened fire again, the 8mm rounds slamming into the limestone wall. With an anguished cry, Redman dropped to his knees, a bullet which had ricocheted off the wall buried in his chest.

Cursing aloud Yates loaded the Bren gun with a fresh magazine.

"I´ll see if I can get a better shot." said Clark, and slipping out of the bedroom, he hurried down the stairs to the room below. Spotting a door in the back wall, slinging his rifle over his shoulder, he yanked it open.

Stepping outside Clark found himself in a small, paved yard covered by a timber lean-to with a low fence separating it from the adjoining house. Scrambling over it, he made his way to the back door of the neighbouring property, and with a well-aimed kick with his hobnailed boot, he forced it open.

Once inside, except for the family´s personal effects, and their choice of furniture, he found the room was pretty much identical to the one he had just left. Even down to the remains of a half-eaten meal left on the table.

Where the layout of the two houses did differ however was on the first floor. Although they both had the same dog-legged landing this one was much narrower. The additional space having been partitioned off by a stud wall to create an additional room at the end of the building. Its construction was cleverly masked by strips of flower-patterned wallpaper.

Climbing up to the landing, spotting the partially concealed door in the false wall, hoping that the room behind it might have a window giving him a better view of the MG´s position, Corporal Clark pushed open the door.

The moment he stepped inside, Clark was greeted by an explosion of beating wings, and being a Yorkshireman, he knew immediately that he had just walked into a Pigeonnier, a pigeon loft. After allowing the twenty or so birds to settle back on their perches, indulging in a moment of nostalgia, he looked around at the dowel-fronted nesting boxes and roosting posts set at intervals along both walls. Although he wasn´t knowledgeable enough to identify the breed, Clark could see that all the birds were ringed. Sadly, though with war having put an end to racing, and food hard to come by no doubt some of the birds, especially the older ones would provide a welcome meal for the family.

His late father had kept racing pigeons, and as a boy, he would be out in the garden with him on race days waiting anxiously for them to return to their loft. Watching with excitement as his, Dad clocked them in, always hoping for a winner. Sadly, when he was laid off from the steelworks due to poor health, with less money coming in, the birds had to go. After a while, probably because she was tired of seeing the look of dejection on his face every Saturday, his mother did give in and allowed him to keep a few tumblers. They were no trouble to look after and with the chaps at the Redcar Racing club helping out by donating a few bags of corn now and then, they didn´t cost much to keep. But for all that you could tell that he still missed his beloved racers.

Returning to matter in hand, unfortunately for Corporal Clark, the window he'd hoped to find had been replaced by a trap and landing board through which the birds could fly in and out when it was opened. Setting his disappointment aside, pleased to see that whoever owned the birds had thought enough about them to leave a bowl of seed and water, something his dad would have done, making sure the door was shut, Corporal Clark made his way to the main bedroom.

Skirting around the neatly made double bed with its ornately carved headboard, he made his way across to the window. Pulling aside the half-drawn curtain his earlier disappointment was quickly forgotten. Not twenty feet away, framed in the first-floor window of the house opposite were two German soldiers manning an MG 42.

Carefully raising the lower section of the sash window about six inches or so, un-slinging the Lee Enfield, Clark gently pulled back the well-oiled bolt. Allowing the spring-loaded magazine to deposit a bullet into the breach, he eased it back into place, and resisting the urge to rest the rifle's barrel on the windowsill, nestling the butt of the rifle into his shoulder, he took aim at the unsuspecting German soldier in the house opposite. At this range, it was like shooting fish in a barrel.

The bullet from the Lee Enfield struck the soldier manning the machine gun in the neck, toppling him sideways. The second bullet was not quite so lethal, hitting the loader in the shoulder. But as far as Corporal Clark was concerned the MG 42 was no longer a problem.

Reassured by the sound of the Lee-Enfield McCormack sprinted across the street, and grabbing hold of Redman's backpack, he dragged him into the recessed doorway. Safe from incoming rounds, releasing his hold on the pack Private McCormack turned his attention to the door. Thankfully the owners of the house were trusting souls, and with a quick twist of the handle, he pushed it open.

Relieved, taking hold of Redman's arm, he dragged him into the hallway.

In the house next door, with the MG 42 silenced, Private Yates' attention was drawn to the building on the opposite side of the street. Alerted by a sudden movement in a first-floor window before he could react the pane of glass in the upper half of the window shattered, showering him in shards of broken glass. More shots followed, and as he reached out to retrieve the Bren, a bullet slammed into his left shoulder.

Unaware of events, positioned behind the wall of the house that Corporal Clark and Yates had entered Sergeant Clemens allowed himself a quick look into the deserted street. Satisfied that the German machine gun was out of action, he turned his gaze on the house halfway along on the other side of the street. Protruding from both first-floor windows were the unmistakable shapes of rifle barrels, and they certainly didn't belong to a Lee Enfield 303.

Accompanied by Privates Hopkins and Uttley, Clemens sprinted across to the building opposite. Crouching alongside the wall, he issued his orders.

"Go around the back. It looks like Jerries holed up in the end house."

Without a word, Hopkins and Uttley moved away. Disappearing around the end of the stone building, with their hearts pounding the two soldiers cautiously made their way behind the row of houses. Their eyes scanning each window in turn, their fingers resting on the triggers of their rifles.

Concerned by the absence of fire from the Bren, and not sure where Redman and McCormack had got to, keeping his back against the wall of the house Sergeant Clemens made his way towards the enemy position. The reassuring Crack! Crack! of Corporal Clark's Lee Enfield music to his ears.

Approaching the first of the ground floor windows in one unbroken movement, using the butt of his Thompson submachine gun Clemens smashed the pane of glass, the sound masked by the gunfire from the rooms above. Propping the gun up against the wall, he unclipped a Mills grenade from his belt. Holding down the safety lever with one hand, slipping the middle finger of his other hand into the ring of the firing pin, he pulled it out. Counting to three, he lobbed it in through the broken window. Quickly repeating the process with a second grenade.

Seconds later the two grenades exploded, the twin blasts, just seconds apart blowing out the doors and windows, sending clouds of dust and debris spewing out into the street. The shock waves rippling outwards and upwards in an expanding arc of destruction reducing furniture to matchwood. The low plaster ceiling blown upwards, the supporting beams snapping like twigs. In the room above floorboards were wrenched from the joists and hurled into the air like drinking straws.

Caught in the blast, two of the German soldiers died instantly. One was thrown headfirst against the stone wall, the impact snapping his neck like a wishbone. The other speared in the chest by a length of splintered floorboard, the dark stain on his jacket ebbing outwards as the coarse material soaked up his blood. A third soldier was more fortunate, the force of the explosion sending him tumbling head-over-heels down the open staircase to the room below. Uninjured, climbing unsteadily to his feet, he staggered out through the open back door. Sadly, it was then that his good fortune deserted him, for unarmed or not it didn´t stop Hopkins and Uttley from shooting him.

Back in the devastated room, slowly dragging himself to his feet, with rivulets of blood running down his face from the deep gash in his forehead, clambering over the piles of rubble the fourth German soldier staggered drunkenly towards what remained of the landing. Wiping away the blood from his eyes with the back of his hand, thankful to discover that the flight of stairs, were still intact, he began making his way down to the room below, and if he was very lucky into captivity.

He had made it halfway down the stairs when Private Hopkins burst in through the back door, and it was then that his luck ran out. Seeing the German soldier, poised on the stairs like a burglar caught in the act, without blinking an eye Hopkins raised his rifle and fired. Although barely nineteen, the apprentice tool maker from Swindon had quickly learned that in war if you don´t shoot first, you could be the one getting shot. And he most definitely didn´t want that to happen to him. No Private Pete Hopkins had other ideas, and they included a wife and kids and, a very long and happy life.

Outside, as the report from Hopkin´s rifle died away an eerie silence settled over the hamlet. Broken moments later by the sound of Sergeant Clemens´s voice.

"Report!"

Emerging from the house with the pigeon loft, Corporal Clark was the first to respond.

"We´ve got a wounded Jerry in the end house."

No sooner had he spoken when the front door of the house in question opened, and the German

soldier Clark had wounded appeared in the doorway. With one arm raised in the air as a token of surrender, the other arm hanging limply by his side, blood trickling out from his jacket sleeve, ashen faced the German soldier stumbled into the street.

"Hilf mir, bitte. Nicht schiessen."

Whether Clemens understood what the young soldier was saying or not, it didn´t make any difference because he shot him anyway. The short burst from the submachine gun hitting the soldier in the chest and knocked him backwards into the doorway. Blood seeping into the ragged holes in his uniform jacket made by the forty-five calibre bullets.

Since landing in France this wasn't the first time Corporal Clark had witnessed his fellow NCO kill an enemy soldier in cold blood and sadly, it didn't look like being the last either. What had triggered this sudden change in him, Clark had no idea. In all the years they had served together in Palestine, North Africa, and Egypt, he had never seen him act like this. It was as though he had turned the war into a personal vendetta.

Clark had first noticed a change in Albert when they both got back from the seventy-two-hour pass, they were given after being discharged from hospital. He couldn't put his finger on it but there was certainly something different about him. A kind of cold indifference, and although Clemens was never a chatty sort of bloke at the best of times, he'd found it difficult to get a word out of him. Clark had put it down to things not being too good between him and his missus and left it at that. These things sometimes happen on leave. A blazing row over something that shouldn't have been said. Simmering tensions coming to the boil due to the long periods of separation. It wasn't all hugs and kisses for soldiers coming home on leave, even Clark himself had had a few ups and downs with his wife over the years. He had thought about broaching the subject but changed his mind. Even though he had known Albert Clemens for the best part of ten years, it still wasn't something you stuck your nose into unless you were asked to, not personal stuff like that. Especially when you were crowded together on the upper deck of the good ship Waveney, a converted pleasure steamer which had spent much of its life taking holidaymakers on trips around the Isle of Wight, heading for France together with the rest of the seventh battalion.

So, with his hands gripping the ship's iron-rails as the Waveney's V-shaped bows ploughed through the choppy waters of the English Channel, its six coal-fired boilers spewing out clouds of black smoke from its twin funnels, Corporal Clark had focused his mind on other things instead. Like what was awaiting them beyond the wide, sandy beach they were about to set foot on. A beach where sixteen days earlier the men of the first battalion had scrambled ashore from their landing craft together with the other regiments of the fiftieth Northumbrian Infantry division into what must have seemed to them like the jaws of hell.

And so, unfortunately for the young German soldier, thanks to nothing more than a recurring bout of malaria, instead of being with the first battalion landing on Gold Beach on the morning of the sixth of June, Company Sergeant Clemens was waiting to greet him outside a house in a French hamlet armed with a Thompson sub-machine gun. Funny old thing fate. Well not for the young German soldier of course. I am sure if he had his way, he would have been far happier if this particular English soldier had never set foot in Egypt at all.

To give Clemens and Clark their due, their resentment at being posted to the seventh battalion was nothing personal. It was just that as regular soldiers finding yourself assigned to a battalion made up of men from the Territorial army like the seventh, was a bit of a kick in the teeth. And while it had nothing to do with bravery or a lack of it; a regular soldier or not if you were not scared by the thought of going into battle, then you had something seriously wrong with you, it was still a bit disconcerting. Fighting alongside seasoned soldiers was one thing, fighting alongside a load of bloody amateurs was another thing entirely. Especially the officers. Accountants one minute with their ledgers and booking keeping, and the next thing you know they are leading troops into battle. Total bloody madness. But it was what it was, and after coming ashore at Le Hamel on the 22nd of June they had just had to put that behind them and get on with what they were there for, killing Germans.

Held in reserve along with the 4th and 5th Dorset´s, the 7th Hampshire´s first taste of action came on the 8th of July when as part of Operation Charnwood, together with regiments of the 129th and 130th Infantry Brigade supported by the 7th and 44th Royal Tank Regiments they were tasked with capturing the strategically important village of Maltot situated on the east bank of the Odon River.

After seven days of bitter fighting, supported by the Churchill tanks of the 7th Royal Tank Regiment, the Hampshire´s eventually fought their way into the village. Sadly however, their success was short-lived, and with eighteen of their officers and two hundred and eight other ranks either killed or wounded, following a counterattack by soldiers of the SS Panzer-Division Leinstandare, and tanks of the 101st Abteilung Panzer Battalion they were forced to withdraw.

Pulled out of the line for a period of rest, and reorganisation, six days later with Maltot successfully taken the 7th Battalion was once more called into action. As part of Operation Bluecoat, along with units of the 129th Infantry Brigade, they soon found themselves locked in battle with elements of the 12th SS Hitlerjugend Division around the village of Cahagnes, twenty-two miles to the Southeast of Maltot. After several days of fierce fighting, despite suffering heavy losses themselves, eventually, the resistance of the German defenders was broken, and Cahagnes was taken.

Another village laid to waste, its homes and buildings reduced to rubble in the process of liberation.

With their strength further depleted, barely able to muster one hundred men, the four companies of the 7th Battalion Royal Hampshire pressed on southwards into the heavily wooded countryside. In a terrain dominated by high hedgerows and narrow lanes, Normandy had quickly become an infantryman's worst nightmare. Pitted against an enemy determined to push them back into the sea, fighting for every field, and every village they paid a terrible price for every yard of France soil they liberated. With casualties mounting companies which had once numbered twenty to thirty soldiers were soon reduced to a handful of men. Men like those under the command of Sergeant Albert Clemens where each day was a fight for survival.

"Redman's wounded Sarge." said McCormack, suddenly appearing in the doorway.

"Right Hopkins, come with me."

"I'll go and see what's happened to Yates," said Clark, concerned by the Scotchman's absence.

"Right-Ho," said Clemens, and with Hopkins at his heels, he made his way towards the open door. "Uttley, you go and collect Jerrie's weapons. But be careful now, okay?"

Removing Redman's helmet, brushing the crockery and uneaten food onto the tiled floor, with Clemens's help McCormack hauled the young soldier up onto the table and sitting him upright, supported by his arm, he watched anxiously as Clemens began unbuttoning Redman's uniform jacket.

With Clemens readying his patient, placing his backpack down on one of the chairs, unbuckling one of the pouches Hopkins removed the company's first aid kit. This was the third occasion when he had been called on to treat a wounded comrade. Unfortunately, the previous two attempts had not gone well, with both men dying on him. One of them had been their commanding officer Captain Joyner a well-respected officer despite being what regulars like Clemens and Clark would call an amateur. He hadn't blamed himself though, he had done the best he could, but their wounds had been too serious. It did however make him reflect on why he had been given the job in the first place. Coming to the conclusion that perhaps volunteering the information that he was a member of The Saint John Ambulance Brigade, (and more used to treating sprained ankles at local football matches than administering to bullet wounds), had not been the wisest of decisions he had ever made.

Carefully removing the wounded soldier´s bloodstained shirt Clemens looked down at Redman´s pale, hairless chest. The bullet had entered his lower abdomen just below the rib cage, away from vital organs. Thankfully, the bleeding had virtually stopped. The only worrying thing was that there didn´t appear to be an exit wound.

"Looks like you´re a lucky lad, Redman," said Clemens, staring down at the young soldier´s ashen face. "A little more to the left and I wouldn´t have fancied your chances."

"That´s a relief, Sergeant," Redman replied through gritted teeth. "Only I just bought an engagement ring before we shipped out."

"Bloody Nora," said McCormack, "don´t tell me you found some poor girl daft enough to marry you?"

"I´m a good catch I am," replied Redman indignantly, feeling a lot better now he knew he wasn´t about to die,"

"I´ll be taking over my old man´s business when I get home. Best grocery shop in Poole."

"Ah, that´s a relief then," said McCormack grinning, "because let´s face it no girl is going to marry you for your looks now, is she?"

Redman didn´t bother replying, his attention was firmly focused on Hopkins´s hand as he placed the padded gauze dressing over the wound. Grimacing with pain as the medic held it in place.

"Right let´s get you bandaged up," and with Redman obliging by holding his left arm out of the way, Hopkins began winding the roll of bandage tightly around his body. Whatever regrets Private Hopkins may have had about letting on that he was a member of the Saint John Ambulance Brigade, as far as Private Peter Hopkins was concerned, he was jolly glad he had.

"Reckon you´ll be able to walk lad? Asked Clemens, as Hopkins helped Redman back on with his shirt.

"Yes Sarge, I´ll manage just fine." replied Redman, swinging his legs off the table.

It was then that Corporal Clark entered the house. The Bren gun tucked under one arm, his other arm around the waist of Private Yates.

"Jocks caught one in the shoulder."

"Ah dinnae fash yerself it´s just a wee scratch." said Yates, trying to make light of it.

"Sit him down on a chair Nobby, young Hopkins here will take a look," said Clemens.

Guiding Yates to the nearest chair, the corporal began to help him off with his jacket.

"Right then Jock, let's see the damage, shall we?"

Moments later with the blood-stained shirt removed, after washing the wound with the last of the water from McCormack's water bottle the young medic began examining the hole in the Scotsman's left shoulder made by the bullet fired from the Karabiner 98K.

"Well, I wouldn't say it was a scratch, more like a hole." said Hopkins, wiping away the blood from around the wound with a wad of cotton wool. "But the good news is the bullet has missed the bone and come out the other side, clean as a whistle."

"Aye, better oot than in laddie," replied Yates, grimacing a little as Hopkins applied iodine to both of his wounds.

"Right less of the chatter," said Clemens, "this is not a bloody doctor's surgery. Get Rob Roy here patched up and let's be on our way." And leaving Hopkins to finish bandaging Yates's shoulder, he stepped outside into the late morning sunlight.

Pulling the cigarette packet from his top pocket, Clemens offered one to Clark who had followed him outside.

"Cheers," said Clark, removing a cigarette and putting it between his lips.

"We got lucky there, Nobby," said Clemens, flicking his lighter into life. "If that Kraut hadn't opened up when he did, we would have been in for it."

"Now better than a bit of lady luck." replied Clark philosophically, "So, what do we do now?"

"Yates should be okay," said Clemens, dragging in a lungful of smoke, "but I'm a bit worried about young Redman."

"We could always stay here for a while," Clark ventured, "rest up for a bit."

"No, we had better push on."

"Not much point in going further south," said Clark, "We would be better off heading east towards Caen. There's bound to be some of our lot over there."

"Yeah, you're probably right," said Clemens turning his attention to the pile of German weapons Uttley had stacked up against the side of a house.

"Is that the lot Uttley?"

Yes, Sarge. Do you want me to put them out of action?

"Yeah, better not leave them laying around for some Frenchie to get his hands on. Never know what them buggers might get up to."

As instructed, picking up the MG 42, a gun the Allied soldiers had nicknamed "The Meat Grinder" because of its prolific rate of fire, lifting it above his head, the former fairground boxer slammed the barrel onto the rim of the stone horse trough. Well, at least there was one they didn't have to worry about anymore.

Chapter Three

Convent Notre Dame De Lourdes – La Cabosse

"What do you reckon, a church maybe?"

"No, too big for a church," replied Corporal Clark, "more than likely a monastery."

"Well, whatever it is it´s got to be better than spending another night under a hedge."

"Aye that´s true enough," replied Clark, "Young Redman looks about done in."

"Right then," said Clemens, let´s go and pay our respects."

It took them over ten minutes to find the entrance to the building, a wooden gate set in the high stone wall. And even after Corporal Clark had rung the bell hanging beside it several times, it was another five minutes before the letterbox-size grill set at head height was eventually pulled back to reveal a pair of eyes. Moments later, much to his relief the gate swung open and standing before him was a young nun.

A convent. Well, at least he had almost got it right, thought Clark after overcoming his initial surprise. Let´s hope it´s not one where they are bound by a vow of silence, or they could be in trouble. After a strained silence, judging from the fixed expression on her face that she had no intention of saying anything, Clark decided he had better take the plunge.

"Bonjour mademoiselle parles-vous anglais?" Good day miss, do you speak English?

Sadly, the fixed expression remained, and the young nun s lips stayed firmly pressed together.

Undeterred, Clark pressed on. "Entrer s´il vous plait?" Can we enter please?

"Oui, suivez-moi, s´il vous plait." The nun replied brightly, turning away quickly so that the soldier wouldn´t see the amused look on her face.

Completely unaware of the humorous effect his attempted impersonation of Maurice Chevalier had had on the nun, while not understanding what she had said, but confident that there had been a "Yes" in there somewhere, Clark stepped through the open gate. With her composure restored, and the remainder of C Company safely inside, after ensuring that the gate was firmly shut, turning on her heels the young nun set off along a wide gravelled path.

Once inside the grounds of the convent, with its huge granite walls inset with rectangular arched windows towering over them, the building itself appeared even more imposing. At one end, rising above the vast expanse of tiled roof was an open-sided bell tower topped by a stone cross. Hanging from its belfry was a solitary bell.

Judging by their lengthy stares, even though none of the soldiers were what you might call keen gardeners; not even McCormack who had worked for Bedford Corporation Parks Department with his uncle Fred before being called up, they appeared just as impressed by the convent´s gardens.

Segregated by the gravel path two manicured lawns ran the entire length of the building, each edged by a wide border planted with an abundance of summer flowers; Marigolds, Dahlias and Iris, lantern-headed Peonies, and lavender, a dazzling array of colour set against the grey, granite facade of the convent walls. Their scent, together with the humming of industrious bees as they moved from plant to plant in search of pollen permeated the air.

"You´re a bit of a dark horse," said Clemens, "when did you learn to speak their lingo?"

"Don´t get your hopes up, said Clark, smiling ruefully. "Seeing as I was going to France, Ena our youngest taught me a few words when I was on leave. One of her teachers is French, and she´s been helping her learn the language. The only trouble is I´ve already forgotten half of what she taught me."

"Not to worry, at least you got us in. I´m sure we can get by with hand signals if we have to."

Ahead of them the young nun had already reached the main entrance to the convent, its two huge arched doors with their ornate metal hinges and rows of blackened bolt heads more in keeping with a medieval castle. With a backward glance, satisfied that everyone was present, taking hold of the circular barley-twist handle, and rotating it anticlockwise she pushed open one of the heavy doors.

Climbing the short flight of stone steps, following Sergeant Clemens´s example by removing their helmets, the soldiers followed the nun inside, the last one pushing the door shut behind them, the sound as it slammed shut echoing in the cavernous vestibule.

Ahead of them, its walls bathed in sunlight, a wide corridor led into the first of four arched cloisters. Surrounding the stone walkways were rows of equally spaced stone columns with a lawned quadrangle crisscrossed by paved pathways at its centre. At the point where they crossed was a small ornate fountain, the sound of trickling water adding to the sense of solitude.

With their hob-nail boots clattering on the worn flagstones, gazing around at their surroundings Clemens and his men followed their guide along the wide colonnade. Reaching the point where the cloister dog-legged to the right, pushing open a door set into the end wall, the nun ushered them into what turned out to be the convent´s refectory.

Rectangular in shape, its barrelled timber roof supported by colonnaded alcove walls towering some twenty-five feet above the tiled floor, illuminated by two vertical glass windows the room resembled a medieval banqueting hall. The illusion was quickly shattered by the large wooden cross, secured to the end wall by iron nails.

Seated four to a bench on either side of the three wooden tables running down the middle of the room, ignoring the bowls of broth in front of them, the convent´s occupants turned their gaze towards the open door. Although having their mealtime interrupted by seven heavily armed British soldiers was hardly an everyday occurrence, they appeared completely unfazed by it.

Seeing the nuns seated at the tables, it was obvious to Sergeant Clemens and his men that they had called at a bad time. Crowded together in a group just inside the doorway, wishing the floor would open and swallow them up, they were quickly put at ease by the warm smile on the face of the woman making her way towards them.

After pausing for a brief, whispered conversation with the young nun, with a nod of the head she continued towards the group of soldiers. Like the other nuns, she was dressed in an ankle-length white, cotton frock worn under a long black apron pulled in at the waist by a wide leather belt. With her hair hidden by a veiled white linen coif, blessed by a youthful complexion although certainly not a young woman it was difficult to judge her exact age. What distinguished her from the others, however, was the simple gold cross hanging from a chain around her neck. Worn not as an adornment but as a symbol of her authority.

Having identified Clemens as their leader from the chevrons on the sleeve of his jacket, prolonging her smile she walked up to him. The look of apprehension on Clemen´s face, quickly replaced by one of relief when she addressed him in perfect English albeit with a French accent.

"Welcome to the Convent Notre Dame De Lourdes."

"Thank you, Sister," said Clemens recovering his composure.

"It´s Reverend Mother Sarge," whispered McCormack, tugging the sergeant´s sleeve. "She´s called Reverend Mother." As the only Catholic among them, although if you asked him when was the last time he went to communion, he would have a hard time remembering, McCormack thought it only right to speak up.

"Err sorry, Reverend Mother," said Clemens, throwing McCormack, a filthy look, "it looks like we are interrupting your meal?"

"Nonsense! Come you must join us. I am sure you and your men must be hungry, nest-pah? Isn´t it so?"

"Well, if you are sure," Clemens replied, conscious of the fact that they were down to their last few tins of bully beef, "that would be very kind."

With her invitation accepted, clapping her hands together, in a firm voice the Abbess sent several nuns off to the kitchen while at the same time, instructing the other nuns to fetch an additional table and benches and place them in the centre of the room.

"Well don´t just stand there you lot," shouted Corporal Clark, angrily, watching the nuns struggling with the heavy furniture, "lend a hand."

Stacking their rifles against the wall three of the soldiers hurried across to give their assistance, and gesturing the nuns aside, taking hold of each end of the long table McCormack and Hopkins carried it into the middle of the room. Left to his own devices, after stacking one bench on top of the other, slipping his arms under the lower one, much to the astonishment of the watching nuns, Uttley proceeded to carry them across the room.

With the additional furniture now in place, following the example of the two NCOs the remaining soldiers seated themselves at the table. Their eyes eagerly observing the progress of the four nuns as they re-entered the room carrying bowls of broth. Struggling to contain their giggles, placing a bowl and spoon in front of each soldier, conscious of the Abbess´s disapproving look, the nuns hurried back to their respective benches.

With the assembly seated, after administering the blessing, with a promissory nod from the Abbess nuns and soldiers alike turned their attention to the midday meal. Some of the younger nuns taking the opportunity to steal a surreptitious glance at the soldiers under the pretext of reaching for a slice of bread. While several of the older nuns found themselves staring out of concern at Redman´s ashen face.

Taking a seat alongside Clemens, after allowing him to finish his meal the Abbess indulged her curiosity.

"So, what has brought you to our door?"

"Two of my men are wounded," replied Clemens, "nothing too serious but it would help if they could rest here for a while." Adding hopefully. "Perhaps there is someone here who could look at them?"

"You are most welcome to stay," the Abbess replied, "but sadly there is no one here who can treat their wounds. Alas, none of us is a doctor."

"Perhaps I can be of help."

Seated on the next table, Clemens hadn't noticed her before. Which was surprising considering she was the only woman in the room not wearing a nun's habit.

"If you could that would be appreciated Madame," replied Clemens, both surprised and delighted that she spoke English.

"Actually, it's Mademoiselle. Mademoiselle Joliane Cabouret," said the woman, getting up from the bench and walking towards him.

"My apologies Mademoiselle," said Clemens quietly observing her as she drew nearer. Her smile told him he was forgiven.

She was probably no more than five feet four inches in height, her well-proportioned figure, accentuated by a close-fitting flower-patterned dress. Facially, she reminded him a little of the actress Margaret Lockwood. She was probably about the same age too, in her mid to late twenties. Both had the same dark hair, although the style was different. Unlike the actress's flowing locks, her hair was cut quite short, with a fringe falling across her forehead. Something else which set her apart from the actress was the pair of utilitarian ankle-length boots she was wearing. Which were not at all in keeping with her pretty knee-length dress and powder blue cardigan.

"You say their wounds are not serious?"

"I've seen bullet wounds that were worse," replied Clemens, conscious that Redman was in earshot, "but I would be grateful if you would take a look at them all the same."

"My uncle was a doctor, Sergeant, and as the men of Normandy have a great love of hunting, there are also many accidents you understand, so as his nurse, I have experienced many gunshot wounds."

Sensing that he had just been politely put in his place, Clemens nodded apologetically.

"Better look at this one first," said Clemens, beckoning Redman forward, "he's got a bullet lodged in his chest."

"Very well, as you wish."

"Come on lad don't be shy now," said Clemens, sensing the young soldier's reluctance, "let's have that jacket and shirt off."

While Redman fiddled with his buttons, Joliane turned towards the Abbess.

"Puis-je avoir de l´eau chaude et des serviettes s´il vous plait? May I have hot water and some towels please?"

"Certainement" The Abbess replied, and turning to Sister Claudine she relayed Joliane´s request.

With a slight bow of the head Sister Claudine hurried away to the kitchen. Behind her, anticipating the young Frenchwoman´s needs, several of the nuns began clearing the empty bowls and bread baskets from one of the tables.

Having stripped to the waist, Redman watched nervously as the young Frenchwoman began removing the swathe of bandage from around his chest. With the binding removed, carefully peeling back the padded gauze dressing Joliane began examining the wound in the young soldier´s lower abdomen. After exploring the edges of the elongated gash with her index finger, encouraging Redman to turn around, a quick look confirmed that there was no exit wound.

"May I see his clothing please?"

Handing her Redman´s battledress jacket first, Clemens watched as she examined the hole the bullet had made in the material, repeating the process with the young soldier´s shirt.

"I think the wound is how you say... Contamine?"

"You mean contaminated?"

"Oui. Here, I show you." And holding up Redman´s shirt she pointed to the hole in the khaki material. "You see, here there is no tear but a hole, yes? And here also," pointing to Redman´s jacket, "so, when the bullet goes in there is also some material."

"And that´s bad, is it?" asked, Clemens.

Oui. It means in time there can be an infection."

"So, the bullet has to come out, right?"

"Of course, but without instruments, it is not possible" said Joliane, shrugging her shoulders.

"What if the hole was bigger?" Clemens replied, looking down at the Frenchwoman´s hands, "you

have very small fingers."

"You wish me to remove the bullet with my fingers?" said Joliane, clearly shocked by the Sergeant´s suggestion. "C´est impossible! It´s impossible."

"Why?" asked Clemens. "Look how thin he is," throwing a look at Redman, "the bullet can´t have gone in too far."

Absurd though the idea was, much to her amazement, Joliane found herself considering doing as Clemens had suggested. Was it perhaps because of the look of distress on the young soldier's face as he came to terms with the realisation that his wound was serious enough to kill him? Or was it the challenge? Whatever it was, something was telling her that she must at least try.

"First, I must make the wound bigger. Perhaps I can use a knife from the kitchen?" said Joliane, looking enquiringly at the Abbess.

"No need for that," said Clemens, before the Abbess had time to reply, and reaching down, he pulled out a dagger from inside his gaiter. "This little beauty should be sharp enough."

The dagger in question was a Fairbairn–Sykes fighting knife, its seven-inch double-edged blade ending in a sharp point. Issued mainly to Commando's and certain airborne troops, Clemens had removed it together with a Thompson submachine gun, and two magazines from the body of a dead Canadian paratrooper they had discovered in the corner of a field near Maltot. His unopened parachute lay beside him like a faithful hound.

"Right lad, up on the table," said Clemens.

Redman's initial reaction was to stay exactly where he was. Strangely enough, it wasn't the prospect of being cut open by the vicious-looking dagger Sergeant Clemens was holding that contributed to his lack of mobility. No, it was more the thought of someone's fingers, no matter how small and delicate they were, and Mademoiselle Cabouret's fingers were certainly that, feeling around inside his body. Surely this was something that happened in horror films for heavens' sake, not on a table in a convent.

"Come on now, you heard what the lady said. There's no point in wasting time, it could be days before we can get you to a field hospital."

Something did move this time but it wasn't Redman's legs just his facial muscles as he tried unsuccessfully to remove the look of terror on his face.

"Look, I've lost enough men already without you dying on me Redman, now get on that bloody table, and that's an order." Barked Clemens, running out of patience.

The Sergeant's tone of voice did the trick, helped by another of Joliane's reassuring smiles, and with an encouraging push from Corporal Clark, Private Redman found himself propelled towards the table where minutes before he had sat enjoying a meal. Resigned to his fate swinging himself up onto its wooden surface, Redman fixed his gaze on the pair of winged angels carved into the arching roof above his head. Silently praying that if there was indeed a God, he would bless Joliane with a steady hand.

No sooner had Redman stretched himself out on the table when Sister Claudine and another nun entered the room. One carrying a bowl of hot water, the other holding a tray containing several folded towels.

With everything ready, anxious to get on with things, with a wave of his hand Clemens signalled to three of the watching soldiers to take up a position around the table.

Well known for his strength; he had once lifted the front of an army lorry off the ground single-handed when a bloody-minded NCO had refused to let him move it, Uttley made his way to the head of the table, and giving Redman an upside-down wink, he placed the palm of his hands on the young soldier's bony shoulders. Moving to the other end of the table McCormack and Hopkins took up a position beside one of Redman's legs, gripping them firmly with both hands.

With the refectory transformed into a temporary operating theatre, pushing up the sleeves of her cardigan, Joliane began washing her hands in the bowl of hot water.

Standing next to her, flicking his lighter into life Clemens held the point of the dagger in its flame for a few moments; a crude but effective method of sterilizing the blade. Satisfied, waiting until Joliane had finished her ablutions, he handed her the dagger.

After wiping off the traces of soot from the tip of the blade with the towel Joliane stepped up to the improvised operating table. Nodding her head to indicate that she was ready to begin, she waited while the three soldiers tightened their grip on Redman's body.

Satisfied that her patient was immobilised, positioning the tip of the blade at the upper end of the wound, exerting just enough pressure to penetrate the layers of Redman's skin, Joliane began making an upward incision, the steel blade slicing effortlessly through the exposed flesh. After making a cut some two inches in length, she repeated the procedure at the other end of the bullet's entry point creating an opening roughly five inches long in the soldier's abdomen.

Happy that the aperture she had made was large enough, handing the dagger back to Clemens, with the fingers of her left hand Joliane carefully peeled back the flap of skin. Pausing for a moment to allow Corporal Clark to insert a wooden spoon between the young soldier's teeth, ignoring the sudden feeling of apprehension which threatened to engulf her, extending the fingers of her right hand she slowly inserted them into the open wound.

After what must have seemed an eternity to Redman but in reality, was less than a minute, with the deformed head of the 8 mm round from the

German machine gun gripped between her index and forefinger, with a sigh of relief Joliane withdrew her blood-soaked fingers.

Smiling, she dropped the bullet into the bowl of water, watching with satisfaction as a piece of Redman´s jacket the size of a postage stamp detached itself from the piece of metal. With her fears vindicated, as she watched the blood from the piece of material permeating the water, turning it a pinkish colour, Joliane was reminded of a story her mother had told her. A teacher at a local school, when conducting a lesson on religion, she asked the class to write their interpretation of how Jesus had turned water into wine. While most of the children spent the entire lesson on the task, she noticed that one boy, in particular, had completed the assignment in a matter of minutes. Keen to expose his apparent lack of effort she asked to see what he had written. The profoundness of the boy´s words had stayed with her mother for the rest of her life. He had simply put "And Jesus removed his sandals, and the water blushed."

Freeing herself from the reminiscence, anxious to discover if the bullet had damaged any of the internal organs, in particular to the spleen which it had come close to hitting, Joliane inserted her fingers into the wound once more. Removing them a few moments later, relieved that her investigation had found no signs of tissue damage or any internal bleeding.

Rinsing her hands in the bowl, she turned to Sister Claudine.

"Puis-je avoir une aiguille et du fil s´il vous plait? May I have a needle and thread please?"

"Is everything okay?" Clemens enquired, as Sister Claudine hurried away.

"Oui, your young soldier has been very fortunate," replied Joliane, drying her hands on a towel. "Now I must stitch up the wound."

Equally relieved by the news, Clemens quickly turned to his other casualty "Let´s have your flask, Yates."

Not best pleased by the request, at first Yates simply ignored him.

"Come on man I´m not that stupid that I can´t smell whiskey on a man´s breath."

Put out by the Sergeant´s request, but with little choice but to comply, un-buttoning a jacket pocket, Yates removed a silver hipflask.

Having spent a solitary life on a croft in the Highlands, where your only friend was a bottle of malt whiskey over the years, he had become a heavy drinker. Even after moving to Fareham to live with his sister when his stewardship was terminated by the landowner, his reliance on the amber liquid continued. Like most alcoholics, he did his best to hide his addiction but most of the men he was billeted with were well aware that he had a drinking problem. Some even joked that if Yates ever ran out of whiskey, they wouldn´t put it past him to drink the anti-freeze in the lorries.

Taking the flask from Yate´s outstretched hand, ignoring the man´s dirty look, unscrewing the cap, Clemens handed the flask to Joliane.

Smiling ruefully, holding the flask over the Redman´s chest Joliane began pouring a liberal amount of Yate´s Glenfiddich malt whiskey over the wound. Experiencing a slight twinge of guilt when she saw the tears forming in Redman´s eyes as the fiery liquid made contact with the exposed flesh.

With the wound suitably disinfected, she turned and handed Clemens the flask.

"Why don´t you have a drink, you have earned it?" said Clemens, smiling.

"Merci," said Joliane. But before she was able to accept the invitation, Sister Claudine appeared carrying a needle and thread in her hand.

With a philosophical shrug of the shoulders, she handed the flask back to Clemens and relieving the nun of the needle and length of course thread used by the nuns for their embroidery, Joliane set to work. Starting at the top of the incision, after pinching the two edges of the flesh together with the fingers of her left hand, ensuring each of the sutures was neatly spaced she began sewing up the wound.

"Voila! said Joliane, stepping away from her patient. "Now you must get down please," smiling at the look of relief on Redman´s face. "I must apply bandages."

Only too happy to oblige, free from his manual restraints, swinging his legs over the edge of the table, Redman gingerly placed his feet onto the tiled floor.

Prompted by the word "bandage" having relinquished his hold on Redman´s left leg, Hopkins hurried across the room to where the soldiers had stacked their backpacks, helmets, and rifles. Retrieving his backpack from the pile, he strode across to where Joliane was standing.

"I have some bandages, Mademoiselle," said Hopkins, holding up the pack. "Field dressings too if you need them."

"Ah! Merci," Joliane replied, slightly surprised by Hopkins´s revelation. "So, you are the doctor, no?"

"No," said Hopkins, a little taken aback by the question, "I´m … "

"Hopkins here is our medic," said Clemens, interrupting the young soldier before he had a chance to elaborate on his time in the Saint John´s Ambulance Brigade. "Right lad, let the lady see what you´ve got for her."

"Yes Sarge," muttered Hopkins, quickly unbuckling the two straps, and reaching inside he began removing the contents of the pack: several packs of field dressings each containing two sterilised bandages, a half-empty bottle of iodine, a packet of safety pins, and a pair of scissors, placing them on the table.

After selecting one of the field dressings, tearing off the outer wrapping of cellophane, and the protective layer of hessian, Joliane removed one of the bandages. Undoing the safety pin attached to it, she then unrolled the dressing to where a sterilised gauze pad had been stitched into it. Carefully placing the pad over Redman´s wound, winding the remainder of the cotton bandage around his body, she secured it with the pin. As a precaution, and to give the wound more support she then repeated the process with the second bandage.

"There, it is done." said Joliane, allowing herself a self-satisfied smile.

"Thank you, Mademoiselle." said Redman sheepishly. "I am very grateful."

"You are welcome, Mon Ami, my friend. You were very brave. Now everything will be fine." Her words of reassurance doing wonders for Redman´s morale.

With Corporal Clark helping Redman back on with his shirt, Joliane turned to Clemens in search of her next patient.

"There is another you wish me to look at?"

"Yes, but I´m not sure the miserable devil deserves it," said Clemens staring at Yates, "but I am sure he would appreciate it all the same."

Taking her smile as confirmation, he turned back to Yates. "Right Jock, your turn."

Having refused the offer of a sling from Hopkins, with his arm, pushed into the opening in his battledress jacket like some modern-day Napoleon Bonaparte, Yates stepped up to the table. While not convinced that he should be letting a pretty wee lassie tend to his shoulder, after hesitating for a moment, he began unbuttoning his tunic.

After stripping to the waist, resting his backside on the table Yates watched as Joliane cut through the bloodstained bandages. Her fingers gently peeling away the gauze dressing from the wound.

"Tres bien, very good", said Joliane, handing the scissors and strips of soiled bandage to Hopkins. "You have done well." Smiling, as the young soldier tried unsuccessfully to hide his delight from her compliment. It was by far the nicest pat on the back Hopkins had ever received.

Turning her attention to Yate´s wound, her diagnosis was delivered swiftly, and confidently.

"You have been very fortunate the bullet has done little damage. Some antiseptics perhaps?" Joliane inquired, glancing at the flask in Clemens´s hand.

"Nay lassie, a wee drop of yon iodine will do nicely," Yates replied, nodding towards the bottle Hopkins had put on the table. "Be a shame to waste any more good Scotch whiskey."

"Very well then I shall leave you to your comrade," said Joliane, shrugging her shoulders, "you will be in good hands."

"Thank you," said Clemens, as she turned away from the table.

"You are welcome," replied Joliane wearily, "now if you will please excuse me." And before Clemens could say another word she hurried away.

In two minds whether to go after her or not, before Clemens could make up his mind, he found himself confronted by the Abbess.

"It would be best to let her rest," said the Reverend Mother smiling up at him benignly. "Perhaps you could express your thanks another time."

"Yes, you are probably right," replied Clemens, "I wasn´t thinking."

"So, now that you´re wounded are attended to what will you do?"

"I know it´s an inconvenience Reverend Mother but I was hoping we could stay until the morning."

"But of course," said the Abbess, extending her arms in a welcoming gesture, "it is the least we can do for such brave men as yourselves. I will see to your accommodation." And with that, gathering the remaining nuns around her like a mother hen, she left the room.

"Right, listen up," said Clemens, turning to where his men had gathered in a group, "we´ll be staying here tonight so be on your best behaviour, understood? And if you want a smoke then go outside."

"What about grub, Sarge?" asked McCormack, whose stomach was beginning to think his throat had been cut.

"I´m not sure if they have enough food for themselves to give us another meal," Clemens replied, "if not you will just have to eat up the rest of your rations."

"Perhaps," said Clemens, ignoring the groans of disappointment, "as our corporal here is such a dab hand at the lingo, he could organise some boiling water so at least we can have a brew up?"

Sarky bugger, thought Clark, knowing he had been put on the spot.

"Alright, I'll see what I can do."

"Good man," a cup of char will do us all a power of good."

With Corporal Clark sent off on his mission of mercy, as the soldiers began gathering up their equipment, Clemens called Uttley to one side.

"See if you can get up into that bell tower and keep an eye out."

"Will do Sarge," and retrieving his rifle from against the wall, Private Uttley set off in search of an entrance to the bell tower.

Shortly after Clark and Uttley had left the room, the Abbess returned with news of their accommodation.

"We have an empty dormitory where you can sleep. Sadly, there are no beds but there are mattresses." Adding by way of a warning. "The floors are very hard.

"You are very kind," said Clemens. "Right, you lot grab your kit, thanks to the Reverend Mother we've got a bed for the night." And following on the heels of the Abbess, Clemens and his men left the refectory.

The dormitory was larger than Clemens had anticipated but then given the sheer size of the convent, it was hard to imagine it having any small rooms. Although there was just a single window, set high up in the end wall the room was quite light and airy. True to her word, spaced out on the tiled floor, were two rows of straw-filled mattresses.

After muttering their thanks, wasting no time in claiming a palliasse, leaving the ones nearest to the door for the two NCOs the soldiers were soon stretched out, and although they were a bit lumpy to them this was pure, unadulterated luxury.

Yet more luxury arrived five minutes later when having found his way to the kitchen, Corporal Clark returned carrying a large two-handled copper pan filled with boiling water.

"Right," said Clark, setting the pan down on the floor, "let's have some of your rations."

Without needing to be asked twice, the soldiers quickly began rummaging through their packs in search of packets of tea, lumps of sugar and milk tablets. Placing their finds onto one of the mattresses.

Scanning the accumulated ingredients, after mentally calculating how many of each would be required to provide the desired result, tearing off the waxed wrappers from four packets of tea Clark set to work crushing the compressed blocks in the palms of his hands. This done, sprinkling the tea leaves into the steaming water, after adding sixteen cubes of sugar, and six milk tablets, he slowly stirred the contents with the blade of his bayonet.

Moments later, the transformation was complete, a gallon of the finest tea this side of London´s Lyons corner house.

"Right, let´s have your mess tins," said Clark, and using his mess tin as a ladle, he began dispensing the tea to the eager soldiers.

"Bloody marvellous, Corporal," enthused Redman, after sampling the amber nectar.

"Should have been in the catering corps," McCormack remarked, as he dipped a wholemeal biscuit into his mess tin.

It was then, just as Clemens was about to take a second swig of tea that Uttley appeared in the doorway. Sensing that something was amiss, putting down his mess tin Clemens stepped outside.

"What is it, Uttley?"

"There´s a couple of Frenchie´s hanging around outside the gate Sarge, and one of them has got a rifle."

"Right, let´s take a look," said Clemens," and with Uttley leading, the pair made their way back along the cloisters towards the entrance hall, and crossing to an arched opening in one of the walls, the two soldiers began climbing the narrow staircase. The sound of their hobnail boots on the ancient stone steps was amplified by the enclosing walls.

Reaching the top of the stairs, stepping out onto a wooden gallery landing, hidden from below by the corner pillar of the bell tower, Clemens peered down at the gated entrance.

Although both men looked like peasants in their rustic clothing, and berets they were most definitely members of the Resistance, thought Clemens. Even during a war, French farm labourers don´t normally go around carrying rifles.

"What do you reckon they want Sarge?"

"Search me. Probably harmless enough. You go and get yourself a cuppa, I´ll keep an eye on them for a while."

Having been relieved from sentry duty, with the prospect of a nice cup of tea to look forward to Uttley made his way back down the steep staircase. Relishing the opportunity for some solitude, resting his back against the wall, Clemens helped himself to a cigarette. Thankfully, things had worked out pretty well after their brush with Jerry, especially for young Redman. Finding someone like Mademoiselle Cabouret to attend to his wound might just have saved the lad´s life. It was then that he began wondering what she had been doing in the convent in the first place. Even if she were a novice, surely, she would still have had to wear some kind of habit. And now there was the arrival of the two Frenchmen. Was there a connection he wondered? It hardly seemed likely, but something was nagging at him. Some little warning bell inside his head was ringing and he knew it wouldn't stop until he got to the bottom of it. If it wasn't a coincidence, then what was it? Time to find out and stubbing out the cigarette on the wall, he made his way towards the stairs.

Clemens found the Abbess in what he assumed was her office, her private retreat. An austere room, similar in size to the dormitory he and his men were billeted in. The starkness of its grey unadorned walls softened by the rays of late afternoon sunlight allowed in through the large plain-glass window in the west wall. With a hand-painted statuette of the Madonna and Child on display in a shallow alcove providing a meagre oasis of colour. Seated on a high-back chair behind the impressive desk positioned in the middle of the room, sensing Clemens's presence, the Abbess looked up from the document she was reading.

"May I have a moment of your time Reverend Mother?"

"But of course, my son," said the Abbess, beckoning him forward. "Please sit down."

Seating himself on one of the two chairs fronting the desk, not one for beating around the bush, Clemens came straight to the point.

"What is Mademoiselle Cabouret doing here in the convent?"

Although she was not expecting the question, the Abbess was not surprised by it.

"The convent has given her sanctuary."

"Who from? The men outside your gate?"

"Ah! So, they have returned?"

"They've been here before then?"

"Oui," said the Abbess, unwilling to elaborate.

What do they want her for?"

"They believe she has betrayed members of the Marquis to the Gestapo."

"And has she?"

"She says that this is not true."

"And do you believe her?"

"I am not here to judge, only to give sanctuary to those who ask for it. Only Mademoiselle Cabouret herself can know the truth." The Abbess replied, unwilling to pardon or condemn.

"So, these Marquis, do they have any proof, or is it just their word against hers?"

"I am told that she was interrogated by the Gestapo, and the next day four of their members were arrested and shot."

"Not what you might call proof though is it?" said, Clemens. "Maybe the Gestapo already knew about these others."

"Perhaps, who can say." the Abbess replied, with a slight shrug of her shoulders.

"It seems to me," said Clemens, a hint of anger in his voice, "that the only people who know are the Gestapo, and my guess is they are not around anymore are they?"

With no reply, forthcoming, placing his elbows on his knees, Clemens rested his chin on his clenched hands. Thoughts racing through his head.

"Will she be safe here?"

"Who can say? We are merely women my son, what can we do against armed men?" replied the Abbess resignedly.

"But surely if you have given her, sanctuary they must respect that?"

"I fear that in times of war, men can forget their obligations to God, my son."

So, when we are gone, they will come and take her then?" said Clemens, watching as the Abbess nodded in confirmation.

"Will they give her a fair trial?"

"Sadly, I think judgement has already been passed."

"In England, a person is innocent until proven guilty," Clemens blurted out, angrily.

"In France also, and when our Grande Humiliation is over, I pray that such justice will return," said the Abbess, making the sign of the cross with her hand. "But until then I fear even those who are merely suspected of such things will be punished. Innocent or guilty."

Stung by the Abbess´s words, little knowing that what he was about to do would change his life, it was then that Clemens decided to take matters into his own hands. He couldn´t say why, it was just something he knew he must do. As had recently been proved to him in the cruellest of ways, in life there are always things over which you have no control. Events which couldn´t be altered or changed no matter how much you wanted them to be. He accepted that. But this time it didn´t have to be like that. This time there was something he could do something about. And he was bloody well going to.

Unaware of unfolding events, having drained the pan of Corporal Clark´s delicious tea, and wolfed down most of the hard-tack biscuits, for the first time since landing on French soil the men of C company had time for a little relaxation. Stretched out on a mattress, with their backpacks as a pillow, Uttley and Corporal Clark were already fast asleep. Meanwhile, having promised the Corporal that he would put in a good word for them all, McCormack had made his way to the convent´s chapel.

Hesitating for a moment in front of the open door, hoping he would be forgiven for his previous lapses in attendance, filled with trepidation, Private McCormack stepped inside. Overawed by the candle-lit surroundings, pausing for a moment at the foot of the statue of the Madonna and Child, he made his way between the two rows of long wooden pews towards the altar. Dropping onto his right knee, with his clenched hands resting on the alter-rail, Michael, Fergal McCormack began a long overdue conversation with the Almighty. Most of which concerned what he would, and wouldn´t do if God were to get himself and the rest of the lads back home in one piece.

Back in the dormitory, forgoing the chance to get some rest, Redman, Hopkins, and Yates were locked in conversation. The topic of their discussion was Mademoiselle Cabouret.

"Do you reckon the sergeant is trying to get his leg over?" said Hopkins, purposely keeping his voice down. "She´s a bit of a looker alright."

"No." Replied Redman, "he´s not like that, feeling he had to come to the NCO´s defence. "Besides he´s a married man."

"Well, she´s not going to know, is she?" commented Hopkins.

"Nae, but he´s ganna ken," Yates replied knowingly, the sobering remark bringing the conversation to an abrupt end.

As Yates, Hopkins and Redman made their way to their mattresses, seated on a stone seat beside the fountain smoking a cigarette, Clemens´s thoughts were also focused on Mademoiselle Cabouret. Having already made up his mind about what he was going to do. The only thing that concerned him was what to do if she refused. It seemed unlikely that she would but there was always that possibility. This however wasn´t the issue. No, the real issue was understanding why her decision had become so important to him.

"May I have one of your cigarettes please?"

Caught off guard by her sudden appearance instinctively, Clemens held out the packet of Player´s Navy Cut. "Help yourself." Watching as she removed one of the cigarettes and placed it between her lips. After accepting a light, seating herself beside him, Joliane inhaled a mouth full of smoke.

"Merci," said Joliane, allowing the cigarette smoke to escape through her parted lips.

"Feeling better now?"

"Yes, it was quite an experience for me. I did not know such a thing could be possible."

"I saw a cowboy do it in a film once," said Clemens, grinning, "so I knew you could do it."

"Ah! So now I am a cowboy, n"est-ce pas? Isn´t it so?"

"A very pretty one," said Clemens, smiling at her display of feigned indignation.

"And you Monsieur are a charmer, I think" said Joliane, before blowing cigarette smoke into Clemens´s face.

Dispersing the smoke with a wave of his hand, refusing to confirm or deny Joliane´s assumption, the pair lapsed into silence.

"It is peaceful here, no?" said Joliane, made a little uneasy by the prolonged silence.

"We are leaving tomorrow," said Clemens, calmly "and I want you to come with us."

Taken aback by his words, Joliane just stared at him, struggling to know how to respond.

"I know why you are here. The Reverend Mother has told me everything."

"Then you will know that she has given me sanctuary," said Joliane, defensively.

"Is that right?" said Clemens, "then you had better come with me." And stubbing out his half-finished cigarette, he got to his feet.

Both perplexed and intrigued, tossing her cigarette butt into the fountain, Joliane hurried after him as he made his way towards the cloisters.

Struggling to match his stride, uncertain where he was taking her before Joliane realised it she was climbing the stairs up to the bell tower.

When they reached the top of the staircase, taking her by the hand Clemens led Joliane along the narrow landing towards the end wall.

"Is that why you are here, because of them?" asked Clemens, looking down at the gateway below.

Even in the late evening light, the two men were visible. The features of the one who was smoking, illuminated by the glow from the tip of his cigarette.

Alarmed Joliane stepped back from the parapet, the colour draining from her face.

"What do they want with you?"

Still shocked by the men´s presence it took her a moment before she could answer him. "They think I am an informer."

"And are you? Are you an informer?"

"No!" said Joliane, her voice tinged with anger. "I did not do what they are accusing me of. Please you must believe me."

"It doesn´t matter what I believe", Clemens replied.

"But I am innocent, I would never do such a terrible thing. I would rather die than betray my friends," sobbed Joliane. "Please you must believe me."

"I believe you."

"You do?"

"Oui," said Clemens, grinning.

"You are very trusting."

"That´s because I am a good judge of character", said Clemens, reaching out and taking hold of Joliane´s hands.

Despite herself, Joliane smiled. Reluctant to free her hands, she looked into Clemens´s eyes.

"It is true that I was taken by the Gestapo, but I said nothing. One of them, a rough-looking brute hit me with his fist a few times but that was all, and then they let me go."

"But those two down there didn´t believe you, did they?"

"No."

"Well then, I think the best thing to do is for you to come with us."

"Is that possible?"

"It is if I say so."

"And what will happen to me?"

"Well for one thing you will be safe."

"You promise?"

"Yes, I promise," said Clemens, reaching out, "You will be safe with me Mademoiselle," and putting an arm around her shoulder, he pulled her towards him. His whole being wanting nothing more than to comfort her. To assure her that all would be well. Unwittingly she had become his anchor. An antidote against the venom flowing through his veins. A reason for living rather than just staying alive.

For her part, locked in Clemens´ arms, the haunting events of the past few weeks, seemed far away. Just like the fairy stories her father used to read to her as a child, it seemed there really were knights in shining armour after all. The fact that the one who had come to her rescue was a tall, handsome English soldier with blue eyes didn´t seem to matter in the least.

Returning to the dormitory, with all six soldiers awake, Clemens broke the news of their impending departure.

"Right lads, now that Yates and Redman have been patched up, and you´ve all had a nice rest, we´ll be leaving in the morning, bright and early. And just so you know Mademoiselle Cabouret will be coming with us."

Although the Sergeant´s last statement was rhetorical, it didn´t stop Redman from replying.

"Fine by me, Sarge."

"Planning on getting shot again, are you?"

The remark generating a few chuckles from the others and leaving Redman blushing like a schoolboy after his first kiss.

It was then that Clemens noticed Clark gesturing towards the door. Time for a chat.

"You might have told me earlier, Albert," said Clark once they were outside the room.

"Sorry Nobby, I just thought now was a good time that´s all.

"And what´s all this about taking the Frenchwoman with us?"

"It´s a long story, said Clemens, removing a cigarette packet from his pocket. "The bottom line is she´s taken sanctuary here because the Resistance are after her."

"Why, what´s she done?" asked Clark, helping himself to a cigarette.

"They think she´s betrayed some of them to the Gestapo." Clemens replied, lighting both cigarettes.

"And has she?" said Clark, drawing in a mouthful of smoke.

"She says she hasn´t."

"And you believe her, do you?"

"Yes, I believe her."

"But you don´t know if she´s telling the truth or not?"

"No, I don´t but I´m giving her the benefit of the doubt, okay?"

"And why´s that," said Clark giving Clemens a dubious look.

"Let´s just say it´s because she´s still got some fingernails. Only from what I hear they are the first thing these Gestapo-type like to remove when they are after information."

"Hardly what you´d call evidence," Clark remarked, "her having nice nails."

"Well, it´s good enough for me."

"Good-looking woman," ventured Clark, brushing cigarette ash off the front of his jacket. "You sure she hasn´t turned your head, Albert?"

Stung by the remark, Clemens waited a moment before replying.

"After all the years we've served together, and you think I would put men's lives at risk because of some woman.? I might have expected better than that from you."

"Sorry Albert, that was out of order." said Clark, instantly, regretting the remark.

"You're damn right it was," said Clemens, angrily.

"Alright, let's suppose she is innocent, surely she's safe enough here?"

"Yes, I thought so as well until two of them turned up outside the gate.

"They mean business then?"

"Yeah, and as soon as we leave, they will come for her."

Clark remained silent for a moment, mulling things over in his mind before replying.

"Look I know it's hard on her Albert but it's still a hell of a risk, taking her with us."

"Risk or not I'm not leaving her here to be shot for something she didn't do."

"Who says they are going to shoot her?" asked Clark, stunned by the revelation."

"The Abbess. It seems the Resistance doesn't go in for trials much. A bullet in the head is their way of dealing with things.

Not sure how to respond, Clark stared down at his feet.

Not a nice thought, is it? And after what she's done for Redman and Yates, I reckon the rest of the lads won't mind her coming along with us, do you?"

"Alright, I take your point," Clark replied, stubbing out his cigarette on the wall. "Anyway, it's your call, Albert," knowing full well that no matter what he said, Clemens wasn't going to change his mind.

Even at six in the morning, and despite Clemens's protest, the Abbess insisted that they stay and eat breakfast, and not wishing to offend, he finally agreed. Fortunately for him, it turned out to be a wise decision, because had they had to forgo the generous helping of golden omelette, infused with herbs, and topped with a sprinkling of grated cheese which was placed before them, his men would probably have strung him up.

After thanking the Abbess for her kindness, and receiving her blessing in return, guided by Sister Claudine and his men made their way out through a back door, and into the vegetable gardens at the rear of the convent. Despite the early hour, several nuns were already at work with their hoes and weeding forks. Just as industrious were the chickens in the enclosed area around the hen house, each forlornly scratching for worms in the compacted ground. Reaching the little-used gate in the wall, after a further round of "Thank You" to Sister Claudine, the men of C Company accompanied by Mademoiselle Cabouret returned to the war.

Chapter Four

Marshalling Area on the outskirts of Villers-Bocage

During the first two hours the only evidence that there was a war going on was when six P-51 Mustangs flew overhead, the roar of their Packard V-1650 Merlin engines shattering the tranquillity of the Normandy countryside. Half an hour later they received further proof when Hopkin´s ears picked up the distant rumble of vehicles on the move. The sound gradually becoming louder, confirmation that at least they were heading in the right direction. That´s assuming the noise wasn´t being made by German vehicles of course. Because if they were, then things could become decidedly dodgy.

Luckily, when they caught sight of the road, the convoy of vehicles travelling along it were British, lorries, and Bren gun carriers mainly. The bulk of the vehicles were Bedford QLs crammed with troops, interspersed by a few Humber armoured carts, and armoured personnel carriers.

Thankful to have reached their own lines, no sooner had Clemens and his men reached the road, when, a Bren gun carrier pulled up beside them.

"Do you chaps need a lift, sergeant?" asked the young officer seated beside the driver, a Green Howards cap badge fixed to his beret.

"No, thank you, sir but I´ve got some walking wounded who need medical treatment", said Clemens.

"Well, just keep on this road for a couple of miles, and you´ll come to a marshalling area, there´s a dressing station there, and they´ll take care of them."

"Thank you, sir," Clemens called out, as the Bren Gun carrier raced away along the convoy of vehicles crawling along the un-made-up road.

Setting off in single file, cursing the clouds of dust thrown up by the caterpillar tracks and tyres of the seemingly endless flow of vehicles, C Company made its way towards the marshalling area. Redman and Hopkins responding to the wolf-whistles and catcalls directed at Joliane by the soldier in the back of the trucks by giving them the customary two-finger salute.

Three-quarters of an hour later, and with the traffic on the road reduced to the occasional despatch rider on his BSA M20 motorcycle, Corporal Clark caught sight of a line of canvas bell tents.

Pitched in orderly rows down one side of the road, judging by the number of soldiers milling around them it looked like many of them were already occupied. Across from them on the opposite side of the road, partially hidden by a stone wall was a two-story building. The gatehouse to a much grander building judging by the two columns, each topped by a heraldic shield positioned on each side of the overgrown driveway. The four rusting hinges embedded in the stonework were all that remained of the ornate wrought iron gates that had once hung between them.

Structurally, the building appeared undamaged, suffering more from neglect than the vagaries of war. The tiled roof and both chimneys were intact, and at first glance, it appeared most of the windows still had glass in them. The letters "HQ" painted on the front wall was an indication that after standing empty for many years someone, namely, the British Army had now found a use for it.

"Right lads, hang around here while I go and find an officer", said Clemens, smiling reassuringly at a very nervous-looking Joliane, and crossing the road he made his way towards the requisitioned building.

Positioned on either side of the front door like a couple of nightclub bouncers the two Military Policemen in their distinctive red caps and white webbing didn't exactly look welcoming. But an old soldier like Clemens knew it was just part of their persona, and that unlikely as it seemed lurking beneath that hard exterior there was probably a likeable human being. Of course, he could be wrong.

"I need to speak to the officer in charge," said Clemens, addressing the MP with a lance corporal's stripe on the sleeve of his jacket.

"Oh, do you know," replied the MP, his tone of voice matching the unfriendly expression on his face. "Well, we'll have to see about that, won't we? Can't have any old Tom, Dick, and Harry waltzing in when they feel like it. What's your regiment?"

"That's for him to know." Clemens replied, stepping past the dumbstruck MP, and grabbing hold of the door handle.

"Hey now, just you..."

But before he could finish, Clemens had the door open and was already halfway through it by the time the MP completed the sentence, his words, most of which were expletives already falling on deaf ears.

Shutting the door behind him, quickly taking in his surroundings, Clemens began scanning the epaulettes of the room's occupants.

Of the twelve soldiers scattered around the room, only two bore the insignia of an officer; a fresh-faced lieutenant seated at a desk with a phone pressed against his ear, deep in conversation, and a grey-haired major standing in front of a large-scale map of Normandy. Choosing the more senior of the two, Clemens crossed the busy office towards him.

"Excuse me, sir."

Ignoring the interruption, with his eyes firmly focused on the map the officer began tracing a line with his index finger. Reaching a point where two roads converged, removing a small red flag from between his teeth, he pinned it to the map. Satisfied that he had positioned the marker correctly, he turned around.

"Sergeant Clemens, C Company 7th Battalion Royal Hampshire's, sir." said Clemens, saluting.

Removing his steel-rimmed spectacles, with thumb and forefinger the officer rubbed the bridge of his nose, the dark circles under his eyes a testimony to a lack of sleep. "Any news on the rest of the battalion?"

"No, sir we lost touch with them at Cahagnes when our signaller stepped on a mine. We moved south after that. Then a couple of days ago we ran into Jerry, and two of my men were wounded."

"How bad are they?"

"Walking wounded, sir."

"I see," said the officer, "Well, thankfully we have a field hospital where they can get some treatment."

"Thank you, major."

"You and the rest of your men can billet yourselves in one of the tents across the road. You're a bit late for a meal I'm afraid but no doubt the field kitchen can rustle you up some tea and sandwiches."

"We've also got a civilian with us, sir, a Frenchwoman. She helped patch up my men, so I brought her along with us. "She's a trained nurse," said Clemens, "and she speaks good English."

"It's highly irregular, sergeant," replied the officer, pausing to reflect on the matter. "Although I suppose at times like this, we can never have too many nurses."

"Very true sir."

Very well, take her with you to the hospital. Ask to see Sister Green, she's in charge. Tell her if she can make use of her, she has my blessing."

"Thank you, major."

"Oh, and I will also want a full report from you, sergeant. See that Lieutenant Langhorne has it on his desk first thing tomorrow." Nodding towards the young officer, the telephone still pressed to his ear.

"Certainly, sir."

"We have some reserves coming through tomorrow, part of a push towards Falaise, I'll have you and your men assigned to them."

"Very good, sir. Any news of the 1st Battalion, Major?"

"Yes, they went through a few days ago, so you might very well be meeting up with them."

"I look forward to it," said Clemens, smiling at the prospect of being reunited with his old battalion.

Located on the outskirts of the busy marshalling area, with its circular white hoops inset with a red cross painted on the roof and sides, the large marque housing the field hospital was easy to find. Happily, for C Company it wasn´t far away from the field kitchen either.

Leaving Corporal Clark and the remainder of his men to the mercy of the cook´s goodwill, together with Redman, Yates and Joliane Clemens made his way across to the infirmary, and pulling aside the canvas flap at the entrance, the four of them stepped inside.

In front of them was a wide aisle flanked on both sides by rows of beds, the majority of them occupied by a wounded soldier. Taking a moment to accustom themselves to the artificial light, Clemens spotted a woman walking towards them. Without wishing to be unkind, to say that she was well-built was a bit of an understatement. Perhaps if her khaki battledress uniform with a small watch pinned to it like a medal, had been a size larger it might have diluted the overwhelming impression of bulk a little. Thankfully beneath the white nurse´s cap, she had a kind face. And she was smiling, too which was a good sign.

"Sister Green?" Clemens enquired, hopefully.

"Yes." The nursing sister replied, her voice as warm as her smile. "I see you have brought me some patients?" Eying Yates´s blood-stained jacket.

"A couple of walking wounded." said, Clemens. "Mademoiselle Cabouret here," turning towards Joliane, "has taken very good care of them. She has experience as a nurse, so the major said it would be alright if you could use her help."

Turning to Joliane, Sister Green extended her hand. "Bonjour Mademoiselle Cabouret."

"Bonjour," replied Joliane, "if it is better for you, my English is quite good?"

"Excellent!" replied Sister Green, "sadly my French is very poor, and yes, Mademoiselle, your help would be most welcome."

Relieved that he had found Joliane a place of safety, and with Redman and Yates in good hands, Clemens took his leave. Pausing at the entrance to the marquis, he looked back at Joliane. Inside there were a thousand things he wanted to say to her. But in the end, all he could manage was a weak smile.

And that as they say should have been that. One good deed in exchange for another. But as Albert Clemens was soon to discover, things don't always work out like that.

In the meantime, while Clemens was away attending to medical matters, thanks to Corporal Clark, and the fact that the head cook just happened to come from his home town of Middlesbrough, instead of a round of cheese sandwiches, the men of C Company enjoyed a mouth-watering fry-up of eggs, bacon, sausages and fried bread all washed down with a cup of army tea. And if that wasn't enough good fortune, after scouring the rows of tents, McCormack had managed to find a vacant one, complete with cots and blankets. And it was there, an hour later that Private Redman found them.

"They've taken her Sarge," Redman blurted out, a swathe of clean bandage visible through his open shirt front.

"What are you on about," said Clemens, jumping up from his cot, "who's taken who?"

"Mademoiselle Cabouret Sarge. Two Frenchies have taken her away." Said Redman, clearly agitated. "The Sister tried to stop them, but they just marched off with her cool as you like."

"Shit!" said Clemens, steering Redman out of the tent. "Did you see which way they went?"

"No, Sarge, but one of the buggers had a rifle."

"Good lad," said Clemens, placing a hand on the soldier's shoulder. "Now you go back to the infirmary, I'll deal with this, okay?"

"I'll come with you if you like Sarge?" Redman volunteered.

"No, thanks all the same but I reckon I can handle a couple of Frenchie's."

He could too, thought Redman as he made his way back towards the field hospital. He could handle the whole bloody German Army if he had to.

Clemens's first thought was to go and see the Major. His second thought was to forget it. What was he going to say anyway? "None of our business, Sergeant, it's better if we don't get involved in these local matters" or words to that effect no doubt. Besides, he had obviously given them his blessing because the bastards wouldn't have dared to just waltz in here and take her without his permission.

"You're not thinking of doing anything stupid, are you Albert?" asked Clark.

"Like what?" Snapped Clemens.

"Like going after them."

"I have too Knobby. I can´t just stand by and do nothing."

"Look, you did all you could, it´s out of your hands now."

"Is it?" said Clemens, staring into Clark´s face. "Well, I don´t happen to think so."

"Jesus Christ! Are you off your rocker?", fumed Clark. "What are you going to do, walk up and tap them on the shoulder and say sorry can I have her back please?"

"Don´t be bloody sarky, Nobby. It doesn´t suit you."

"Look, all I´m saying is ..."

But Clemens was already pushing him aside.

"Right lads," said Clemens, running his eyes over the slightly bemused faces of the three privates. "I´ve just got an errand to run so while I´m gone Corporal Clark is in charge, okay?" and retrieving his submachine gun, without another word Clemens slipped out of the tent.

The easy part had been making up his mind on what he had to do. The hard part was going to be finding them. His first thought was that they would probably make their way back towards the convent. It wasn´t far from the village of La Cabosse, and that was where the two Frenchmen were bound to be taking her. What he would do when he finally caught up with them had already been decided. He would simply kill them.

Leaving the road at the spot where hours earlier he had encountered the Bren gun carrier, Clemens set off across the open countryside. Blessed with an inbuilt sense of direction it wasn´t long before he found himself retracing C Companies´ footprints.

Being cooped up in an office five days a week, at weekends his late father had always enjoyed getting out into the countryside. With the New Forest on their doorstep, and assuming Mrs Clemens didn´t have any urgent jobs that needed doing. Or if she and his elder sister Esther had something "girlie" they had to do, like clothes shopping. Outings he was not allowed on because they might involve them buying brassieres or some other items of feminine underwear, things an eight-year-old boy wasn´t supposed to know about (didn´t want to, was more likely). Equipped with an old two man-tent and enough provisions for a couple of days they would enjoy many happy trips together exploring the woods.

Of course, his dad always forgot to bring the compass, even though he swore blind that he had packed it. Which in hindsight was probably how he developed a knack for finding their way back to the tent when they got lost. His dad disagreed of course. Swearing it was all down to the fact that his Great, Great, Great, Grandfather's mother had been an Apache Indian, a tribe well renowned for their tracking skills. All a load of nonsense really, but even so, a small part of him secretly hoped that it was true and that he did have Indian blood in his veins, no matter how diluted it was.

It took less than an hour for him to catch up with them. Fortunately, they were following a path lower down the hillside than the one he was on, one probably used by local hunters. Which meant that he saw them before they saw him. Always an advantage when the one thing you want in your favour is the element of surprise. Fortunately, due to the wooded terrain, they were also being forced to walk in a single file, something else which suited Clemens down to the ground.

Keeping parallel with the lower path, hugging the edge of a tall hedgerow Clemens quickened his pace. Satisfied that he was well ahead of them, camouflaged by the dappled sunlight filtering through the leafy canopy, he began making his way down the wooded slope to the path below.

Taking a moment to catch his breath, resting the Thompson machine gun against the trunk of the tree, Clemens pulled the commando knife out of his gaiter. Although there was a war going on, with the possibility that the sound of gunfire might attract unwanted attention, using the machine gun would be a last resort. Gripping the dagger in his hand, he didn't have long to wait for his unsuspecting quarry to appear. Still walking single file, with Joliane positioned between the two men. Allowing the leading man and Joliane to pass by him, as the second man drew level stepping out from behind the tree, clamping his left hand over the man's mouth, Clemens plunged the dagger into Frenchman's neck. The razor-sharp blade slicing effortlessly through flesh and tissue and severing the man's jugular vein. Alerted by the desperate choking sound made by the dying man, the leading Frenchman spun around, his hand reaching for the Luger tucked into the waistband of his trousers. Alert to the danger, wrenching the dagger free from his victim's neck, Clemens raced towards him. With the man still struggling to free the pistol Clemens plunged the blade deep into the Frenchman's chest, stabbing it into his body five or six times, before taking a step back. With blood dripping from his mouth, fatally wounded, the man's legs gave way.

Cleaning the blood of the blade on the dead man's jacket, Clemens straightened up. A faint smile appearing on his face when he saw Joliane running towards him.

Sobbing with relief, she flung her arms around his neck, clinging to him like a frightened child. "Albert! Albert!"

Waiting until her sobbing had subsided, holding her at arms-length, Clemens stared into her tear-streaked face.

"I promised I would keep you safe, didn´t I?"

They could have left the bodies to be found by scavenging animals but as the path was likely to be used by local hunters Clemens decided the prudent thing to do was hide them. No point in asking for trouble.

Catching sight of what appeared to be a stream or a river below them in the valley bottom, working together, Clemens and Joliane began dragging the bodies of the two men down the wooded slope. Exhausted from their efforts, when they finally reached the river frustratingly, they found that the ribbon of water was barely deep enough to paddle in. Thankfully, after a short excursion downstream at a bend in the river, the flow of water had worn away the riverbed to form a deep pool. A pool which turned out to be deep enough to accommodate the bodies of two dead Frenchmen and a Mauser rifle.

With the men´s bodies concealed, Clemens and Joliane made their way back along the narrow path. If he felt any guilt over what he had done it didn´t show. As far as Clemens was concerned when the two men had discovered that Joliane had left the convent they should have just called it a day. Perhaps if they had, they wouldn´t be laying at the bottom of a river. For Joliane of course it was different. Both men had been her comrades in the Marquis. They had fought together against the Boche, the Germans. But at the end of the day, what mattered most was that without any real proof that she had indeed collaborated with the Gestapo these so-called comrades were about to put her up against a wall and shoot her. No, just like Clemens her conscience was clear they had deserved to die.

Even though Nobby Clark wasn´t really surprised to see Mademoiselle Cabouret and Clemens standing in front of him when the tent flap was pulled back, just for a moment he was still lost for words.

Clemens didn´t know what to say either, so both men just stared at one another. Leaving the pleasantries to Hopkins.

"Hello Miss, here come and sit down," said Hopkins, pointing to a vacant camp bed.

Touched by his concern, conscious not to expose too much of her legs, Joliane seated herself beside him.

"I need a word, Nobby." said Clemens.

And leaving Joliane in the care of a delighted Hopkins, both NCOs stepped outside.

"I see you found her then." said Clark. "So, what happens now?"

"A Jeep, I need a Jeep," said Clemens.

"Oh, riding off into the sunset, are we," Clark replied before he could bite his tongue.

"You could say that", said Clemens, ignoring his friend´s sarcastic remark. "I just need to get her to somewhere where she will be safe, Nobby."

"And what about the two Frenchie´s?"

"They won´t be bothering her again."

Silly bloody question thought Clark. Poor buggers never stood a chance.

"So, where are you going to go? I mean there is a war going on or had you forgotten?"

"There´s bound to be a town that´s not too far away. Somewhere where nobody will know her."

"Well, it´s, worth a try I suppose," Clark replied, even though he had his doubts.

"I´ll just drop her off and be back here before you know it." said Clemens.

Try as he might, Clark couldn´t stop himself from grinning. Lord knows why because inside he was angry. Very bloody angry, because despite what Clemens had just said, deep down Nobby knew he wouldn´t be coming back. He had seen the looks Clemens had given her, the growing attraction between them, and he knew this wasn´t about helping the Frenchwoman escape the clutches of the Marquis. But what made Clark´s blood boil was that Clemens could just go off and abandon his wife and child like that. And over what? Some stupid argument they had, had when he was on leave. No, you don´t go running off with another woman because of something like that, not in his book anyway. There was also the small matter of desertion. Because if he did get got caught, Clemens would almost certainly end up spending the rest of his life in prison. Yet despite all that, he couldn´t bring himself to hate him for what he was doing. In fact, if he did say anything to him right now, he would probably call him a silly bugger.

As it was, Clemens wasn´t fooled by the grin either. He knew what Clark must be thinking of him. How much he must despise him for what he was doing. Yet despite that, he still couldn´t bring himself to tell him the real reason for going off with Joliane. To tell him the truth. To explain why helping this woman had become so important to him. To share the feelings of grief and anger which were eating away at him, day after day. He knew if he did Clark would understand, and he would forgive him. Support him even. But sadly, the words wouldn´t come. One day perhaps but not today.

As it turned out the real sadness for both men, was that because of Clemens´s reticence to confide in him, Clark would never discover what had driven Clemens to do what he did that day. Or atone for the false judgment he had made which would blight their friendship for the rest of his life. And for two men who had been comrades in arms for so many years, this was a terrible price to pay for something so simple as a missed opportunity.

"Well, if it´s a Jeep you need, I am told Uttley is your man. There´s not much he doesn´t know about vehicles, even Yankee ones."

After holding a meaningless conversation with a REME mechanic busy stripping down the engine of a Bedford QL with a blown head gasket, after wishing him luck, Uttley wandered across to the row of parked Jeeps on the far side of the vehicle park. One, in particular, caught his eye; the census number stencilled on the side of the bonnet was M5844677 and as seven was his lucky number he took it to be a good omen.

With its canvas roof folded back, the layer of dust on the jeep´s seats could mean one of two things; that it was a "non-runner" or that it wasn´t being used very much. Hoping for the latter, Uttley eased himself into the driver´s seat. Normally, his first job would have been to check the vehicle´s oil and water but on this occasion, he thought it best to skip the inspection, and just get down to the business at hand, namely stealing it.

A simple enough layout, thought Uttley, running his eyes over the instrument panel, and after easing out the hand throttle and the choke, turning on the ignition, he pressed his right boot down on the foot start. The sound made by the L 134 "Go Devil" as it spluttered into life music to his ears. And after making some adjustments to the throttle, and choke, he soon had the 6-horsepower engine purring like a kitten.

Bearing in mind the object of the exercise, the fact that the vehicle park was a hive of activity suited Uttley perfectly. The busier the better as far as he was concerned. Unfortunately, it was also being patrolled by MPs. With this thought in mind, as a precaution, Uttley had applied some "mechanics make-up" to his arms and face; smudges of oil gleaned from the engine block the mechanic had been working on. With the Jeep´s engine ticking over nicely, spotting a couple of lorries driving towards him, slipping the Jeep into gear Uttley edged his way out from the line of parked jeeps. Falling in behind the two lorries, keeping to the ten-mile-an-hour speed limit, he followed them out onto the road.

It was hard to tell who was pleased the most when the Jeep pulled up at the prearranged spot half a mile north of the marshalling area, Uttley or Clemens.

"One Jeep all present and correct," said Uttley, applying the handbrake. "She´s got a full tank and there´s a full Jerry can on the back."

"Good man, Uttley."

"All in the line of duty, Sarge."

Merci, Uttley mon cher ami," said Joliane, smiling warmly at the English soldier who had risked so much for her.

Blushing slightly, totally unfazed by the fact that she was now wearing Hopkin´s spare battledress jacket and McCormack´s beret, Uttley watched as Joliane climbed into the passenger seat.

"Take good care of her, Sarge," said Uttley, hoping the NCO didn´t think he was referring to the Jeep.

"I will," Clemens replied, staring up at the young soldier. Looking back, he had always thought that by ending up in the seventh battalion along with a load of territorials, he had drawn the short straw. Now he knew just how wrong he had been. And how proud he was to have served with them.

"Get home safely, lad," said Clemens, fighting back the first real pang of regret. "And that´s a bloody order."

Although Private Uttley was well aware that one didn´t salute non-commissioned officers, as the Jeep sped off down the dusty road, he saluted anyway.

Chapter Five

Avranches – Normandy

Having driven in silence along a road devoid of traffic for just under an hour, Clemens was suddenly faced with a decision. Bringing the Jeep to a stop, staring through the grimy windscreen he fixed his gaze on the make-shift signpost. The first thing that struck him was that although there were four possible directions for them to take the signpost only had three arms. One pointed northwest with Saint Lo daubed on it in white paint, another pointing southwest with the name Avranches painted on it, with the third pointing in the direction they had just come from. Thankfully, this didn´t present too much of a problem, and with Saint Lo not an option, ignoring the unmarked road leading off to his left, Clemens slipped the Jeep into gear.

"It looks like we are going to Avranches Mademoiselle."

"C´est parfait. That´s perfect" said Joliane, smiling at his mispronunciation of the town´s name.

An hour later, as they climbed out of the densely wooded Vire valley, and into the bocage countryside Joliane spotted the tower of the Saint Gervais Basilica away in the distance like a welcoming beacon. She had visited the town on three previous occasions, the most memorable being when accompanied by her parents she had taken her first communion at the Cathedral Notre-Dame-Des-Champs. Now, approaching it for the fourth time, for reasons she couldn´t quite understand, she found herself filled with a strange sense of foreboding.

A mile further on, with the feeling persisting, Joliane suddenly found herself thrown sideways in her seat as yanking on the steering wheel, Clemens pulled the Jeep off the road.

"Looks like a military roadblock up ahead, you had better hide in the back."

Without a word, squeezing between the two seats, Joliane clambered into the rear and pulling the bedding roll which she found on the floor on top of her, she curled up on the narrow back seat.

With a quick glance over his shoulder, satisfied that Joliane was hidden from view, Clemens pulled back onto the road and frantically searching his brain for a reason that would explain his journey, he drove towards the roadblock.

As he approached the barrier, with the germ of an idea forming in his mind, Clemens´s first stroke of luck was that judging by their uniform the two soldiers manning the temporary roadblock were American. Had they been British soldiers, explaining why he was driving across France on his own would have proved a hell of a lot more difficult. Even more encouraging was the fact that both of them appeared to be Privates. Well, thought Clemens, bringing the Jeep to a halt in front of the barrier, let's see if he could bullshit his way out of this one.

"Howdy sergeant," said the young GI, taking in the chevrons on the sleeve of Clemens's jacket, "what brings you to this neck of the woods?"

Although Clemens wasn't too familiar with American dialects, at a guess, he would have said that this particular soldier was more corn on the cob than a city slicker. He would have been right too. Born and raised in Nebraska Private Levi Nelson was a Cornhusker through and through. Yes, Siree.

"A mission of mercy soldier," said Clemens, offering up a broad smile.

"Say, you ain't a padre, are you? Only if you are then maybe you oughta be wearing one of them their dog collars so folks would know."

"No, I'm not a padre," replied Clemens, puzzled as to why the GI should assume that the two things were somehow related. "Maybe what I should have said was I'm on a rescue mission."

"Yeah, that sure sounds a whole lot better. Ain't that right Ed?

Ed, or Edward as he preferred to be called, didn't bother replying. After standing beside this God-forsaken patch of road for close to three hours now, he was too bored to care. Not to mention being driven crazy by his fellow Americans' corn-fed philosophy on how they should go about winning the war. A topic which had dominated the conversation ever since they had come on duty. No, this particular Bostonian was leaving everything in the hands of his fellow sentry. And with his sympathies on the side of the British soldier, who unless he was lucky could be spending a very long time enduring the ramblings of "Nebraska man," he strolled away towards the shade of the trees.

"It seems my colonel has gone and got himself lost in Rennes," lied Clemens, having previously learned that the city had been liberated on the 4th of August, "and I've been sent to fetch him."

"Shucks, how did he manage to do that?"

"If I knew that, Private, believe me, I would tell you." said Clemens, hoping that by reminding the GI of his inferior rank it might somehow help to bring their conversation to an end. "All I know is if I don't get there soon, I'm going to find myself in a whole lot of trouble. You know what I mean?"

Thankfully, he did, and without another word, Levi Nelson walked across to the barrier, and putting his weight on the counterbalance, he raised the red and white striped pole into the air.

Waving his arm as a "thank you" with a sigh of relief, Clemens pulled away, glancing in the rear-view mirror as the roadblock slowly faded into the distance.

"Are you alright back there?"

"Oui Monseigneur," said Joliane. "Perhaps when we are alone you can take my confession, no?" Her voice infused with piety.

"Perhaps, but then again I might just put you over my knee instead."

"Such a punishment is permitted in your church?" replied Joliane, in feigned amazement. Secretly delighted that her knight in shining armour also possessed a sense of humour.

"Oh, yes," said Clemens, a mental picture of Joliane´s shapely bottom flashing before his eyes. "It is most definitely permitted."

Driving on in silence, it wasn´t long before the reason for the roadblock became apparent. They had entered what appeared to be an American supply depot. A big one too, judging by the number of large canvas tents erected down both sides of the road. Conscious that they had nothing in the way of food, having safely negotiated the roadblock Clemens decided to chance his luck once more.

Continuing past the lines of GIs ferrying boxes of supplies to the waiting trucks he pulled up outside one of the tents.

Seated at a trestle table just inside the tent flap, the Corporal looked up as Clemens stepped inside.

"Howdy."

"Hello," ventured Clemens, hoping that the cheery smile on the soldier´s face was a good omen.

"Something I can do for you, sergeant?"

"As a matter of fact," replied Clemens, glancing at the rows of crates and boxes. "I was hoping to scrounge some food from you?"

"You guys run out already, have you?" joked the corporal.

"No," replied Clemens, smiling, "just me. I left in a bit of a hurry."

"So, where you headed, only I thought we were supposed to be handling things in this sector."

"That´s right, only somehow one of our bloody officers has managed to end up in Rennes," said Clemens, repeating the lie. "And I´ve drawn the short straw."

"Wouldn´t you just know it," said the corporal, sympathetically. "They go getting themselves in a fix and it´s left to us NCOs to get them out of trouble."

"Something like that," replied Clemens, encouraged by the man´s attitude towards officers in general.

"So, do you think you could help me out?"

"Sure, no trouble." said the corporal, pointing towards the stacks of crates and boxes which filled the tent. "A couple of the crates on the end have been opened, just take what you need."

"Good man," said Clemens, and like the proverbial kiddie in a sweet shop he made his way towards the two opened crates. Whatever else their soldiers might die of thought Clemens it certainly wasn´t going to be starvation. Pushing aside the lid of the first crate, he stared at the neatly stacked rows of cardboard boxes, each stamped "12 Rations KS". The second crate, its lid propped against the side, also contained a layer of boxes, two of which he noticed had been opened. These were simply labelled "canned fruit." While not sure what K-rations were, assuming that the twelve probably meant twelve days of meals, returning to the first crate Clemens helped himself to one of the cardboard boxes. Tempted by the cans of fruit but not wanting to abuse the corporal´s generosity by taking a whole box. Clemens solved the dilemma by stuffing four of the tins from an opened box inside his battledress jacket.

Having transferred his bounty to the passenger seat of the jeep, keen to express his gratitude, Clemens returned to the tent.

"Thanks again, you´ve been a lifesaver."

"Glad to help out." said the GI. "Say, are you a coffee drinker, Sarge?"

"Yes, not that we ever see any mind you. Coffee is as rare as hen´s teeth in our lot." said Clemens, hoping the corporal was familiar with the idiom.

"Here you go then." And like a magician pulling a rabbit from a hat the NCO placed a sealed package on the table. "Courtesy of the 83rd Division."

"That´s kind of you corporal. I´m much obliged."

"Be my guest," said the NCO, watching as Clemens stuffed the packet of ground coffee into a trouser pocket. "Good luck on getting to Rennes."

"Thanks, I might need it." Clemens replied. "Say, can I still get through Avranches?"

"I guess it´s possible. Only from what I hear your fly-boys sure made one hell of a mess of it."

"We bombed it?"

"You sure did. Made a pretty good job of it too, not much of it left standing."

"But you reckon I can still get through?"

"Well, our armoured guys have cleared most of the main streets with their bulldozers, so as long as you stick to them you should be okay. The Pontaubault bridge is still in one piece so you can still get across the river okay."

More disturbed than relieved by the soldier´s revelations, with the prospect of Avranches providing a safe haven for Joliane thrown into doubt, Clemens made his way towards the entrance to the tent.

"Have a good war, Corporal," Clemens called over his shoulder, "and thanks again for the rations."

"You, too, Sarge, I sure hope this officer appreciates the trouble you´re going to, to save his butt."

"I doubt it", said Clements pushing aside the tent flap, and leaving the Corporal to his paperwork, stepping outside into the warm sunshine, he made his way back to the Jeep.

"We are not far from Avranches," said Clemens in a low voice, as he climbed into the driver´s seat. "I´ll let you know when it´s safe for you to come out, okay?"

"Oui, Albert."

Smiling, Clemens fired the engine into life and praying that the Corporal´s assumption was correct, he pulled away. Having resisted the temptation to top up with fuel from one of the fuel tankers parked alongside the road, after driving for about five miles, turning onto the N176 Clemens made his way towards the town of Avranches.

Fifteen minutes later, with very little traffic on the road, military or civilian, pulling into the roadside, Clemens brought the Jeep to a stop.

"It´s safe for you to come out now."

Delighted by the prospect of breathing fresh air again, freeing herself from the roll of bedding, Joliane climbed out of the back seat. Stretching her arms above her head, she watched with interest as Clemens began transferring the rations he had acquired onto the backseat.

"We have food!"

"Yes, but first we need to find somewhere safe to stay," said Clemens, as Joliane climbed into the passenger seat beside him. "Avranches here we come."

Whatever she had expected to see, it wasn´t this. A town in ruins. Laid to waste as if some angry giant had trampled through it tearing off roofs and crushing the buildings with his fists. The sight of burnt-out vehicles and the bloated corpses of horses, some still in their shafts littering the road should have served as a warning. Should have prepared her for the worst. But it hadn't.

Following the Corporal's advice, by sticking to the recently cleared main road with all hope of the town being a safe place for Joliane to stay gone, Clemens began looking around for a bolt hole in one of the side streets. Somewhere among the pulverised landscape of windowless facades of houses and shops where they could hide out for a while, and plan what to do next.

Moving along the rubble-lined street, they came across small groups of people standing on street corners, huddled together like lost sheep. Touched by their plight, Joliane waved at them as they passed by, but none responded, simply staring back at her with hollow eyes. Their minds and bodies were numbed by the destruction which surrounded them.

As they passed one old man sitting on a wooden chair beside the side of the road, he suddenly began shaking his fist at them. The same fist he had shaken on the 7th of July at the waves of Lancaster bombers as they rained down death and destruction from the sky. The same old man who had watched without a grain of pity as the stricken bomber, its starboard engine ablaze, had begun its death spiral. The same old man whose wife's body was still entombed in the ruins of what had once been their home. The same old man who, like the seven-man crew of the doomed bomber, had paid a high price for Avranches so-called liberation.

With many of the narrow roads leading off from the main street clogged with fallen brick rubble, after finding one that looked as though it might be passable, Clemens turned into it. Navigating through the heaps of fallen masonry, he suddenly found himself confronted by a tall double-fronted building. It seemed that what he thought was a side road was really a cul-de-sac.

Faced with the unenviable task of reversing back down the rubble-strewn length of road, spotting a pair of tall wooden doors set into the wall alongside the building, Clemens walked across to them. Judging them to be wide enough to accommodate the vehicle, putting his shoulder against one of the doors, he forced it open. With the second door proving just as accommodating, returning to the Jeep, he drove through the narrow gateway into what appeared to be a large courtyard, surrounded on three sides by a three-story building.

Switching off the engine, Clemens stared out at the towering buildings. Two of them were little more than windowless facades, their gutted interiors clogged with rubble. The third however looked more promising. One of its chimney stacks and part of the roof had collapsed but the majority of the windows were still intact, some even had glass in them. Although the brickwork showed evidence of structural damage, unlike the other two buildings, it didn´t look in danger of collapsing.

Having convinced himself that the house was habitable, and with room in the courtyard to turn the jeep, helping Joliane down, Clemens walked towards the door at the back of the building.

Thankfully, just like the gates, it was also unlocked and pushing it open Clemens stepped into what appeared to be the family kitchen.

"This should do nicely," said Clemens, looking around the spacious room.

"But what of the family who lives here?" asked Joliane, a little concerned that they might have just broken into someone´s home.

"If they had any sense they would have left," said Clemens, and leaving Joliane to discover what the kitchen had to offer in the way of amenities, he made his way towards the door. "I´ll bring in the things from the Jeep. Why don´t you try the tap and see if we have any water?"

Reassured by his words, picking her way through the lumps of ceiling plaster which had fallen onto the tiled floor, Joliane walked across to the deep porcelain sink set under the window.

"We have water, Albert," said Joliane, as Clemens returned, the box of K-rations tucked under one arm, and the bedding roll under the other.

"See!" exclaimed Joliane excitedly, pointing at the steady flow of water coming out of the tap.

"That´s good." said Clemens, dumping the K-ration on the table, and the bedding roll onto the floor. "Maybe we should fill a few of those," pointing towards a collection of copper pans hanging below a wall shelf, "just in case."

"You are always so sensible," said Joliane, smiling brightly.

For the next half an hour, wielding the broom they had discovered in one of the cupboards, with Joliane having filled all but two of the pans with water, together they set about transforming the kitchen into something more habitable. Pleased with what they had achieved, motivated by the prospect of a hot meal, they turned their attention to the stove.

Having reassured Joliane that the smoke from the fire was unlikely to attract attention, Clemens focused on finding some fuel. The kitchen chairs were obvious candidates. Two of them had already been badly damaged by the collapsed ceiling, so it wasn't as though they were of much use anyway. And of course, there was always the table. Although, thankfully, the need to turn that particular piece of furniture into firewood was to prove unnecessary when Joliane discovered a scuttle filled with coal in another of the cupboards.

Placing the broken pieces of chair, and several lumps of coal into the firebox, setting alight to the old newspaper they had discovered in a cupboard drawer, Clemens watched as the flames took hold. Satisfied with his efforts, he turned his attention to the exciting part, at least it was for Joliane, of opening the box of food kindly donated to them by the US Army.

Already seated at the table, with her chin resting in her cupped hands like an inquisitive child, Joliane watched intently as Clemens tore open the lid of the cardboard box. The expression on her face changing from curiosity to delight as he removed three oblong packages, each with its distinctive colouring and placed them on the table.

"C'est merveilleux, really wonderful", said Joliane, staring at the lettering on each of them. "And so clever to prepare food this way."

"Well, at least we won't be going hungry," said Clemens. "Which one do you think we should try?"

"Perhaps, as it is late, we should have that one, Joliane replied, pointing at the green box with the word Supper printed on it.

"Supper it is then", said Clemens, and tearing open the package, he emptied the contents onto the table, a tin of beef and pork loaf, a bar of chocolate, a bouillon cube, a packet of Chesterfield cigarettes, and a stick of chewing gum.

"And people eat such things for supper?" Joliane enquired, staring at the items in disbelief.

"Well, I guess Americans do," replied Clemens, "maybe we should open another one?"

"Oui, perhaps that one", said Joliane pointing to another of the boxes.

Happy to oblige, tearing open the box marked Dinner Clemens tipped out the contents; a tin of cheese and bacon, a packet of biscuits, four caramel bars, more Chesterfield cigarettes, a book of matches, packets of salt and sugar, and more chewing gum.

"For me, this is very strange", said Joliane, sitting back in the chair.

"Yes, but you have to remember that these are for a soldier. A way to survive when he is on his own."

"I suppose," said Joliane, shrugging her shoulders.

"Maybe this will cheer you up", said Clemens, suddenly remembering the coffee the American corporal had gifted him, and unbuttoning his pocket, he removed the packet of coffee.

It did too, as the pout on her face was instantly replaced by a beaming smile.

"So, what would Mademoiselle prefer? Beef and pork loaf or cheese and bacon?"

"I think for me the cheese."

"Good, then I´ll have the beef and pork," said Clemens, and retrieving the two tins, and the bouillon cube, which was in with the dinner option, he made his way across to the stove. Minutes later, after diluting the bouillon cube in hot water, and emptying the contents into two small pans, he placed them onto the stove.

Eager to contribute in some way, with the aroma of cooking wafting through the kitchen, abandoning her seat at the table, Joliane began scouring the cupboards for items of crockery and cutlery.

She located the crockery first. Plates and dishes of varying sizes all neatly stacked in one of the wall cupboards. The cutlery she found in one of the drawers. What Joliane also discovered in another of the cupboards was a wine rack. Better still, it was full. All classic vintages judging by the labels on the bottles. Whoever the owners of the house were they certainly had a taste for fine wine. Plus, a healthy bank account too. Bottles of Chateauneuf-du-Pape, Rothschild Chateau Lafite, and Chateau Latour were not cheap.

Selecting a bottle of Chateau Latour, a vineyard renowned for producing one of France´s finest Cabernet Sauvignon Merlots, Joliane returned to the cutlery drawer in search of a corkscrew. Frustrated by her lack of success, with Clemens about to serve up their meals bottle in hand, she returned to the table.

"Here give it to me", said Clemens reaching for the bottle.

Curious to know how he intended to open it she followed him across to the sink. Having repeated the trick countless times, holding out the bottle, striking downwards with the dagger, Clemens succeeded in decapitating without spilling a drop.

Smiling up at him as he poured the wine into two glasses, once again Joliane found herself amazed by the ingenuity of the man; was there anything he couldn´t do?

The meal was eaten in silence, and while it was not something they would have chosen to cook for themselves, helped by several glasses of wine, and supplemented by the oatmeal biscuits, the meal exceeded all their expectations.

"Merci Albert", said Joliane, "So, now my knight in shining armour is also a chef."

"Perhaps I should open a restaurant?" joked Clemens.

"Oui. Le Café Albert," said Joliane, raising her glass. "It sounds good, no?"

"And perhaps you could be my waitress? I would even give you your very own corkscrew", teased Clemens.

"So, now you make fun of me", Joliane replied, pouting her lips.

"Time for some coffee", said Clemens, ignoring her performance and pushing back the chair he made his way across to the sink. Filling a small pan with water, he walked across to the stove. "Maybe we should try some of that chocolate too?"

Quickly forgiving him for poking fun at her, with the aroma of coffee in her nostrils and spurred on by the mention of chocolate, an extravagance she had not indulged in for a very long time, Joliane made her way to the crockery cupboard in search of cups and saucers.

"Merveilleuse, wonderful", said Joliane, licking the melted chocolate from her fingers like a cat cleaning its paw. Oblivious to Clemens gaze, and the pleasure, he was getting from watching her. With all trace of chocolate removed, seducing Clemens with a beguiling smile, holding out her cup, she watched as he topped it up with the remains of the coffee.

Having smoked the last of his Player Navy Cut cigarettes back at the convent, Clemens reached for one of the packets of Chesterfields lying on the table. Removing two of the cigarettes, handing one to Joliane, he flicked his lighter into life.

"My first American cigarette", said Joliane, inhaling a mouthful of smoke. Quite surprised to find that it was not as strong as she was expecting, surprisingly mild in fact, and very enjoyable.

With the daylight outside beginning to fade, seated across from each other at the table, wreathed in smoke the pair retreated into their thoughts. Two people who until a few days ago were complete strangers, thrown together by a chance encounter.

What would her Pere, her father think of her now? Joliane wondered to herself, and of the woman, she had become. And what would he think of this beautiful English soldier to whom she owed so much? Deep down she knew he would have approved of her decision to join the Marquis. Even though he was not a young man anymore, she knew he would have done the same thing had he been alive. She also knew that he would have given Albert his blessing. After all, he had been a soldier himself in the Great War. Although she had only been five when he returned, she could still remember the bandage across his eyes where he had been blinded by an exploding shell. He had never complained. I am one of the fortunate ones he would tell her. Thousands of his fellow soldiers would never be coming home he said. Besides, he could still feel the rain and the sun on his face. Still hear the birds sing and the sound of our voices. Best of all he told her in secret, something he swore she must never tell her mother, was that he would never see his wife grow old. That she would always be the beautiful young girl he had married.

"You look tired", said Clemens, interrupting her thoughts. "Why not lie down, and get some sleep?"

"And you will wash up the dirty plates?" asked Joliane, stubbing out her cigarette.

"No, you can wash them up in the morning."

"So, now I am to be a housemaid," said Joliane, threatening to throw her cup at him while at the same time trying unsuccessfully not to smile.

"Okay, we´ll do them together", said Clemens. "Or better still, let the owners do it when they come back."

It was the last remark, spoken in all innocence which brought Joliane back down to earth. Just what would tomorrow bring? What was to become of her when he left? Filled with uncertainty it was then that she knew she had to ask the question she feared most, regardless of what the answer might be.

"Tomorrow you will leave, yes?"

"I don´t have to leave." Clemens replied, looking into her eyes. "I don´t want to leave".

"But you are a soldier", said Joliane, taken by surprise at his reply.

"I am also a man. A man who is sick of war, sick of all the killing."

"But what will you do?"

"That depends a lot on you."

"I don´t understand?"

"I want a new beginning, Joliane, I want a new life. Would you share it with me?"

It was the first time that he had called her by her Christian name, which surprised her almost as much as the statement he had just made. Could he really mean what he had just said? That he would turn his back on everything just to be with her? And, if he did what would this new life mean for her? So many questions. But only one answer. YES! YES!

"Oui," I too would like a new beginning, Albert, un nouveau depart," said Joliane, tears trickling down her cheeks. "Yes, I would like that very much."

Reaching out, Clemens placed his hand on hers. A physical link between two strangers who were about to embark on a new life together.

"But do you not have a family in England?" Joliane asked.

"No, there is no family." Clemens replied pulling his hand away. "Now no more questions, okay? We can talk about things tomorrow." And getting up from his chair he walked over to where he had left the bedding roll.

"It´s not a proper bed, but it´s better than a tiled floor", said Clemens, unrolling the bedding.

"And where will you sleep?"

"I´ll use the seats in the Jeep. Now get some rest." And picking up the packet of Chesterfields lying on the table he walked towards the door.

Stretched out full-length on the bedroll, filled with a sense of contentment, Joliane stared up at the damaged ceiling. A few days ago, all that lay ahead of her was the prospect of her imminent death. Her life forfeited for a crime she didn´t commit. But now thanks to this English soldier she had the chance of a new life. What that life would be only time would tell. For now, all that mattered was that she was safe, and whatever the future had in store, at least she now had someone to share it with.

Sitting behind the steering wheel, a cigarette between his fingers, although more profound, Clemens was also reflecting on the decision they had made. This new life they were both about to embark on together. He hadn´t lied to her. There was no family for him to go back to. No wife and child waiting to welcome him home when the war was finally over. He had simply chosen not to tell her why. What good would it have done anyway, none. No, that part of his life would always remain a secret. Hidden away, just like the small black and white photograph tucked in his wallet, a photograph he still couldn´t bring himself to look at.

Perhaps if he had found the courage to tell Nobby things might have been different. He had wanted to confide in his old friend, not knowing why he wouldn´t. After all the years they had spent together they were almost like brothers. "Laurel and Hardy" their old Regimental Sergeant Major used to call them, Nobby being the short, skinny one of the pair. They had even come down with malaria at the same time for goodness' sake, for which Nobby blamed him of course. Swearing blind, that it had been Clemens's idea to visit the brothel in Cairo in the first place. They had laughed about it afterwards of course. I mean how many blokes come out of a brothel without catching a dose of syphilis but end up with malaria instead?

Where would he have begun? How do you tell somebody about something like that? To go over it again in your mind, to relive the moment in words. To experience the horror, and the pain all over again. Even now, if he closed his eyes, he could still visualise it. Like watching a homemade film projected onto the living room wall, the short walk from the station up to their little house in Windmill Road. The look of surprise on Lizzie's face when she opened the door. He hadn't told her he had been given forty-eight hours leave after the spell in the hospital, wanting it to be a surprise and young Sam running down the hall towards him, with the teddy bear Albert had brought home for him on his last leave clutched in his arms.

It had been such a lovely sunny day, that they had visited the local park in the afternoon. With Sam making a beeline for the swings as always, and Lizzie chastising him for pushing the boy too high. Then stopping off at Mrs Mobbs Corner shop on the way home for ice cream. Precious moments shared as a family.

Then had come the chance encounter with their neighbour Mr Berryman which was to change everything.

He had just finished cutting his front lawn when they arrived home. "Hello Albert." Berryman had called over the fence that separated the two houses, "I'm just off down the pub, you fancy coming for a pint?"

Clemens hadn't wanted to go. Oh, he enjoyed a drink as much as the next man but Mr Berryman wasn't exactly good company. Somehow, he always seemed to find something to belly-ache about. A spell in the army would have soon sorted him out but somehow, he had managed to fail his medical. Anyway, Lizzie said he should go. She wanted to bath young Sam before bedtime and then she had dinner to see too. So reluctantly, he accepted the man's invitation.

They had been on their second pint when they heard the explosion. The blast rattling the windows in the saloon bar. Slamming down their glasses they dashed outside. "The shelter" Berryman shouted but Albert was already running as fast as he could down the street.

He had found Sam's red tricycle standing in the road outside the house without a scratch on it. Except now there was no house. Number 43

Windmill Road, the end terrace that, he and Lizzie had lived in since they were married was now just a smouldering pile of rubble.

In the eerie silence, he could have sworn he had heard them calling out to him as he tried desperately to scramble over the mound of shattered bricks. But in reality, it was just the sound of his voice ringing in his ears as he called out their names. Hours later when the A.R.P (Air Raid Precaution) wardens eventually brought out their bodies, each wrapped in a blanket they wouldn't let him look at what they were carrying. He hadn't argued with them. There was no point really. All he had wanted to know was that there was no hope of them being alive.

Most of the people living in the street wondered why the sirens hadn't gone off. Herbert Wilson the local ARP warden said it was probably because it was just the one lone aircraft. A Heinkel most likely, dumping the last of its bombs before crossing the channel.

As it turned out, he couldn't have been more wrong. The plane responsible for dropping the 500-pound bomb on Clemens's house had been English, not German. An RAF Mosquito from the 627 Squadron based at an airfield in Woodhall Spa in Lincolnshire.

The Mosquito had been part of a pre-D-Day raid on the bridges over the river L'Orne where three of its 500-pound bombs had successfully found their target. It was on the return flight, when the fault with the mechanism for releasing the bomb which had previously malfunctioned chose to rectify itself, a cruel twist of fate which would change Albert Clemens's life forever.

Joliane woke to the unmistakable aroma of coffee brewing, and the sight of Clemens, his sleeves rolled up standing beside the stove with a frying pan in his hand.

"Bonjour Albert", said Joliane, pulling herself upright and stretching her arms above her head.

"Bonjour to you too. Did you sleep okay?"

"Oui", said Joliane, climbing to her feet. "Are we having breakfast?"

"Yes, breakfast American style", said Clemens, picking up the can he had just opened. "According to the label we are about to enjoy chopped ham and eggs."

"But how is that possible, there are no eggs?"

"I think they mean dried eggs."

"Sacre Bleu, I think perhaps Americans are crazy in the head."

"Well," said Clemens, "let's see how it tastes first, shall we? Now go and sit down, I'm hungry even if you are not."

Deciding not to pursue the matter further, pulling out a chair, Joliane seated herself at the table.

"Bon Appetit", said Clemens, scooping a portion of the cooked food onto her plate.

"Merci Monsieur", Joliane replied, applauding his use of French, "soon perhaps we will make you a Frenchman, Oui?"

Well, that´s the plan, thought Clemens as the pair began tucking into the K-ration breakfast.

Although neither of them admitted it, they had both enjoyed the meal. But what impressed Joliane the most was the tin of peaches Clemens had remembered to bring in from the jeep.

With breakfast concluded, sitting across from each other, a Chesterfield in one hand and a cup of coffee in the other, both knew that now was the time to get down to business. Clemens had spent much of the previous night pondering over what lay ahead of them, and he was under no illusions that it was going to be easy. On the plus side, they did have a few things going for them. The most important of which was that they both wanted the same thing. They had transport, although he knew that at some point driving around in a Jeep was not going to be practical. They had a supply of food which if they were careful would last quite a while. More importantly, they had the confusion created by the war. On the downside, his inability to speak the language could be a major issue. Plus, where would they go to? And what would they do when they got there?

It was Joliane who came up with an answer to the language problem.

"It is quite simple, Albert, you must not speak. You must be, how you say, dumb."

Actually, it was quite a brilliant idea. The only downside was knowing what to do if somebody asked him something, especially when he wouldn´t know what the hell they were saying anyway.

"Then we must make little signals between us," said Joliane, determined not to be beaten. "If someone asks if you are hungry, I will rub my tummy. If somebody asks if you are weary, I will yawn. See, it is easy."

Clemens smiled, loving her positivity. Next came the question of their relationship. And once again, she had the answer.

"We should be brother and sister it is how you say not so compliquee, not so complicated.

"So, I am going to be your older brother?"

"Oui, Albert Cabouret, it sounds good, no?"

"I have never had a baby sister before," said Clemens, quite liking the idea. And actually, he quite liked the name too, Albert Cabouret. It had a nice ring to it.

The issue of where to go was a relatively simple one to answer, their only option was to go south. What happened after that, they decided to leave it to chance. As a soldier, especially an NCO thinking on his feet had become second nature to Clemens, so he didn't see why it should change now just because he was a civilian, albeit a French one.

One thing that couldn't be left to chance, was the question of money, and the fact that they didn't have any. This time it was Clemens's turn to come up with a solution. He would rob a bank.

Although Joliane pulled a face when he suggested it Clemens wasn't deterred. The town was bombed to hell, surely there had to be a bank with its front door missing.

"I won't be gone too long," said Clemens, pulling on his jacket. And picking up the Thompson submachine gun he walked towards the door.

As expected, the war-torn town was devoid of people. Those he did come across either ignored him or hurried away. It seemed his uniform had turned him into some kind of pariah. A gang of young boys he came across picking through the rubble of a house had proved a bit of a problem. Thankfully, a threatening gesture with his machine gun soon sent them scurrying away like feral cats.

The first bank he found was quite literally a shell. The brass plate engraved with its name was the only evidence that the building had ever been a bank at all. Shrugging off his disappointment, Clemens moved deeper into the heart of the town. Entering a narrow street, identified by a metal wall plaque as Place Littre, he found himself confronted by the town's War Memorial; a statue of winged victory supporting a wounded soldier. Although it had suffered some superficial damage thankfully the statue had survived the bombing. More importantly, so too had the building on the far side of the square. True, its stone frontage had not escaped unscathed, but the words Bank De France carved into the baroque façade were still visible, and that was all Clemens needed to know. Despite the outward signs of damage, this one definitely had possibilities.

Inviting though it was Clemens decided against gaining entry through the half-open door. With the stonework surrounding it so badly cracked, any attempt to open it would probably have brought the whole frontage crashing to the ground. Undeterred, discovering a narrow passageway which separated the bank from the neighbouring building, Clemens decided to investigate.

Forcing open the wrought-iron gate barring the entrance, hoping for better luck, he made his way towards the rear of the building. Halfway along he found just what he was looking for, a hole in the wall of the building. Judging by the lintel above it, the section of the wall that had collapsed had once been an old doorway. Probably bricked up when it was of no further use. With the supporting lintel undamaged, clambering over the heap of brick rubble, Clemens squeezed his body through the resurrected doorway.

Once inside, the damage to the interior of the building appeared more extensive than he had hoped. There was also evidence of a fire which didn´t bode well. A large part of the roof had collapsed bringing down the ceilings, and leaving a gaping void crisscrossed with the charred remains of beams and rafters. The floor below was littered with lumps of plaster and piles of broken terracotta tiles. Picking his way through the rubble, Clemens made his way towards the front of the building. Even though they were covered by a layer of debris, and badly burned the row of teller´s booths were still recognisable. If there was any chance of finding some money, this is where it would be.

Although it wasn´t all bad news, he still swore. SHIT! The fire had beaten him to it, and where there had once been drawers filled with rows of neatly stacked banknotes all that was left were ashes. Millions of francs were devoured by its all-consuming flames. Looking on the bright side, there were still the coins, thousands of them. Some were still in their drawers; others were scattered on the floor like confetti. Ah well, Beggars can´t be chooser, thought Clemens and without even bothering to check their denomination, he began stuffing handfuls of them into each of his trouser pockets.

With his pockets bulging with coins, as he was making his way towards the narrow opening, a panelled door hanging open like a flag at half-mast caught his eye. Intrigued, scrambling over the remains of the ornate ceiling, Clemens made his way towards what appeared to be an office of some kind. Would this prove to be a lucky find, or more disappointment he wondered? As it happened, it turned out to be a little of both.

Pushing aside the damaged door, Clemens stepped into what turned out to be a vault. A small, windowless room specifically designed to accommodate safety deposit boxes. Two of the three walls were lined with them, floor to ceiling. Neat rows of identical oblong boxes, each with twin keyholes.

The majority had been badly damaged, crushed and buckled by falling masonry. But not all of them. A few had survived and although a little bent out of shape they still appeared salvageable. And that was all the encouragement Clemens needed.

It was a struggle but eventually, using the dagger as a lever, he managed to prise one open. Disappointingly, all he found inside were bundles of old documents tied together by a faded ribbon. The next two boxes contained much the same, some old photographs and what he assumed were more legal documents but nothing in the way of valuables. Frustrated by his lack of success, determined not to be beaten, Clemens set to work on another of the boxes.

After, a quick inspection the fourth box also looked like being a disappointment. But then just as he was about to hurl it against the wall, Clemens spotted what appeared to be a small bag or purse tucked into a corner. After retrieving it from the box, Clemens found that it was a pouch made of what appeared to be velvet. Eager to see what was inside, pulling open the drawstring, he emptied the contents onto the palm of his hand. Diamonds! Twenty of them at least. Maybe more. Sparkling in the sunlight flooding in through the hole in the roof. Hardly daring to believe his luck, Clemens stared at the stones. All were identical in size and colour and appeared to have been cut in the same way. What a find. They may not be hard cash but Clemens wasn´t too concerned. Diamonds were diamonds, and he was pretty sure somebody would pay good money for these little beauties.

Trying his utmost not to smile, weighted down by the coins, Clemens entered the kitchen. Sitting on one of the chairs nursing a cup of coffee, Joliane looked up at him, expectantly. Unable to keep up the pretence a moment longer, dipping a hand into his trouser pocket, grinning like a naughty schoolboy, Clemens began emptying the contents onto the kitchen table.

Several handfuls later, with every coin removed from his uniform pockets, pulling out a chair Clemens seated himself at the table.

"Ah! So now you are a bank robber n´est- pas?"

"Guilty," said Clemens, raising his arms in mock surrender. "It looks a lot but I´m not sure how much it´s worth?"

"But are there no banknotes." said Joliane.

"All burned I´m afraid, this was all there was," said Clemens gesturing towards the pile of coins. "Shall, we count them and see how much we´ve got?"

"Oui, but first I will make you coffee, the robbing of banks is how you say, thirsty work, no?"

Watching as she made her way to the stove, eager to do his bit, Clemens turned his attention to the coins, and spreading them out across the table, he began sorting them into their respective denominations.

"Bravo!" said Joliane, returning to the table with a steaming cup of coffee, and placing it in front of Clemens, she began piling the separated coins into stacks of ten, counting them as she went.

"Nuef mille sept cent cinq francs – Nine thousand seven hundred and five francs", said Joliane, sitting back in her chair, quite exhausted by her coin counting.

To Clemens, this sounded like quite a lot of money. However, judging by the look on Joliane´s face he had the feeling that, he could be wrong.

"I also have a surprise," said Clemens, deciding that now was a good time to play his trump card, removing the velvet pouch from his jacket pocket, pulling open the drawstring, he tipped the diamonds onto the table.

At first, Joliane just stared at them, speechless.

"I know It´s not money," said Clemens, a little unsure of her reaction, "but …"

"Oh, Albert, they are beautiful," she cried, brushing her fingertips over the cluster of diamonds. "Do you think they are real?"

"Well, I found them in a bank, so I think the answer to that is yes."

"So, we are rich," exclaimed Joliane, jumping up from her chair and wrapping her arms around Clemen´s neck.

"Not quite, first, we need to find someone who wants to buy them."

But Joliane´s enthusiasm wasn´t to be denied that easily.

"Poof!" said Joliane, relinquishing her hold on Clemens´s neck. "It will be easy, no? Everyone loves diamonds, n´est-pas?"

"Yes, but before we sell them," said Clemens, "we need to know how much they are worth, and that´s not going to be easy."

"As always you are right," said Joliane, disappointedly.

"Always," Clemens replied, drinking the last of his coffee. "Just you remember that."

At first, he thought she was going to throw her cup at him but thankfully she settled for a withering look instead.

"Well, that just leaves one other thing, said Clemens, "I´m going to need some clothes."

Logically, as they were already inside the house anyway, providing it was safe to do so, they decided that it was probably as good a place as any to start looking.

There was just one door leading off from the kitchen, so praying that he didn´t bring the wall down, Clemens pushed it open.

Cautiously, they entered what was the house´s main entrance hall. Off to the right, at the end of a long hallway was the front door. Although getting to it now would mean clambering over the remains of the missing chimney breast which now filled much of the hallway. To the left, miraculously still intact was a wide balustraded staircase leading up to the floor above.

Staring up at the gaping hole left by the chimney breast, cautiously, Clemens began making his way up the flight of stairs, testing each tread as he went. But even before he had reached halfway it became obvious that if he attempted to go any further there was a strong possibility that the stairs would come away from the wall. Disappointed, he slowly retraced his steps.

"You are too big," said Joliane, the word heavy escaping her. "I will go." And pushing Clemens aside, with one hand gripping the banister, she began climbing the stairs.

"Be careful," shouted Clemens when she had reached the half-landing.

"Oui," Joliane called back, her gaze focused on the second flight of stairs.

Surprisingly, apart from missing a part of its ceiling, the first-floor landing was virtually undamaged. Beyond it, on the side of the house facing onto the street, it was a different story. Although the inner walls of the two bedrooms were still intact, beyond them, their windows and much of the outer wall were gone, exposing the furniture to the elements.

With two doors on the other side of the landing to choose from, selecting the one towards the front of the property which she hoped might be the main bedroom, Joliane made her way inside.

Thankfully, she was right and from the size of the bed, and the quality of the furniture the people who lived here did so in some style. Judging by the unmade bed, and the discarded clothing on the floor, they had obviously, left in a hurry. Confident that the room would provide her with all she needed, walking across to the large double-fronted wardrobe, Joliane began her search.

Standing at the foot of the staircase Clemens counted off the minutes. What the hell was she doing up there? Exasperated, just as he was about to call out to her, Joliane appeared on the landing, half-carrying, half-dragging a large leather suitcase. With visions of both her and the suitcase tumbling down the flight of stairs, praying that the treads would stand his weight, Clemens made his way up to her and relieving her of the suitcase, hugging the wall, they made their way safely back to the hall.

"So, what did you find," asked Clemens as he hoisted the suitcase up onto the kitchen table.

"Some clothes for you, and for me also."

"Clever girl," said Clemens and before she could stop him, throwing open the lid, he began rummaging through the contents. The jacket and trousers were obviously for him, as was the drab-looking shirt. The remaining items though were most definitely not.

"Non, Albert. Pour Moi! Pour Moi!", cried Joliane, horrified as Clemens held up a pair of lace panties.

"Not sure I can get into these," joked Clemens, trying not to laugh as Joliane snatched them from him, and quickly pushed them out of sight under what looked suspiciously like a woman´s dress.

"Now you must try them on," said Joliane, pointing at the jacket and trousers, her cheeks still flushed with colour.

Obediently, Clemens removed his battledress jacket and retrieving the tan-coloured jacket out of the suitcase, he slipped it on. It wasn´t a bad fit. A little short in the sleeve but at least he could fasten the two buttons.

"Now these," said Joliane, holding out the pair of men´s trousers, an impish grin on her face.

"Merci," Clemens replied, and draping the trousers over the back of a chair, he began removing his gaiters.

"You can turn around now," said Clemens, unbuckling his webbing belt.

"You are a little shy, Monsieur?" replied Joliane as though butter wouldn´t melt in her mouth.

Ignoring the question, stony-faced, Clemens began unbuttoning his flies. A smile creasing his face as she quickly averted her eyes.

"Well, Mademoiselle?"

"Now, you are too tall."

"My mother used to say the same," said Clemens, looking down at the gap between the trouser bottoms and the tops of his boots.

"You must stand on a chair, and I will see if they can be made longer."

Watching as she removed his dagger from its scabbard, with a shrug of the shoulders, Clemens did as he was told. Whatever she had in mind, now was not a good time to argue about it.

Dagger in hand, kneeling on the floor in front of him, using the tip of the blade Joliane began carefully unpicking the stitching around the trouser bottoms.

Although not very wide, the additional material gained by removing the turn-ups made quite a difference, and while not in keeping with the fashion of the day, at least Clemens no longer looked like a Pennsylvanian hillbilly.

Bright and early the next morning, with the problem of his clothes resolved, aware of the ever-present threat of detection, Clemens decided that it was time for them to leave. After burning the opened K-ration cartons, and wrappers in the stove, returning the cutlery and crockery to their respective cupboards they loaded the bedding roll and suitcase onto the jeep. Thankfully, as well as their clothing the case had also proved large enough to accommodate the flour sack containing the coins, and the remaining K-rations. After a final inspection, with the diamonds hidden away in a pocket of his battledress jacket Clemens made his way to the jeep. Having a road map would have been the icing on the cake but, he wasn't too worried. There was only one direction for them to take and knowing the names of towns and villages en route wasn't that important. Where they eventually ended up would be decided by fate, not a map.

Chapter Six

La Chenaie – Pays De La Loire

Their departure from Avranches was much like their arrival two days earlier. Ruined buildings lined every rubble-filled street. People staring at them as though they were from another planet as they drove past. As a precaution, Clemens had changed back into his uniform trousers, and Joliane had put on Redman's battledress jacket. That way if they were stopped, they could stick to the same fabricated story as before, with Joliane playing the part of his interpreter. Although it was a pretty flimsy subterfuge it had worked so far, and given the reason for his journey, the presence of an interpreter shouldn't appear that unusual.

As the GI Corporal had predicted the Pontaubault bridge over the river Selune had escaped the bombing, and once across it, Clemens and Joliane breathed a collective sigh of relief. Although they were far from out of the woods, at least things were looking a whole lot brighter. Now it was just a case of keeping their wits about them and taking each day as it comes.

Without the aid of a map, and with the majority of the roads missing their signposts, Clemens decided that to put as much distance between themselves and Avranches they would take the more direct route. Unfortunately, while the logic was sound what he had not envisioned was the volume of refugees with the same idea. Hundreds of them, all with their possessions packed into boxes and suitcases or piled onto handcarts, and by mid-afternoon, they had barely managed to cover twenty miles.

Conscious of the fact that at some point they would have to complete the transformation into civilians, Clemens also knew that the jeep would have to go. With the importance of remaining as inconspicuous as possible paramount, the sight of two civilians driving around in a British Jeep was bound to look suspicious.

With this in mind, although it slowed their journey even more, whenever they came across an abandoned car or van, in the hope that it was driveable, Clemens would stop and check it out. None of them were of course. Most were riddled with bullet holes after being strafed by the RAF. But he kept looking anyway, just on the off chance. The last thing either of them wanted was to end up on foot. Especially as it involved lugging around a suitcase which seemed to weigh half a ton.

Finally, frustrated by the lack of headway, in the hope that by tomorrow the exodus of people and vehicles would have eased, Clemens decided to call it a day. Although not the start, he had hoped for, at least their journey to a new life together had begun, and that was what mattered most.

Located just far enough away from the road to discourage any refugees with a similar idea, the derelict barn proved the ideal lodgings for the night. Although the flames wouldn't have been seen from the road the smoke would have been a dead giveaway, so Clemens had waited until it was dark before lighting a fire. Puzzled by the need for one on such a warm night, it was only when he produced a frying pan and a small saucepan from the backseat that Joliane realised why. Her rescuer clearly had no intention of them eating cold food. His resourcefulness hadn't ended there either, as much to her delight, among his illegal requisitions was a bottle of wine. Two bottles as it happened. His excuse being, that one of them might have got broken.

The next morning having enjoyed a good night's sleep they were awoken by the unmistakable sound of engines. Hidden from sight behind what remained of the barn's wall, they stared across towards the road. Far from being less congested than they had hoped, it was busier than ever. Only this time it wasn't refugees who were the problem, it was trucks. American ones judging by the white, five-pointed star emblazoned on their doors. A seemingly endless convoy, all heading south towards Rennes. It seemed that day two of their new life had not gotten off to a good start.

With the main road definitely "off limits" the temptation was to stay where they were and wait things out. But the idea didn't appeal to Clemens; far too risky. So, while Joliane began preparing breakfast, a cold one under the circumstances, supplemented by a can of peaches, he set out on foot across the field at the rear of the barn. Hopefully, as the track they had followed to get to the barn continued along the edge of the field, it might just prove to be their salvation.

Half an hour later, he was back. "We're in luck," said Clemens, catching his breath. "There's a track over there which looks like it runs parallel with the road. It might just lead to a farm, but I think it's worth giving it a try."

"You think it is safe Albert?"

"It's safer than staying here."

"But first breakfast, yes?"

"Yes, we'll eat first," said Clemens, eying the opened tin of chopped ham and eggs, and dry biscuits without too much enthusiasm. A nice cup of coffee would have made all the difference but lighting a fire was out of the question.

With the meal over, and everything packed away in the Jeep, keeping the barn between them and the road, Clemens steered the jeep across the un-cultivated field towards the newly discovered track.

As it turned out, the track was, in fact, a made-up road. The compacted earth covered in a layer of tarmac, greatly reduced the risk of the Jeeps" wheels kicking up clouds of dust. Something which might well have brought them to the attention of the American convoy moving along the Avranches road two hundred yards away. Better news quickly followed, when quite unexpectedly, the narrow road veered sharply to the right, taking them away from the main road before doglegging to the left half a mile further on.

Surrounded by open countryside, with the sound of the "Go Devil" engine humming in his ear and the imminent threat of discovery removed, filled with a sense of optimism Clemens continued driving south. No matter what lay ahead of them they were safe enough for now. That was until he rounded the next bend and saw the tank with a black cross painted on its side.

Although he had never come face to face with one before, given its enormous size, Clemens knew right away that straddling the road, less than fifty yards ahead of them was a German Tiger tank.

Slamming his foot down on the brake pedal, Clemen brought the jeep to a juddering halt, and praying they hadn´t been seen, he stared out through the windscreen, his eyes glued to the tank´s turret. Relieved that it showed no sign of swinging towards them, he slammed the Jeep into reverse. But then, just as he was about to accelerate away, he noticed something strange. It appeared the tank had acquired a new crew, and they were most definitely not German. He also noticed that one of its members had something hanging around his neck that he would dearly love to get his hands on.

After giving Joliane a reassuring smile, selecting a forward gear Clemens continued driving towards the tank. Drawing nearer, he noticed the furrows gauged out of the road by cannon shells. Caught out in the open, the Tiger tank appeared to have been strafed, and with one of its caterpillar tracks shattered, it had become a sitting duck. Miraculously though, apart from the damage to the track, the rest of the tank appeared to have escaped unscathed, its heavy armour providing effective protection against the aircraft´s 20 mm shells.

Abandoned by its five-man crew, the tank had now been requisitioned by four local farm boys. Three about the same age, their skinny arms and legs sticking out of rolled-up shirt sleeves and cut-off trousers. The fourth was a couple of years older, probably about twelve, and instead of a shirt and trousers, he was dressed in an old V-necked jumper and a pair of baggy shorts. All had the same pudding-basin style haircut.

Bringing the Jeep to a halt, under the watchful eyes of its new owners; two of them sitting astride the barrel of the 88 mm gun like a pair of bare-back riders, another half-in half-out of a hatch cover, and the older boy, clearly the tank´s new commander seated on top of the Gondola, Clemens and Joliane walked towards the tank.

"What am I to say to them, Albert?"

"Just ask the one with the map case what he wants for it. Offer him some chocolate and chewing gum, that should do the trick." And leaving Joliane to initiate negotiations, Clemens made his way back to the Jeep. Returning moments later with the "trade goods."

"He says if you want it then you must give them cigarettes."

"Tell him we don´t have any cigarettes," said Clemens, sorely tempted to climb onto the tank, and grab the cheeky little bugger by the scruff of the neck.

"Nous n´avons pas de cigarettes a vous donner", Joliane shouted up at the boy.

Unimpressed by her answer, he responded by sticking up his middle finger.

Angered by the boy´s rude gesture, striding back to the jeep, throwing the chocolate, and chewing gum onto the seat Clemens picked up the sub-machine gun.

"Right, get down all of you," shouted Clemens, striding menacingly towards the tank. "Now!"

Terrified by the sight of the machine gun, the four boys scrambled down the tank´s superstructure like a troop of monkeys, forming a line in front of it like naughty schoolboys.

With a face like thunder, Clemens approached the older boy, and slinging the Thompson over his shoulder, he removed the map case from around his neck.

Relieved to discover that there was a map inside, after spreading it out on the bonnet of the Jeep, he turned to Joliane.

"Ask him to show me where we are."

This time there was no rude gesture, just an immediate willingness to comply with Clemens´s request.

With their location on the map pin-pointed Clemens´s mood softened, and succumbing to Joliane´s wishes, he watched as she handed each of the boys a bar of chocolate and a packet of chewing gum from the K-rations. Working on the assumption that young French boys, especially ones living out in the countryside had probably never even heard of chewing gum before, let alone eaten it, he did think about giving them a demonstration. But then decided against it as it would take up valuable time. Besides, even if they did just swallow it, which they probably would it wouldn't kill them.

Thanks to the map, Clemens was now able to plan a route which avoided going through Rennes. A place they certainly needed to steer clear of judging by the number of military vehicles they had seen on the road from Avranches. The town he decided to aim for was Vitre, about twenty-five miles to the east of Rennes. It was far enough from the city to avoid running into American troops but not too far east where there was always the possibility of encountering advancing Allied troops. The only drawback was that to get to Vitre meant crossing the main highway. They could have waited until it was dark of course but that would mean driving with the headlights on, and Clemens wasn't keen on that. With night fighters prowling the skies the sight of a pair of headlights might prove too tempting a target.

To get around the problem he decided to take the bull by the horns and make the crossing through one of the small towns located on the main Avranches road. There were a couple of candidates but in the end, the one he chose was Saint-Aubin-du-Cormier. According to the map, the track they were on now would eventually bring them quite close to it anyway, and if they stayed on the main road through the town, it would take them directly to Vitre.

An hour after leaving the boys to enjoy their chocolate and chewing gum, they reached the road Clemens had identified on the map. Conveniently placed by the roadside was a sign informing them that Saint-Aubin-du-Cormier was four kilometres away. The journey through the miles of open fields had proved uneventful. The only people they encountered were an old couple on a horse-drawn cart piled high with freshly cut alfalfa. The woman had given them a cursory glance from under her wide-brimmed bonnet but other than that they had paid them no attention. Now as they neared the junction with the main highway Clemens suspected all that was about to change.

For once in his life Clemens was happy to be proved wrong. Because as it turned out the main road was completely devoid of traffic. As was Saint-Aubin-du-Cormier itself. Not a vehicle to be seen, and if they hadn't passed the occasional pedestrian, Clemens would have sworn the town was deserted. What was also pleasing, was that the people they did come across also turned out to be friendly. Smiling and waving at them as they drove passed. Still, it was not surprising thought Clemens. Judging by the pristine condition of the houses and buildings, unlike Avranches, Saint-Aubin-du-Cormier's liberation appeared to have been quite painless.

After a short drive, with the evening sun lowering in the sky, and the church tower of Saint-Aubin reflected in the driver's mirror, they once again found themselves heading into the open countryside. Relieved that what could have been a potential hazard was behind them, the priority now was to find some lodgings for the night. Another empty barn would be perfect.

Five miles from Saint-Aubin-du-Cormier they found what they were looking for. A small hamlet of

stone-built houses. Or at least the remains of them. One or two still had a roof but all of them were missing walls. Buildings which had once been peoples' homes were reduced to piles of rubble. Scattered among them were wrecked vehicles; A Sherman tank with its turret torn open like a tin can, a line of burned-out trucks, their canvas covers turned to ash, and an M3 howitzer reduced to a twisted heap of metal. All bearing the same symbolic marking, a white five-pointed star. Whatever had taken place here had not only sounded the death knell for the hamlet, but it had also claimed the lives of countless American soldiers.

Having taken up residence in one of the least damaged houses, with his back against the stone wall, nursing the saucepan containing the remains of the coffee Clemens inhaled a mouthful of smoke. Beyond the dying fire, Joliane was already asleep, curled up like a child on the bedding roll, his jacket covering her legs. Having enjoyed another meal courtesy of their supply of K-rations, with a half-smoked Chesterfield pressed between his lips, his thoughts were focused on one thing: the Jeep. Or more importantly, what to do with it.

Just like the uniform he was wearing, the vehicle had now become a liability, and it had to go. Preferably by tomorrow. Or if not the next day at the latest. Regrettably, if they were unable to find a suitable replacement it would mean them having to walk. Not an ideal situation, especially as it meant having to carry the large suitcase which now, thanks to its contents, weighed a ton.

Kean to leave the ruined hamlet, and the reminders of the war, which was still raging across France, a war they were no longer a part of, they set off early next morning. If he intended to get rid of the offending vehicle, Clemens wanted to get as far south as possible first. By keeping to the back roads, after several wrong turnings, it was midday before they crossed the bridge over the river Semnon and entered the town of Martigne-Forchaud.

"Where is everybody?" asked Clemens,

"It is La pause de midi Albert, the pause for lunch. You do not know this?"

"No, it´s news to me."

"In France, Albert lunch is between noon and two o´clock."

"Two hours seems a long time just to eat a meal?"

"It is the custom."

"And everything stops?"

"Oui."

"What about the shops, do they close too?"

"Oui, they must also eat."

Two hours for lunch. Maybe living in France wasn´t going to be so bad after all, thought Clemens as he navigated his way through the streets of the picturesque town.

"Perhaps we should also eat, Albert?"

"Soon," replied Clemens," turning the corner into the Rue De Chateaubriant. "Let's get through the town first." and slipping into third gear, he gunned the engine.

Fifteen minutes later, with the rooftops of Martigne-Ferchaud disappearing into the distance, and the road running ahead of them straight as an arrow, given the way things were turning out, it seemed Lady Luck was on their side after all.

"I am hungry, Albert."

It wasn´t that he didn´t sympathise with her. He was feeling a little peckish himself. No, the reason Clemens didn´t respond was because something far more important had just piqued his interest. Something which just might be the answer to their transportation problems.

Although he wasn´t too familiar with French cars, as they drew nearer Clemens had no trouble identifying the one parked at the side of the road. It was a Citroen Avant. He remembered seeing them in old cops and robber films. The mystery was, what was it doing out here in the middle of nowhere? Kean to discover the answer, pulling the jeep in behind it, he killed the engine.

Even before getting out of the Jeep, from looking through the car's rear window, he could see that both the driver and the passenger seats were empty.

"Wait here while I go and take a look."

Joliane nodded, and with all thoughts of food forgotten, she watched as Clemens walked across to the car and peered in through one of the windows. Well, it was empty. Even the back seat, where he thought the driver might have been taking a nap. Perplexed, looking around him, Clemens spotted the outline of a building partially hidden by trees about a hundred yards from the road.

"Stay in the Jeep Joliane, I'm just going to see if there's anybody in the house over there."

Watching as Clemens walked away along the narrow dirt track leading to the half-concealed building, Joliane suddenly had the urge to go running after him. Having had to depend on herself for so long, having that burden lifted from her shoulders, she had exposed her vulnerability.

Thankfully, in a matter of minutes, he was back. "Nothing there, the place is deserted."

"Perhaps it is abandoned?" said Joliane, her voice tinged with relief.

"Maybe," replied Clemens, turning his attention to the car. Outwardly, it looked undamaged. There were no bullet holes in the bodywork, and the tyres were all inflated. No, if there was a problem, then logically it had to be something mechanical, and with this in mind, walking around to the driver's door, he pulled it open.

The first thing Clemens noticed was the key. Why would someone go off and leave the key in the ignition? Not that he was complaining, at least it meant he could try and start the engine. Sliding in behind the steering wheel, after turning on the ignition, Clemens pulled the starter button. The good news was that at least the engine turned over. The not-so-good news was that it didn't fire up. Thankfully, it only took a quick look at the instrument display panel to discover why. With the needle on the fuel gauge pointing at zero, the only reason the car wouldn't start was because it was out of petrol.

"I think it just needs petrol," said Clemens, elatedly, and striding to the rear of the Jeep, he removed the petrol can that Uttley had assured him was full of fuel. Which of course it was, and shadowed by an excited Joliane, returning to the Citroen Clemens unscrewed the petrol cap. On the off chance that the problem was not entirely due to a lack of fuel, not wanting to waste a drop of the precious commodity, he began pouring in what he thought would be enough to at least start the engine. Satisfied after replacing the cap, he returned to the driver´s seat.

"Here goes," said Clemens, hopefully, as he reached for the starter button.

It spluttered to begin with as the first drops of petrol found their way into the carburettor. Then, with the perfect combination of fuel and air achieved, the engine roared into life.

"Stay here", shouted Clemens, pushing his foot down on the accelerator pedal.

"Where are you going?" asked Joliane.

"I just want to get it off the road," replied Clemens, and selecting first gear, he steered the car onto the narrow track leading to the empty building.

With the Citroen safely out of sight, as he was making his way back to the road Clemens spotted what he hoped would be an ideal place to abandon the Jeep.

"What will we do now?" said Joliane as Clemens climbed in beside her.

"I think I´ve found somewhere we can hide the Jeep," replied Clemens, "but I have to check it out first."

With the two vehicles parked side by side outside the deserted house, eager to show Joliane what he had in mind, taking her by the hand Clemens led her back to the track.

"So, what do you think?" said Clemen, pointing towards a large pond.

"I think perhaps you have too much sun on your head," replied Joliane, staring in disbelief at the muddy pond.

"No, it´s perfect." said Clemens, and before Joliane could say another word, he began unbuttoning his shirt.

"What are you doing, Albert?"

"I just need to find out if it´s deep enough."

She didn´t say another word after that, she just stood watching as he began removing all of his clothes. She should have looked away of course but strangely she found she couldn´t. Or was it that she didn´t want to? Well, whatever it was she carried on looking anyway. Her eyes glued to his naked body as he picked his way through the tall grass towards the edge of the pond. Why was it she wondered, with her gaze firmly focused on Clemens´s buttocks, that women had this fascination with men´s bottoms? Was it some primitive, stimulus designed to produce a reproductive desire perhaps? It was then that she suddenly found herself blushing.

Even though he had only waded out about four feet from the bank the water was already well above Clemens´s waist. Another three steps and it was up to his shoulders, and certainly deep enough to hide a jeep. Delighted that his idea was achievable, Clemens waded back to the bank, and placing a hand over his genitals, he emerged from the water. His attempt at preserving her modesty did not go unnoticed, and as Clemens walked back to where he had left his clothes, he noticed that Joliane had averted her eyes.

Picking up his discarded uniform and boots, Clemens made his way back to the jeep. Now that they had a new mode of transport and found a suitable place to dispose of the Jeep, all that needed to be done was for him to change into civilian clothes.

After drying himself with his army shirt, removing the clothes Joliane had acquired for him from the suitcase Clemens set about transforming himself from soldier to civilian. Although badly in need of a wash, the army issue long johns, and the pair of woollen socks would have to do for now. Moments later, dressed in his new clothes, and with his uniform folded away in the suitcase, Clemens presented himself for inspection.

"Well, how do I look?"

Pursing her lips, she slowly ran her eyes over him. "Parfait, perfect. Now you are truly Albert Cabouret."

Now came the tricky part. Getting the Jeep into the pond. Thankfully, being a left-hand drive vehicle made things much safer as it meant that when the time came to jump clear, he would land on the track. Had it been a right-hand drive, he might well have ended up in the clump of trees on the other side which could have proved fatal. Another thing in his favour was that as the track sloped down towards the pond, he didn´t need to drive at speed.

With Joliane looking on anxiously, having reversed to the start of the track, putting the Jeep into first gear Clemens began his run-up. Gradually picking up speed, reaching the point where the track curved away towards the house, releasing his hold on the steering wheel, Clemens threw himself out of the jeep. Unharmed, scrambling to his feet, praying that the vehicle had stayed on course, grabbing hold of Joliane´s hand, he began running towards the pond.

By the time they reached the pond, the Jeep was already half-submerged. Slowly sinking beneath the murky water until apart from clusters of bubbles rising to the surface, all traces of the jeep were gone. Clemens would have loved to have drained the remaining fuel from its tank but without a length of rubber tubing to syphon it off, he had to admit defeat.

Pleased with what had been accomplished the pair made their way towards the car.

"You are not injured, Albert?"

"No, I´m fine," replied Clemens, feeling quite pleased with himself following his perfectly executed "parachute roll." Strangely enough, he had thought about volunteering for the Parachute Regiment when it was formed in nineteen forty, but Nobby had talked him out of it. His argument being that if the Good Lord meant men to fly, he would have given them wings." After that, the subject never came up again. Just another missed opportunity to add to those already in the "box of regrets." The one we only open when it´s too late to do anything about it. Much like all the things we were going to do one day but never quite got around to it. Even more regrets.

With Clemens´s transformation into a civilian completed, after stowing away the suitcase containing Clemens´s uniform, and the dismantled machine gun in the boot along with the empty jerry can, Clemens and Joliane climbed into the car. They had debated whether or not they should stay in the abandoned house for the night but with the possibility that the owner of the car could return at any time, they decided against it. And besides, it was still early, and like migrating birds they too were gripped with an undeniable urge to fly southwards. Southwards to obscurity, and a new life.

Although it was on the route they wanted to take, still a little uncertain about the roles they had created for themselves, lacking the confidence to put them to the test, they decided to skirt around the town of Chateaubriant. Sadly, the decision turned out to be a mistake. Not only in time and distance but also the fuel they wasted as the inadequacies of the military map began to manifest itself. Leaving them wandering aimlessly along back roads and through small villages without any idea of exactly where they were. The only consolation was that at least they were still heading south.

After a long and tiring day, to Joliane the cluster of buildings up ahead of them looked like the ideal place to stop. Clemens however wasn´t so sure. Outwardly the place certainly appeared deserted. But then so had the others they had passed in the last few hours. Only for them to turn out to be lived in.

"But it is parfait Albert," pleaded Joliane.

Maybe she was right, thought Clemens, conscious that it was getting late. "What does the sign say?"

"La Chesnaie", said Joliane, staring at the hand-carved letters. "In English, it is The Grove of Oak trees."

"Okay, let´s take a look." and tempted by the prospect of a hot meal and a cup of coffee, turning onto the rutted track, Clemens drove towards what they both assumed was an abandoned farmhouse.

Even though it was still quite light outside, clearly it was dark enough inside for someone to have placed a lighted oil lamp in one of the downstairs windows.

"Shit!" said Clemens, desperately looking for somewhere to turn around.

But even before he had completed half of his intended three-point turn, the door to the house swung open, and a very angry-looking grey-haired, old lady began walking towards the car. And if that wasn´t bad enough, the fact that she was carrying a shotgun was not exactly encouraging.

Thankfully, before she began using the Citroen for target practice, Joliane was out of the car and showering her with platitudes. Which, judging by the fact that she had lowered the shotgun, appeared to be working. Having decided that staying behind the wheel of the car was probably the better option, Clemens watched as a conversation developed between the two women. With the window wound down, even though he could not understand a word of what they were saying, at least the old lady didn´t appear to be quite so angry.

Several minutes later, with what Clemens took to be a smile, the old lady suddenly turned away and began walking back towards the house.

"We can stay here for tonight, Albert", said Joliane through the open car window.

"Do you think that´s wise? Only I´m not too happy about that shotgun she´s carrying."

"Oui, she was just a little afraid, you understand,"

"Did you tell her about us?"

"Oui, just as we decided. So, you must just remember not to speak, d´accord?"

"Okay. What about food?"

"We can eat the American food. I have told her they were kind to us."

Well, thought Clemens it had to happen sometime, so we might as well get it over with. "You go in, I´ll put the car in the barn over there."

"You will bring the valise? Our suitcase, I mean?"

"Oui, Mademoiselle," Clemens replied, nodding his head deferentially.

Rewarding his impudence by sticking out her tongue at him, turning on her heels, Joliane made her way towards the half-open door.

Yet another kitchen thought Clemens, as he stepped across the threshold, although this one was much smaller than the one in Avranches. There was also more in the way of kitchenalia; shelves crammed with stacks of crockery, every surface covered in pots and pans. The heavy lace curtains at both of the windows explained the need for the pair of oil lamps, one suspended from the low ceiling on a length of chain, the other in the middle of the table. The warmth from the stove, and the aroma emanating from the pan perched on top of it, the lid half-on half-off gave the room a nice, homely feeling.

"Albert," said Joliane, walking across the room towards him, "c´est Madame Lacagne."

In response to the introduction, putting down the suitcase, Albert gave the old lady what he hoped was a "pleased to meet you" smile accompanied by a deferential nod of the head. Receiving in return a look which was more suspicious than welcoming.

With the formalities over, not quite sure what he should do next, suddenly remembering the two cartons of K-rations he had tucked under his arm, walking across the room Clemens put them down on the kitchen table.

Intrigued by the strange-looking packages with their blue and white markings, following Joliane to the table, the old lady watched her as she emptied the array of cans and packages. The look of amazement on Madame Lacagne´s face as Joliane revealed their contents, was a clear indication that she had never seen anything like it before. For an old French woman in her seventies, such things were unheard of.

With Madame Lacagne´s curiosity satisfied, having decided on the menu, when the meal was eventually served up it looked quite appetising. It smelled good too. It was certainly a meal that the old lady would never forget in a hurry. Although it has to be said, her contribution; a kind of vegetable broth infused with herbs was far tastier. The highlight of the meal though was when Clemens removed the tin of peaches from his coat pocket. Now that did bring a smile to the old woman´s wrinkled face.

After ingratiating himself even more by offering the old lady one of the Chesterfield cigarettes, which she quickly accepted, leaving the two women to clear the table, conscious of the need to spend as little time as possible in the old lady´s company, after excusing himself Clemens headed for the kitchen door.

Once outside, lighting up his first cigarette of the day, with still enough daylight left Clemens decided to take the opportunity to have a look around. From the outside, the house looked to be a good size. With a chimney at both ends it meant that apart from the kitchen there must be at least one more room on the ground floor. Gazing up at the roof, he counted three small dormers which he assumed were bedroom windows. Opposite the open-fronted barn where he had left the car, there were two more barns both with large double doors. Again, despite their great age, they looked in good condition. However, he did notice that the pantile roof on one of them had begun to sag ominously in the middle.

Walking on past the barns, the smell wafting towards him on the evening breeze, instantly brought back childhood memories of days spent on the farm close to his parent´s house. A place where he had enjoyed many happy hours. Mucking out the cow sheds for a few pennies, and hunting for rats with Rex the farmer´s Labrador. It was there that he had kissed a girl for the first time. A local girl from the village called Jean Summerfield. His first childhood sweetheart. How old had he been? Eleven, or twelve, and yet he could remember it as if it had been yesterday. Though mainly a dairy farm, they had also kept a few pigs, so the smell which greeted him as he walked around the end of the barn was instantly recognisable.

Enclosed by a stone wall constructed from local stone, the three Stys were separated from each other by a partition wall. Each pen had a wooden stable door, and just inside the front gate was a wooden feed trough and a water bucket. With room to house two pigs, while there had not been much rain in the past few days the ground was still muddy enough for them to wallow in. They were big pigs too, with enough bacon on one of them to feed a regiment for a week.

"Albert! Albert!"

Turning away from the pig styes, Clemens watched as Joliane came running towards him.

"Come, Madame Lacagne wants to show us our rooms."

Bedtime already thought Clemens. Still, after spending goodness know how many nights sleeping on the ground or on a hard floor, the prospect of a night in a proper bed, regardless of how early it was sounded very tempting.

With a lantern in one hand, her other gripping onto the wooden handrail the old lady led the way up the narrow staircase. Once assembled on the landing, opening the first door on the left, she ushered Joliane inside.

"Pour vous, mademoiselle." before carrying on along the windowless hallway.

Handing Joliane the suitcase, with a fleeting smile, Clemens hurried after the old lady as she continued along the windowless hallway.

"Monsieur", said the old lady gesturing towards the door at the far end.

Transforming his face into what must have looked like a stupid grin, in an attempt to express his thanks, pursing his lips together Clemens somehow ended up making a sound like a baby blowing raspberries.

Seemingly unimpressed by his attempted display of gratitude, with a shrug of her bony shoulders Madame Lacagne turned away, and muttering something unintelligible under her breath, she made her way to the door halfway along the hallway.

After a good night´s sleep, even though they had both risen early, Madame Lacagne was already down in the kitchen preparing breakfast. After a brief exchange of pleasantries between the two women, the remainder of the meal which consisted of freshly baked bread, and boiled eggs supplemented by jars of homemade jam was eaten in silence. Hoping to escape outside for a smoke, as he was making his way towards the door Clemens suddenly found himself confronted by the old lady.

"Pour le cochons", said the old lady, holding out the bucket of leftover vegetables and kitchen scraps from last night´s meal.

Well, thought Clemens, this wasn´t too difficult; mentally adding the word cochons to his growing repertoire of French words. Although there was the likelihood that there was a henhouse somewhere on the farm, judging by the contents of the bucket she had just handed him, he was pretty sure it was meant for the pigs. Contorting his face into what was quickly becoming his method of communicating, Clemens made his way towards the kitchen door. Ah well, at least the pigs would be pleased to see him.

They were too. Although with their snouts buried in the trough, it was pretty obvious that it was the meal, they were pleased with rather than the person who had brought it to them. Leaving the pigs to enjoy their breakfast, after lighting a cigarette, bucket in hand Clemens made his way back to the farmhouse.

He hadn´t gone far when he saw Joliane emerging from the kitchen and judging by the look on her face, he could tell right away that something was wrong.

"What is it?" asked Clemens, holding out the packet of cigarettes.

"Nothing", Jolane replied, removing a cigarette.

Taking out his lighter, Clemens waited for the "but" he was pretty sure was coming.

"She has asked us to stay, Albert."

Now that he wasn´t expecting to hear.

"Let´s go for a walk," said Clemens, "we need to talk."

Strangely, despite having to play the part of a mute, Clemens was in favour of the idea. It didn´t have to be permanent. Just long enough for them to experience some normality. Freedom from the constant fear of discovery. It was pretty obvious that the war would be over soon, so as far as their anonymity was concerned, they had time on their side. Besides, where else were they to go? They couldn´t just keep driving around aimlessly in the hope that something might turn up. No, perhaps by stumbling upon La Chesnaie their guardian angel had come up trumps once again.

Thankfully, after explaining all this to her, despite her reservations, Joliane finally agreed. It seemed that despite her concerns, having come to rely on him so much over the past few days, she found it difficult to question his judgement. So, as they sat down for supper that night, she informed Madame Lacagne that they wished to accept her kind invitation.

Although she didn´t make a great show of it, for Madame Lacagne the couple´s decision to stay was a Godsend. The man who used to help out on the farm had up and left several months ago, and without him, she was finding it increasingly difficult to manage on her own. The animals were no trouble, but without someone to help with all the other day-to-day tasks, she knew that running the farm would soon be beyond her. She was a little suspicious of their brother-and-sister relationship although she couldn´t put her finger on why this should be. It was just a feeling. Not that it bothered her unduly, in times of war many things, and many people were not as they seemed. No, she must count her blessing. Having a man about the place could only be a good thing, and although she didn´t like to admit it, she was beginning to enjoy the young woman´s company.

By the end of the week, a kind of routine had been established. Immediately after breakfast, Clemens would feed, and muck out the pigs, while Juliane fed the chickens, and collected the eggs from the previous day. Lunch was taken around midday, usually outside under the shade of one of the old oak trees. After that Joliane would help the old lady in the vegetable garden while Clemens began making repairs to the wall of one of the barns. Supper was a joint effort by the two women. As it turned out Madame Lacagne was glad of the help, and thanks to the K-rations, she had become a big fan of "American cuisine." Apart from the Chesterfield cigarettes that is, which she found a bit bland, preferring instead her old clay pipe. Where she got the tobacco for it from Clemens was not quite sure, but he guessed it was probably obtained illegally. He was also relieved by her decision. Twelve packs of K-rations contained a total of 144 cigarettes, and as both he and Joliane were smokers it wasn´t an inexhaustible supply. And without meaning any disrespect to Dentyne, none of them seemed to like the chewing gum, although both Clemens and Joliane used it most nights as a way of cleaning their teeth.

The only disruption to this routine came a week later due to the untimely arrival of Monsieur Rene Gautreau the local Charcutier, the pork butcher in his dilapidated Citroen van, its dark green paintwork pitted with rust.

"Bonjour Monsieur, ca va?" The butcher called out through the driver´s window, as he pulled up in front of the pig sties.

Thankfully, when Clemens turned round, judging by the look on his face Rene Gautreau seemed just as surprised to see him, as Clemens was to see the pork butcher.

For what seemed an eternity, but in reality, was probably less than a minute, with Clemens struggling to formulate some kind of sign language to convey to the man that he was unable to talk and the butcher wondering what had happened to the man who had been here the last time he called, the two men ended up staring at each other.

Ironically, although both women had left the house together, it was Madame Lacagne who came to Clemen´s rescue.

"Bonjour Rene," she called out, walking briskly towards the parked van. "il peut t"entendre mais il ne peut pa parler, he can hear you, but he cannot speak."

"Ah, je vois, I see", Rene replied, acknowledging Clemens' efforts with a nod of the head as he climbed out of the van, "une affliction que je pourrais souhaite pour ma femme. An affliction I could wish for my wife." He clutched what appeared to be a walking stick and followed Madame Lacagne across to the pigsties.

Finding himself relegated to the sidelines, breathing a sigh of relief, Clemens looked across at Joliane, who having witnessed his encounter with the pork butcher was having a hard time stopping herself from laughing. It would appear that far from sharing his relief she had found his predicament quite amusing. Her knight in shining armour had a vulnerable side after all.

Having pointed out the sow destined for Monsieur Gautreau´s abattoir, leaving the task of getting it loaded onto the van to the pork butcher, the old lady made her way back to the house, calling over her shoulder, "Albert vous aidera si vous avez besoin de lui." She pointed at Clemens indicating that he would help if needed.

"Ne t'inquiete pas, Madame, Rene Gautreau connait son affaire, I do know my business", he replied, a little put out by the suggestion. After plying his trade for over twenty-five years, there was nothing you could teach Rene Gautreau about handling pigs.

Lifting the tailgate of the Citroen the butcher dragged out a wooden ramp. Engaging the two metal lugs on one end into slots cut in the floor of the vehicle, he rested the other end on the ground. After testing that it was firmly in position with his foot, he made his way towards the end sty.

Intrigued, Clemens watched him as he opened the gate to the pigsty, and making a kind of "clacking" sound with his tongue, he coaxed the sow outside. Once this was accomplished, with skilful use of the stick, accompanied by yet more "clacking" he guided her towards the rear of the van. With the animal now in position, giving it a whack across the hindquarters with the stick, the sow scrambled up the ramp and into the van. Job done.

Denied the opportunity to voice his congratulations, Clemens applauded the butcher's accomplishment by clapping instead. Grateful for the display of appreciation, turning towards him the butcher gave what was presumably meant to be a bow. However, due to the size of his girth, the bow tended to be just a bending at the waist. Yes, if ever a man epitomised his profession, it was Rene Gautreau; with his small pale blue eyes, and rotund physique here was a man who loved pigs so much he was beginning to look like one. Thankfully for those who liked their pork and bacon, it didn't stop him from killing them though.

Clemens had almost fallen asleep when Joliane opened the door. Framed in the doorway, she stood for a moment gazing across at him. Then, closing the door behind her, bathed in the moonlight allowed in through the open window, one by one she slipped the straps of her petticoat off her shoulders, allowing it to fall around her bare feet. Resting on his elbow, Clemens gazed at her naked body. His eyes slowly moving from her small, rose-tipped breasts, down across her slender waist to the triangle of dark hair between her thighs.

Tiptoeing across to the bed, pulling aside the sheet, Joliane slipped in beside him, her lips searching for his, her tongue eagerly exploring his mouth. Placing her left hand on his chest she began slowly brushing her fingers up and down his body. Aroused, Clemens gazed up at her, his mouth as dry as sand, his fingers clawing at the bedsheet. Encouraged by his response, raising herself to a kneeling position she leaned over him, slowly lowering her head towards his manhood. Unable to constrain himself, grabbing a handful of her hair, Clemens forced her down, groaning with pleasure as she began teasing him with her tongue. Sensing he was close to an orgasm, sitting astride him, she guided him into her with her hand. Then throwing back her head, with her palms pressed against his naked chest, she began to move, her body rising and falling. The tempo increasing with every thrust, their bodies as one, speeding towards a final climactic crescendo.

Being a light sleeper, Madame Lacagne had always cursed the loose floorboard in the hallway outside her bedroom. Her late husband: may he rot in hell was always going to fix it. "Yes, Yes I will get around to it woman" he used to say whenever she complained but he never did. While they shared the same bed it hadn´t mattered. It was only when his drinking became worse, and she kicked him out that it became a problem. After that, night after night as he staggered back to his bedroom at the end of the hallway the noise would wake her. Two years of disturbed sleep before the drink took him, and what remained of his liver to the grave before she was free of it. Now, after all those years it had woken her again. At first, she thought she must be dreaming. But no, this was not a dream. It was that damn floorboard again.

Although her initial choice of room was wrong, with her ear pressed against the bedroom door at the end of the hallway she knew the floorboard hadn´t lied. And although it had been more years than she cared to remember since she had experienced the joys of carnal pleasure, judging by the sounds coming from the other side of the door, the two people who had arrived at her farm were certainly not brother and sister.

Cradling Joliane in his arms, Clemens brushed away the strand of hair that had fallen across her eyes. Was it love she felt for him or just gratitude for what he had done, he wondered? Whichever it was he didn´t care. All that mattered was that they were together, and whether it was love or gratitude, he now had somebody who needed him as much as he needed her.

In hindsight, if Madame Lacagne had just stayed in bed things would have worked out so much better for all concerned. But alas, she didn´t. And like many before her, she was about to learn that it is not just cats who get killed by curiosity.

Clemens heard their voices even before he had opened the kitchen door. Predominately Madame Lacagne´s, loud, and filled with anger. Once inside, putting down the bucket he was carrying, he hurried across to the stairs. Reaching the landing, Clemens stared in through the open bedroom door.

Standing with her back to him, clearly agitated, the old lady was still talking, her hand pointing towards the bed. Standing before her, defenceless in the face of her accusations Joliane stared at her. It was then that Clemens saw the opened suitcase lying in the corner of the room. Strewn on the floor beside it were the clothes Joliane had acquired in Avranches.

Even before he turned his attention to the bed Clemens had a good idea of what he would find. So, he wasn't that surprised to see his uniform, and the dismantled submachine gun laid out on the duvet like exhibits A and B in a murder trial. The only mystery was why would Madame Lacagne want to search their belongings in the first place. While he didn't know the answer, one thing he was sure of, she was not at all happy with what she had found.

Catching sight of Joliane's despairing look, her eyes blazing, Madame Lacagne turned around to face him.

"Deserteur! Lache! Coward!", she screamed, jabbing her finger at Clemens accusingly. La police en entendra parler. The police shall hear of this!" She pushed past him hurried out the door.

What happened next was unclear. Did she trip, or was she pushed? As the sole witness, only Clemens could provide the answer, and yet even he wasn't one hundred per cent sure. Yes, he remembered reaching out a hand. What was unclear was his motive for doing so. Was it to stop her from going to the authorities? Or to push her down the stairs? Whatever it was, the next thing he knew Madame Lacagne was tumbling head-over-heels down the narrow staircase. And the floorboard which had caused her so many sleepless nights, had now robbed her of her life.

"It's no use," said Clemens, holding Joliane back, "she's dead."

"Oh, mon Dieu," cried Joliane. "How can you be so sure?"

"Look at her head", Clemens replied, pointing at the body of the old lady at the foot of the stairs, her head laid at an unnatural angle.

Gazing at her as she stared down at the body of Madame Lacagne Clemens could sense the question forming in Joliane's mind. But he knew she wouldn't voice it. Just like him, she knew they would have had to kill her anyway. She did have another question though.

"What are we to do, Albert?"

Ironically, if hadn't been for the visit by the damn pork butcher they could have just packed up and left. Now, that was out of the question.

"We will have to report it."

"But the police will think we have killed her."

"Why would they think that? Anybody can see it was an accident."

"Yes, but they will wonder why we are here."

"Then we´ll tell them the truth, that the old lady wanted us to stay, and help on the farm. She must have said something to the butcher about us, so hopefully he can back us up."

Nodding her head, Joliane smiled, but it wasn´t a very reassuring one.

"Come here," said Clemens, taking her into his arms. "Trust me it will be alright."

"Oui, if you say so," replied Joliane, burying her head in his chest.

Assuming that whatever happened, they would be leaving anyway, after repacking the suitcase, they made their way down the stairs. Taking care not to disturb the old lady´s body, retrieving the last of the K-rations from the kitchen they left the house. With the suitcase safely stowed away in the boot of the Citroen, bidding La Chesnaire farewell they set off for the nearest town. A place not that far away according to the German map named Mouzeil.

On their arrival, the first piece of news they received was quite encouraging, According, to the passerby they stopped in the street, Mouzeil didn´t have a police station. The nearest one the man said was in Ancenis fifteen miles away. However, like all French towns what it did have was a Mairie, a town hall.

Having decided that it was better if Joliane reported the matter without his presence, parking the Citroen outside the building Clemens waited anxiously for her return. No doubt a doctor would have to be involved to establish the cause of death this was to be expected. Their hope was, that if he was satisfied the old lady´s death had been an accident, then there should be no need for the police to be involved.

After half an hour or so, Joliane eventually emerged from the Town Hall, and walking across to the car, she climbed in beside him. Her smile said it all, it had gone well.

"We are to return to the farm. The mayor will inform the doctor, and they will visit as soon as it is possible. We must also disturb nothing."

"Did he mention the police?"

"Non."

"That´s a relief." said Clemens, starting the car. Given their circumstances, they were the last people he wanted nosing around.

Having no doubt observed La pause de midi they arrived at La Chesnaire a little before three o´clock. There were just the two of them,

Monsieur Dumont, the mayor, a portly man in his mid-fifties wearing a crumpled linen suit and an open-necked shirt, and Le Docteur, an elderly gentleman, smartly dressed, with grey hair and a thin, pale face. Retrieving his medical bag from the back seat of the car, he followed Monsieur Dumont into the farmhouse's kitchen.

With formal introductions completed, the doctor walked across to the foot of the stairs, and putting on a pair of steel-rimmed spectacles, he peered down at Madame Lacagne's body. There was little doubt that she was dead. Judging by the abnormal position of her head, it would appear that a broken neck was the most obvious cause.

Putting aside his bag, reaching out a hand the doctor carefully pulled down the old lady's skirt, covering the pair of spindly legs sticking out of her bloomers like a pair of broom handles. Being of the old school, to him preserving a lady's modesty, even in death was a matter of common decency.

With the cause of death established, and his work here done, the only question remaining was why she had fallen down the stairs. Not that it was something he needed to trouble himself with. After all these things were a matter for the police, not a doctor. But like one of those itches that you just have to scratch, the question would not go away.

He had been Madame Lacagne's doctor since arriving in Mouzeil forty years ago, and during all that time, apart from an unfortunate miscarriage, she had never had a day's illness in her life. Perhaps that was why he felt so compelled to look for clues. To see if there had been foul play. Not that he had any reason to suspect the young couple standing behind him in the kitchen. According to Dumont, the reason for their presence on the farm had been confirmed by Rene Gautreau when the mayor had called at the abattoir for his order of pork. There was some suspicion regarding the man's dumbness. But if what the pork butcher had said that he had been caught up in the bombing of Avranches it could well be true. Having served as a doctor during the Great War, he had treated many soldiers suffering from shell shock, and the trauma caused by it, and losing the ability to speak was one of its many symptoms.

Carefully stepping around Madame Lacagne's body, gripping the handrail for support the doctor made his way to the top of the stairs. Finding the door on the left open, he peered inside. The bed was neatly made with a woman's nightdress draped over the pillow. Moving on down the hallway, opening the door on the right, he found himself looking into what was quite obviously Madame Lacagne's bedroom. Continuing to the door at the end, with the door ajar, he pushed it open. Again, the bed was neatly made and hanging over the back of the chair was a man´s jacket. A jacket which had once been worn by the late Monsieur Lacagnes.

It was as the doctor made his way back to the head of the stairs that he noticed the strip of torn lino that Clemens had carefully prised up with the tip of his dagger. Bending down, he examined the potential hazard carefully; was this the culprit? Was this where she had caught her foot and lost her balance? It wasn´t conclusive evidence of course but given the circumstances, there was every chance that it was this which had caused her demise. Having fulfilled his obligation to his late patient, satisfied that there was no evidence of foul play the doctor made his way down the stairs and into the kitchen.

After confirming that Madame Lacagnes´ of death was accidental, leaving the mayor and the young woman to continue their conversation, lured by the open packet of cigarettes in Clemens 'hand, the two men stepped outside. Although suffering from a persistent cough which had plagued him for years, the doctor still enjoyed an occasional cigarette. Especially when it was an American one.

Shortly after lighting up, alerted by the opening of the kitchen door, nipping out the half-smoked cigarette, the doctor tucked it into the top pocket of his jacket. A little treat to look forward to after supper this evening, with a nice glass of cognac, and bidding Clemens Au revoir, he climbed into Monsieur Dupont´s car. With the mayor safely ensconced behind the wheel, filled with a sense of relief, raising a hand in the air, Clemens watched as the car moved off down the dusty drive leading to the road.

Even before the car had disappeared out of sight, grabbing Clemens by the hand, Joliane dragged him into the garden.

"We can stay, Albert," cried Joliane, excitedly. "The mayor has said we may stay."

"What, forever?"

"Non", said Joliane, pulling a sad face, "that is not possible."

"That´s a pity, I was beginning to like it here.

"Non, first he must see if Madame Lacagne has any family. If she does, the farm is theirs."

"How long will that take?"

"Who can say," replied Joliane, shrugging her shoulders.

"So, we are caretakers then?"

"I don´t understand these caretakers. What is its meaning?"

"That we are to look after the place, feed the animals."

"Oh oui, le concierge", replied Joliane. "It is good, no?"

Clemens responded by taking her in his arms and kissing her hard on the lips.

"Yes, it is good. It is very good", he said, holding her at arms-length.

Joliane smiled at him. She had not felt happiness like this before. She had never felt such a longing to be with someone as she did now. No matter what might lie ahead, this was a moment she would remember forever.

"But what about the old lady?" said Clemens, suddenly remembering the body lying at the bottom of the stairs.

"Les Croque-morts will come soon. You understand croque-morts?"

"I think so," replied Clemens, rightly assuming she had meant the undertakers.

An hour later, under instructions from the mayor, the undertaker's hearse, a converted Dodge D-24 with narrow etched glass side windows, and a chrome cross on the roof arrived accompanied by two sombre-faced gentlemen in long black coats. After introducing themselves, with practised efficiency they went about their work, and in a matter of minutes, Madame Lacagne's body was safely transferred to the hearse. Their work completed, having informed Joliane of the time and date of the funeral, after executing a near-perfect three-point turn, the hearse, and the body of La Chesnaire's late owner slowly proceeded back towards the road and the onward journey to Mouzeil.

For both Clemens and Joliane, the days and weeks that followed were idyllic. A life neither of them could have dreamed of a few weeks ago but one they quickly adapted to. Not surprisingly the farm took up most of their time. Contrary to Clemens' expectations, as well as caring for the livestock, there was always something that needed attention. But he enjoyed the work and the satisfaction he derived from re-building a crumbling wall in one of the barns or repairing the door to the hen house. His greatest pleasure however came from looking after the pigs. Joliane even teased him about it. Making oinking noises and calling him Monsieur Cochon which usually ended with her running off squealing like a schoolgirl with Clemens chasing after her with the pitchfork. She would always make sure he caught her though.

Joliane attended Madame Lacagne's funeral. It seemed only fitting somehow, despite how things had ended. In hindsight, perhaps if they had owned up and explained things to her, then she might still be alive. Pushing the recriminations aside, the funeral also allowed her to reacquaint herself with Rene Gautreau who was there together with, a woman who she assumed was his wife; a small elegantly dressed woman with a black lace shawl covering her head. He had kindly promised to help them with the pigs. And that once he had slaughtered Madame Lacagnes sow, just as he had always done with the old lady, he would see they received a share of the meat in payment.

Two months to the day, however, following a visit from Monsieur Dupont, the mayor, their whole world came crashing down. He had located a relative. A distant cousin of Madame Lacagnes on her mother´s side living in Bordeaux. An elderly lady by all accounts. Anyway, the upshot was that having no use for the farm, she had instructed Monsieur Dupont to arrange for it to be sold. The price agreed on was one million francs. Thankfully, there was some favourable news, the mayor had convinced the new owner to allow them to continue living on the farm until it was sold.

It was only after the mayor had left that Clemens remembered the diamonds. Why let somebody else buy the farm when they could purchase it for themselves? They were both happy here, and it was the perfect place to begin their new life together. The big question was, were the diamonds worth one million francs?

Seated at the kitchen table, Clemens and Joliane stared down at the cluster of diamonds. They had counted them properly this time. There were thirty of them, each the same size and as far as they could tell, cut in the same fashion.

"What are we to do, Albert?" asked Joliane, trusting as always that he would have an answer.

"Well", said Clemens, "the first thing we need to do is to find out what they are worth."

"Perhaps someone at a bank would know."

"No, I don´t think so. The only people who will know their real value are diamond dealers."

"And where are we to find such people?"

Lost in thought, Clemens didn´t answer.

"Perhaps there are such people in Paris?"

"Maybe there are, but I´ve got somewhere better in mind."

"Oh," said Joliane, pouting, "and where can be better than Paris?"

"The diamond capital of the world," replied Clemens, ginning. "Antwerp."

At first, Joliane just looked at him as if he had gone mad.

"Mais c´est impossible", said Joliane, "Antwerp is too far away."

"Perhaps," replied Clemens, conceding that she had a point. "But it's worth a try."

"And if it is not possible?"

"Then we try to find somebody in Paris."

Still a little unsure about what he was suggesting, Joliane tried another tact.

"Could we not offer Madame Lacagne's cousin the diamonds in exchange for the farm? You agree they must be very valuable."

"No," said Clemens, half-smiling, "even if they are worth one million Francs, we can't use them to buy the farm, it would look too suspicious."

"I will make us some coffee," said Joliane, a little exasperated by the whole thing, and leaving Clemens to his thoughts she made her way to the stove.

Not that there was much to think about. The truth of the matter was, that they had to find out how much the diamonds were worth because only then would they know if it was enough to purchase the farm. That's assuming they could find someone who would buy them of course. Quite a few ifs and buts.

Lighting a cigarette for each of them, Clemens waited for Joliane to return with the two cups of coffee before telling her what he had decided.

"Okay", said Clemens, having collected his thoughts, "we both agree that we want to stay here, yes?"

"Oui", Joliane replied, nodding her head.

"Good, so here's what we'll do. We will drive to Paris and then see if we can get to Antwerp. Maybe trains are running, who knows? If it's not possible then we'll sell them in Paris, agreed?"

"D'accord", said Joliane, accepting the compromise.

"So, Mademoiselle, all we need is for you to go and see the mayor and ask him to give us some time to raise the money."

"Will we tell him we are selling the diamonds to buy the farm?"

"No, telling him about the diamonds is too risky", said Clemens, rubbing his fingers over his stubbled chin, "we have to make up a story. Perhaps, we could say that we know someone who will lend us the money?"

Although Joliane gave him a quizzical look, secretly, she thought it was quite a good idea.

As it turned out it was an excellent idea. Certainly one, good enough for the mayor, who readily accepted the story Joliane had concocted about a rich relative in Paris; a kindly uncle who she was confident would help them. After all, given how difficult it was likely to be to find a prospective buyer for the farm, what had he got to lose?

"Je peux t´accorder deux semaines mademoiselle Cabouret, tu ne comprends plus? I can allow you two weeks, no longer, do you understand?"

"Merci monsieur le maire, vous etes tres gentil. You are most kind."

With Rene promising to look after the three remaining pigs in exchange for helping himself to as many eggs as he wanted, everything was ready for their departure. Fortunately, Joliane had found a smaller suitcase in Madame Lacagne´s bedroom, plus some clothes for Clemens. Although she had thrown her late husband out of the marital bedroom, apparently, she had kept some of his clothing. Including three pairs of underpants which Clemens was sorely in need of and two short-sleeved shirts which looked to be his size. She would have liked to have given them all a wash to get rid of the smell of mothballs but there was no time. The large suitcase containing Clemens´ uniform and the submachine gun they hid away in the loft.

Before leaving they made one final visit to Mouzeil. A trip to the local bank where, although the elderly clerk was far from happy to oblige, thanks to a heart-rending sob story from Joliane supported by a beguiling smile, he finally succumbed to her request by exchanging the majority of the cumbersome collection of coins for banknotes.

Bright and early the next morning after a quick breakfast they set off. Clemens had planned a route of sorts but with no idea of what might lay ahead, the only certainty was that once again their lives were in God´s hands.

Chapter Seven

Antwerp – Mid-October

After an uneventful journey, turning onto the Boulevard de Denain, Clemens drove towards the imposing, neoclassical façade of the Gare du Nord railway station, its arched windows fronted by six regal statues towering above the columned entrance. Taking a right turn into Place Napolean Third, he pulled up opposite what looked like a workman's hut. On a sign fixed above the door was the word Taxi.

With priority given to the seemingly endless convoys of lorries travelling on the roads southeast of Paris from the supply depots established inland from the Normandy beachhead, their journey had taken longer than they had hoped. Reinforcements, and supplies destined for the ever-moving front line as the Germans were slowly pushed back towards the Rhine. On one occasion they were waved off the road by an MP on a dust-covered Norton motorcycle to make room for a convoy of Bedford trucks crammed with fresh-faced British soldiers on their way to the front line. Watching as lorry after lorry drove past, if Clemens had felt any pangs of guilt it hadn't shown. He was not that man anymore. As far as he was concerned, Sergeant Albert Clemens no longer existed.

After driving through a city virtually unscarred by war, its streets were alive with various modes of transport as people went about their daily lives. A city slowly coming back to life after four years of German occupation, Clemens' hopes began to rise. Now, having reached their first objective, the next thing they needed to find out was if any trains were running to Antwerp.

Leaving Clemens in the car, crossing the road Joliane made her way into the station building. Much to her relief while most of the people thronging the station's concourse were Allied soldiers, scattered among them there were also groups of civilians. And although few in number it was an encouraging sight, nevertheless. After standing in line at one of the few ticket booths in operation, at last, it was Joliane's turn to be called forward. Smartly dressed in his railway uniform and peaked cap, the official, an elderly gentleman with a grey droopy moustache listened intently as she made enquiries concerning the train service between Paris and Antwerp. His reply was not encouraging. It seemed that all train services from Gare du Nord to Antwerpen Centraal were for military personnel only. He did however offer a crumb of comfort; by way of a concession the train leaving at noon each afternoon had been allocated two additional carriages for civilian passengers. The only drawback was that while he was allowed to sell her tickets, with so many people competing for the available space, he could not guarantee that there would be room for her. Thanking the man for his honesty, after confirming that she was willing to take the risk, handing him the required payment, Joliane purchased two return tickets.

Despite the ticket clerk´s pessimism regarding them finding room on the train, after a quick conversation they both agreed that it was worth a try. They had come too far to give up at the first hurdle, and with so much depending on them getting to Antwerp, if they had to fight their way onto the train, then that´s what they would do. That just left them with one small problem, what to do with the car.

As it happens, even before Joliane had disappeared through the station entrance, the matter had already crossed Clemens´s mind and gazing at the taxi rank across the street from the entrance to the station, he thought he might just have come up with a solution. What was staring him in the face right now was a prime example of a supply and demand problem. The demand element represented by the lengthy queue of potential passengers standing in line on the pavement. The supply part of the equation being the lack of cars available to accommodate them. Sensing that this could well be a solution to his problem, it was then that Clemens noticed the man, he had seen standing outside the hut, begin walking across the road towards him. It appeared that although not quite on the same wavelength they had both been thinking the same thing.

"Belle voiture. Nice car."

"Parles-vous anglaise?" Clemens replied, ignoring Joliane´s reproachful stare.

Here in Paris, he wasn´t too bothered about people knowing that he was English. Certainly not the man standing in front of him. Dressed in a double-breasted suit with a collar-bar shirt and patterned tie, his face partially obscured by a black fedora he looked more like an extra from a gangster film than the owner of a fleet of taxis.

"A little", the man replied, his gaze wandering back to the Citroen. "You wish to sell? I can give you a good price."

"Not for sale", replied Clemens, "but you can have it on loan if you like." Letting the words sink in before adding, "free of charge."

The man´s thin lips parted in a smile. "You wish me to take care of it for you?"

"Yes, just for a few days," said Clemens, "it looks like you could find work for another car", glancing over at the long queue of people standing at the taxi rank.

The taxi proprietor remained silent, his mind quickly analysing the pros and cons. Another car, even for a few days would certainly prove lucrative. He would need to change the registration plate but that was easily solved, he had acquired quite a stock of them over the past four years. Petrol was not a problem, although it was only available on the black market, he had some excellent suppliers, British and American who he could rely on. Plus, with a war going on, there was always the possibility the owner might not return. Not a nice thought but still something to consider.

"Okay", said the man, holding out a hand. "Then we have a deal, Monsieur."

After shaking the man´s hand Clemens tossed him the keys, and removing the suitcase from the boot, he began walking towards the station entrance.

"You are very trusting, Albert", said Joliane when he told her about the arrangement, he had made with the taxi owner.

"Oh, I don´t think we need to worry," said Clemens, slipping an arm around her waist. "He´s not likely to run off with it."

As they made their way across the station concourse, outside in the Place Napolean Third a driver had already been found for the Citroen, and while a second man began replacing the number plates, the new driver was already securing a temporary taxi sign to the Citroen´s roof.

Like so many of Europe´s mainline railway terminals, the station hall of the Gard du Nord was built to impress. Located immediately behind the neoclassical façade and enclosed on two sides by stone columns topped by arched windows, with twin rows of slender cast iron pillars supporting the V-shaped roof. The two lines of glass panels at its apex allowing in natural light. At the departure end of the train shed a glass screen added to the illusion of a giant Victorian greenhouse.

Just as the booking clerk had warned, although only five were in use, each of the station´s twelve platforms were crowded with people. Military personnel mostly. British and Canadian troops judging by their insignia. All waiting their turn to board the carriages attached to the five locomotives, standing at the buffers like patient beasts of burden, whisps of steam leaking from their brake valves.

On platform eight things were different. Here, mingled in with the waiting soldiers were groups of civilians, all desperately trying to reach the two carriages at the rear of the train. With the station clock showing five minutes past twelve, not best pleased that his train had not departed on time, a portly station master was desperately ushering soldiers and civilians alike towards the waiting carriages. "Depechez-vous! Depechez-vous! Hurry along!"

Entering the melee Clemens and Joliane began pushing and shoving their way through the crowd. Shouldering aside soldiers and civilians alike in an effort to get to the rear of the train. When they eventually reached the first of the carriages allocated to civilians it was already crammed with people. Peering over the heads of the crowd in front, Clemens could see that the second carriage was also surrounded by a throng of people all desperately trying to board the train. With their chances of boarding the train diminishing by the second, a soldier standing in the doorway of the adjoining carriage unwittingly came to their assistance.

Leaning out of the open window watching the crush of people moving along the platform, spotting Joliane, the soldier called out to her.

"There´s room in here for you sweetheart." Hoping she might take up his invitation.

What he didn´t expect to happen next was some broad-shouldered bloke, grabbing hold of the handle and pulling the door open.

"Merci, monsieur", said Clemens in his best French accent, while at the same time helping Joliane into the carriage.

No, this was not at all what Gunner Evans had in mind. What he had hoped for was some female company with perhaps a bit of a kiss and a cuddle as a reward for his act of kindness.

"Here, what´s your game, I only ..." the protest dying on Evans´ lips. What is the point, he thought, the man who he assumed was French was already closing the door behind him. Thankfully, there was some compensation coming his way.

"Merci, mon brave soldat", and with that Joliane planted a kiss on his cheek.

Blushing slightly, stepping aside to let them pass, Evans watched as the couple moved through into the carriage. While having no idea what she had just said to him, at least he had got his kiss if nothing else.

After drawing inquisitive looks from the remainder of Gunner Evans´s troop, spotting a vacant seat in the corner, Clemens steered Joliane towards it. Ignoring the curious stares, slumping onto the seat, Joliane looked up at Clemens and smiled, they had made it. Seconds later, following a shrill blast on a whistle, the train began to move. Slowly creeping along the platform. Past those who had been unable to find a seat, their dejected faces mirrored in the carriage windows. Once out from under the giant canopy of steel and glass, the locomotive quickly gathered speed. Plumes of smoke drifting past the carriages like fluffy white clouds. Tired after a long day´s driving, lulled by the gentle rocking motion of the carriage Joliane closed her eyes, and moments later she was fast asleep. Although forced to stand, Clemens had also managed to doze off. An art most regular soldiers acquire over time. Grabbing every chance, you could to get a few moments rest while still retaining an awareness of what is going on around you.

Although less than two hundred miles between the two stations, due to the hurried repairs carried out to parts of the track and several of its bridges, damaged by Allied bombing, with the speed of the locomotive dictated by the condition of the track, progress was frustratingly slow. Eventually, after spending half an hour in a siding to allow two goods trains carrying what to Clemens looked like 7.2-inch howitzers to pass, at thirty-seven minutes past five the train finally pulled into Antwerpen Centraal railway station.

After waiting until the detachment of soldiers from the Royal Artillery had left the carriage, eager no doubt to be reunited with their howitzers, stepping down onto the platform, enveloped by the flow of people exiting the rear carriages, Clemens and Joliane found themselves being swept along towards what they hoped would be the station exit.

Emerging from the cavernous interior of the station building with its Beaux-Arts façade, blinking in the late afternoon sunshine, they found themselves confronted by the vast expanse of Koenigin Astridplein Square. The formal gardens, with their horseshoe-shaped flower beds and manicured lawns, remained although large parts of it were now being used as an assembly area for military vehicles. Lorries mainly, their tailgates lowered ready to receive the soldiers who had disembarked from the train. There were also several gun tractors each towing a 25-pounder field gun, and a line of armour personnel carriers. The throbbing of idling engines and the sound of troop sergeants bellowing out their orders intruding on what should have been a place of calmness, and tranquillity.

Off to one side, hoping to take advantage of the flood of passengers exiting the station several street vendors had set up their stalls. The majority of which appeared to be selling food in some form or another. Having not eaten since breakfast that morning, eager to see what was on offer, Clemens and Joliane made their way across the square.

A stall selling pies caught Clemens's eye, and although none of them looked particularly appetising, with his stomach thinking his throat had been cut, he was willing to give them a try. With the labels written in Flemish, he was having a hard time distinguishing sweet from savoury. Being roughly the same size, and texture didn't help matters either. Forced into taking potluck, having decided on a likely candidate, just as he was about to make his purchase, he felt Joliane tugging at his arm. Hoping that she had found something better to eat, he found himself being escorted towards a stall manned by a gangly youth with long legs and skinny arms.

Like most children you came across, he was undernourished. Together with death, and destruction it seemed the war had also spawned a generation of stick insects. To his credit, the boy had done a good job when it came to advertising his wares. The cardboard sign pinned to the table was written in three languages; Flemish, French, and English with the price displayed alongside each of them in their respective currency. The only thing Clemens wasn't too happy about was the fact that he didn't appear to be selling food.

"A map is important, no?" said Joliane, noticing the look of disappointment on Clemens' face.

"Oui, Mademoiselle, if you say so" Clemens replied, a little sarcastically. Something he instantly regretted when she jabbed her elbow into his ribs.

Having made her point, crossing to the table Joliane picked up one of the maps. Unfolding it, she began examining the intricate maze of streets and roads, their names written alongside each of them in black ink. As the wording on the cardboard sign stated, it wasn't a map of the whole city, just a Town Map covering the area around the station. Enough for someone on foot who wanted to explore the old part of the town without getting lost. To go farther afield you would need to take a tram anyway and have a much larger map.

"Do you make these yourself?" Joliane enquired, hoping that the boy would understand English.

"Yes, they are all drawn by me", the young boy replied proudly in perfect English. "I copied them from the map we have in the library."

"They are tres bien" replied Joliane. "You are very clever to do this."

"Thank you", said the boy, smiling with delight. "I like maps, I hope one day it can be my work."

"Can you show me where we are" asked Joliane.

"You are here", replied the boy, indicating a place on the map with his finger. "I will mark it for you." Taking a fountain pen from his pocket, he drew a small cross on the map alongside Antwerpen Centraal.

"Thank you", said Joliane, reaching into the handbag slung across her shoulder; a bag she had found in Madame Lacagne´s wardrobe, and withdrawing a two hundred franc note, she handed it to him.

"I have some change", said the boy, rummaging in his pocket for some French currency.

"No", Joliane replied, holding up her hand, "it is not necessary."

"You are very kind", said the boy, delighted with the extra eighty francs. He had already made five sales, so it was turning out to be one of his best days. Hoping to repay the woman´s generosity, having seen Clemens standing over by the pie stall, he turned towards him. "You wish for some food?"

"Why, can you recommend somewhere?"

"Oh yes, Café Zodiac, it is not far from here and the food is very good. The prices are also quite cheap."

"How do we get there?"

"I will take you", said the boy, eager to help. "It is not far." Quickly gathering up the remainder of his maps, and tucking the small folding table under his arm, he set off.

Ten minutes later after threading their way through several side streets, they entered Rijfstraat a wide road lined on both sides by elegant flat-fronted, three-and-four-story houses with narrow rectangular windows. The grander ones boasting a first-floor balcony enclosed by ornate iron railings. Halfway along tucked away down a cobbled side street, was their destination.

"There", said the boy proudly, pointing with his free arm, "Cafe Zodiac."

"Merci", Joliane replied, smiling.

"The owner is Madame Gevaert, perhaps you could tell her that it was me who brought you?"

"Of course," said Joliane, thankful for his help. Even though the café owner had erected a small neon sign on the wall, hidden away as it was, they might easily have walked right past it.

With the woman´s generosity repaid, and hopefully, a free breakfast from Madame Gevaert to look forward to in return for his recommendation, turning on his heels the boy began running off down the road.

Situated halfway along the cobbled side street, the door to the café was flanked by a pair of rusting iron tables and chairs. The windows on both sides were in no better condition. Encrusted with seagull droppings from the roof above, it was obvious their glass panes hadn´t seen a window cleaner´s shammy leather for years. The yellow net curtains behind them were also in need of a wash. Or better still replaced with new ones. Thankfully, when they ventured inside the interior turned out to be much more pleasing. Illuminated by several brass oil lamps hanging from the white-washed ceiling, their eyes were instantly drawn towards the back wall. Painted to depict a night sky, scattered among the myriads of stars were beautifully hand-drawn images of the twelve signs of the zodiac. There were just two rows of tables, each covered with a spotlessly clean blue and white gingham tablecloth and surrounded by four matching chairs. The only slight concern was the distinct lack of customers.

"Hallo! Hallo!" A cheerful voice called out.

Turning their heads, Clemens and Joliane watched as the woman made her way towards them. A petite, elderly lady with greying hair dressed in a long black skirt and a white blouse with lace edging around the neck and cuffs and carrying what appeared to be a menu.

"Hello", Joliane replied, "you are open, yes?"

"Of course", the woman answered, her voice heavily accented. "You are a little early, but it is not a problem. Come you can sit here by the window."

"We were recommended to you by a young boy at the station", said Joliane, relieved that the woman had spoken to them in English and not Flemish.

"Ah! Young Ralph", exclaimed the woman, smiling brightly, "such a nice boy."

"We bought one of his maps", Joliane added.

"That was kind of you. He sells them to earn a little extra money for the family", said the woman, handing Joliane a menu. "Ever since his Papi was sent away by the Germans things have been hard for them. Hopefully, soon this terrible war will be over, and he can return home."

"We too hope so", replied Joliane. "In France, it is the same."

"Do you have beer Madame?" asked Clemens, keen to focus the conversation on the question of food and drink rather than chit-chat about the war.

"Of course. Good Belgium beer. The Germans didn´t drink it all, you know."

"Two beers then please", said Clemens, glancing across at Joliane for her assurance.

Nodding her confirmation, as the woman who they assumed to be Madame Gevaert hurried away, Joliane turned her attention to the menu.

"So, what delights do we have in store", asked Clemens, hopefully.

"Sadly, Albert, there is no beef and pork loaf; said Joliane ruefully, scanning the menu. "But if you enjoy soup and sausages, you will not be disappointed."

"Oh", said Clemens, smiling at her reference to the K-rations, "that´s a pity. I suppose I will have to make do with sausages then."

By the time their meal arrived, served by a pretty, young girl with braided hair, wearing a flower-print dress, the café was beginning to fill with customers. The buzz of conversation engendering a feeling of normality.

Having enjoyed an experience denied to her for so long, no sooner had Joliane put down her spoon when the old lady appeared beside the table. "You were happy with your food?" A question no self-respecting proprietor failed to ask. "Another beer, monsieur?" eyeing Clemens´ empty glass.

"No thank you", replied Clemens, wiping his mouth with a napkin.

"The soup was delicious, madame", said Joliane, resting back in her chair.

"Homemade", said the old lady proudly, "and the sausages also", looking with satisfaction at Clemens´ empty plate.

"I wonder if you could help us, please", enquired Joliane, as the old lady began collecting up their dishes. "Do you know of somewhere we can stay? A hotel perhaps?"

"Let me see now", replied the woman, pursing her lips.

"Not too expensive", added Joliane.

"The Hotel Van Eyck is not far from here. It´s a little scruffy", said the old woman, "but the rooms are clean, and the owner doesn´t charge too much."

A bit like your café, madame, thought Clemens but he didn´t say so of course.

"It sounds perfect", said Joliane. "Do you have the address please?"

"Schuptstraat 211", replied the old lady, "here let me show you on your map."

Minutes later, after settling the modest bill and thanking the proprietor for her kindness, promising to visit again for their meals, Clemens, and Joliane left the Café Zodiac and set off in search of their accommodation.

Unlike the Café Zodiac, with a large neon sign jutting out from the front of the building with its name illuminated in red letters, the Hotel van Eyck was hard to miss. In case of power cuts of which there had been quite a number recently, there was also a brass nameplate bearing the hotel´s name screwed to the wall. Although with the copper-plate letters so badly corroded it was almost impossible to read. The imposing antique door inset with etched glass panels was in a similar condition. The flaking paintwork suggesting that the last time it had seen a paintbrush was probably around the same time as Johan Van Eyck himself was working on the Arnolfini Portrait way back in 1434.

Unfortunately, unlike the cafe when they entered the hotel´s lobby things didn´t improve. Quite the opposite. Although, to be fair, with most of the electricity supply being consumed by the hotel´s neon sign, the lighting in the small, rectangular foyer was so dim that it was hard to tell if it was green flock wallpaper covering the walls or mould. Mind you, with the threadbare carpet and the thick layer of dust covering the hall-stand, a betting man would have staked his money on the mould.

The lump of lard slouched in the overstuffed armchair half-hidden by the receptionist´s desk reading yesterday´s copy of De Volksgazet didn´t do much for the ambience of the place either. The food-stained T-shirt he was wearing had been washed so many times that what had once been some kind of artwork now looked like one of those faded tattoos you see on the arms of old soldiers and sailors.

With no bell to ping and oblivious to the fact that potential customers had just walked in through the front door, Clemens decided that rather than running the risk of standing here until the man had finished reading his paper it was probably better if he made an effort to attract his attention.

"Hey! What´s this a hotel or a bloody library?"

Although the man didn´t respond, having noticed a slight flickering of the man´s eyelids Clemens was pretty sure that he had heard him. What Clemens didn´t realise however was that concealed behind the newspaper was a pornographic magazine. And that at that precise moment, the man looking at it was far too busy studying the sepia photographs of two lesbians performing cunnilingus on each other to worry about the needs of a potential guest.

With his patience wearing thin, just as Clemens was about to venture behind the desk, and articulate his request more forcibly, perturbed by the man´s tone of voice, begrudgingly, the receptionist, who as it turned out was also the hotel´s owner dragged his eyes away from the erotic images.

"Do you want a room?" he asked, peering over the top of the newspaper.

"Yes", replied Clemens, "a double."

"It´s one hundred francs a night."

"Do you take French francs?"

"Yes, but then the price is two hundred and fifty. Twenty-five francs more if you want towels, said the man, struggling up out of the chair. "Payment in advance."

"We´ll pay for two nights with towels", said Clemens, watching as Joliane withdrew the required payment from her bag, and placed it onto the desk.

Although not too thrilled by the man´s attitude, perhaps Madame Gevaert had done them a favour after all, because going on first impressions, if anybody was likely to know where he could find someone to take the diamonds off his hands, with no questions asked, he was standing right in front of him.

After counting the money for a second time, removing a key hanging on a board attached to the back wall, he placed it on the desk. "Room 101, second floor, the bathroom is at the end of the hall."

Without bothering to thank him, hoping that the café owner´s comment regarding the cleanliness of the room proved to be correct, Clemens led the way towards the stairs. But he wasn´t holding his breath.

To her credit, she was. Although the room was sparsely furnished, it was spotlessly clean. The curtains at the one window looked like they could have been washed and ironed that morning. The duvet which covered the good-sized double bed still retained some plumpness, as did the pair of pillows. A Persian carpet, which if it were genuine was worth a small fortune, covered most of the floorboards. Hidden away behind an internal door was a closet with a washbasin. Delighted with their accommodation, hanging her bag on a hook behind the door, Joliane threw herself full-length onto the bed.

"Oh, Albert it is perfect, no?"

"Pretty good," Clemens confessed, putting down the case. "I´ll just go and check out the bathroom."

Returning a few minutes later after a satisfactory inspection of the bathroom, he found Joliane fast asleep. Curled up like a child, her head buried in the pillow. Carefully removing her shoes and hanging his jacket on the back of the door, Clemens climbed onto the bed beside her. It had been a long, and eventful day, yet despite everything here they were in Antwerp. Something even he had begun to doubt. Now there was just the business of the diamonds, and with the thought uppermost in his mind, he closed his eyes.

Early next morning, leaving Joliane sleeping, Clemens made his way down to the lobby. It was time to put his assumption about the man´s ability to the test.

Thankfully, the same man was on duty. Still slumped in the armchair reading the same newspaper. Perhaps he´s been there, all night thought Clemens, a permanent fixture like the large ornate mirror on the far wall which due to heavy foxing was about as reflective as a windswept pond.

"Good morning."

The man responded quicker this time, and tucking the newspaper down the side of the chair, he climbed to his feet.

"Everything alright?" asked the man, without really caring if it was or not.

"Fine", replied Clemens, quickly changing the subject. "I was hoping you could help me."

The man stared back at him, suspiciously. "Depends on what you want?"

"I´m looking to sell something," replied Clemens, sliding a one-thousand-franc banknote across the desk toward him. "Some diamonds."

If it was a smile, it was lacking something, sincerity perhaps? But at least it was a positive sign.

"For that sort of information, I´ll need another one of those."

Clemens wasn´t going to argue. He had brought five one-thousand-franc notes with him, so he was getting off lightly.

Stuffing the notes into a trouser pocket, reaching for the notepad and pen on the end of the desk, the man began writing. This was an unexpected bonus, and it would also put him in Van Der Broeck´s good books too. Never a bad thing now that the Bosch had been kicked out of Antwerp, and things could begin getting back to normal. Allowing the ink to dry, tearing out the top page, he handed it to Clemens.

"Should I mention who I got this from?"

"No need, he´ll know who sent you", replied the man, and replacing the pen in its holder, he returned to his armchair and the newspaper which he had probably read a dozen times already.

Joliane was just returning from the bathroom when he reached the landing.

"Hello, sleepyhead, are you ready for some breakfast?"

"Oui, but I am only this sleepyhead because you keep me awake with your twitching."

"What twitching?" said Clemens following her into the room.

"Tonight, I will show you", replied Joliane, "but now it is time for breakfast, no."

With no trouble in finding the café again, after a warm welcome from Madame Gevaert Clemens and Joliane tucked into a very un-continental style breakfast of scrambled eggs, thin strips of crispy bacon and fried bread. Having been spoiled by their supply of real coffee, Café Zodiac´s offering left much to be desired but as Madame Gevaert was quick to point out, even though Antwerp had been liberated, there was still a war going on. So, they didn´t dare complain.

The only real discord came when Clemens insisted on going to visit the diamond dealer alone. Thankfully, infuriating though it was Joliane saw that he was right. So, having agreed to spend some woman-to-woman time with Madame Gevaert while he was gone after locating the diamond dealer´s address on the boy´s map, Clemens left the café.

His route took him back past the Hotel Van Eyck and along Schuptstraat before turning left at the junction with Lange Herentalsestraat. Crossing the intersection with Lange Kievitstraat after a ten-minute walk, he found himself in Van Leriusstraat.

Unlike the hotel, the door to Van Leriusstraat 43 was freshly painted, and the brass plate attached to the wall alongside was highly polished. The occupant´s name and the nature of the business clearly defined in black lettering; Van Der Broeck – Diamantaire. Pressing the brass nipple on the doorbell, Clemens stepped back onto the pavement.

He didn´t have long to wait before the door was opened, by a tall, burly man wearing a drab, grey double-breasted suit, and a patterned shirt. His thin cotton tie was so grease-stained that it looked like it was made of leather.

"Ja, wat wil je. Yes, what do you want?"

Clemens didn´t bother replying, instead, he just held up the piece of paper the hotel owner had written the address on.

"Come, follow me", said the man, reverting to English, and closing the door behind them, he led Clemens towards a set of stairs.

Once they reached the first floor, indicating for Clemens to remain where he was the man walked across to a door inset with an opaque glass panel. Knocking once without waiting for a reply, he pushed it open. After a brief conversation with the person in the room, beckoning Clemens forward, he ushered him inside. The gesture revealing the shoulder holster under the man´s outstretched arm. Obviously, he was more than just a doorman.

Located at the rear of the building judging by the lintel running across the ceiling the room had been extended. Two rooms knocked into one by the look of it. Given the room´s original dimensions, it had probably been done to accommodate the over-size antique knee-hole desk which took up half of the available space. Behind it were two windows, the row of iron bars discreetly hidden by half-drawn curtains. The only other furniture was a two-seater sofa pushed up against the opposite wall complemented by a pair of orange velour cushions.

The man sitting behind the desk didn´t bother getting up. Simply waving a hand towards one of the two chairs facing towards him. "Please sit down."

Quite a suave-looking chap our Monsieur, Van Der Broeck thought Clemens, as he lowered himself into one of the chairs. Middle-aged, maybe a little older. Although the tie didn´t match the dark green tweed jacket and white spearpoint collar shirt he was wearing, he took pride in his appearance. Judging by the odd grey hair in his moustache, his dark, slicked-back hair was obviously out of a bottle. Like his voice, his nails were also well-manicured. What also caught Clemens´s eye was the signet ring he was wearing. He had never seen one with a diamond in it before, certainly not one that wouldn´t have looked out of place in the Crown Jewels.

Crossing to the desk the man with the gun placed the slip of paper in front of his employer and without saying a word he left the room, closing the door behind him.

"So, Monsieur?" said Van Der Broeck, enquiringly, glancing down at the piece of paper.

"Smith." Clemens replied, keeping a deadpan face.

"Ah! Smith. Such an uncommon name" Van Der Boeck replied, without a trace of sarcasm.

"Oh, there are more of us than you think", Clemens replied, winking.

"So, Mister Smith how may I help you," asked Van Der Broeck, keen to get to the reason for the man´s visit.

"I have some diamonds I would like to sell."

"Indeed, then you have come to the right place. Do you have the stones with you?"

Reaching into his pocket Clemens took out the small pouch and placed it on the desk´s tooled leather liner.

Intrigued, opening a desk drawer Van Der Broeck removed a piece of green felt cloth, much like the baize used on billiard tables, and laying it out in a square, he smoothed it with his hand.

"May I?" and picking up the pouch, the dealer emptied the contents onto the cloth. Stretching out his hand, he brushed his fingers gently over the diamonds, spreading them out evenly across the cloth.

"There's thirty altogether", said Clemens.

Van Der Broeck didn't answer right away, his attention focused on the collection of stones.

"So, what do you think they are worth?"

"Patience my friend", the dealer replied, "first I must inspect them." And reaching into the drawer once more, he retrieved a folded cloth containing a pair of long tweezers and a jeweller's loupe.

Selecting one of the gems, he gripped it with the tweezers and holding it up in front of him with the loupe pressed against his left eye, Van Der Broeck began examining the stone. The light from the desk lamp reflected off its highly polished facets. Placing it to one side, the dealer selected another diamond, repeating the process until he had examined all thirty of the diamonds.

"One can never be too careful", said Van Der Broeck retuning his tools to the drawer. "There are so many fakes these days."

"But not these", said Clemens, looking at the cluster of stones.

"No, Mister Smith, these are how do you say, the genuine article."

"And you would like to buy them?"

"Certainly, for the right price of course."

"Well, you are the expert, so you tell me what they are worth."

"First I would like to ask where you obtained these beautiful diamonds?"

"A gift from my dear old Grandma", Clemens replied, "God Bless her."

"God Bless her indeed, but to be serious ..."

"I was told you didn't ask too many questions", said Clemens, cutting him off in mid-sentence.

Van Der Broeck looked across at him. He was right of course, part of the reason he was so successful, even during times like this was because of his reputation for discretion. It had brought him a lot of business. Lucrative business too. And this might well be another of those occasions. The stones the man had brought him were top quality. Even without weighing them, he could tell that they were at least a carat in weight, perhaps one and a quarter. The clarity was excellent with barely a blemish, and with each stone so closely matched, whoever cut them must have been very skilled indeed.

"Forgive me", said Van Der Broeck, smiling, "a force of habit I´m afraid. So, how much were you expecting to get for your diamonds, Mister Smith?"

"As much as I can", Clemens replied.

"Of course, you must understand that with the war, things are not good right now", replied Van Der Broeck. "Many people, especially the Jews have been liquidating their assets and flooding the market with diamonds."

Here we go, thought Clemens, the same old sob story. "Look just give me your best price."

"Do you wish to be paid in Belgium francs?"

"No, French francs."

"Very well", said the dealer, "Then I can offer you five hundred thousand francs. In cash of course."

"I was looking for more", Clemens replied, "a lot more."

"How much more?"

"A million francs."

"Forgive me, Mister Smith", said Van Der Broeck, "but such a sum is impossible. Even in a buoyant market, your diamonds are not worth that much, believe me."

He´s got me over a barrel really", thought Clemens. Even if he is trying to swindle me, which he probably is. Having, no idea what they are worth anyway, the only reason he had said one million francs was because that was what they needed to buy the farm.

"How about meeting me in the middle at seven hundred and fifty thousand."

Leaning back in his chair, Van Der Broeck stroked his chin, thoughtfully. He was a strange one this Mister Smith, not his real name of course. He was English, there was no disguising the accent but what was he doing in Antwerp with such a collection of exquisite diamonds he wondered? He didn´t look like a thief but then who can tell? During the last four years, many people, good honest people have turned to stealing just to survive.

"I will increase my offer to six hundred thousand but not a franc more. You can take it or leave it."

He means it, too, thought Clemens, and it was an extra hundred thousand. "Done", said Clemens, relieved that the bartering was over.

"Excellent", Van Der Broeck replied, getting up from his chair, "then we have a deal. Come shake hands."

Having sealed the transaction with a handshake, Clemens´ next concern was the payment.

"Do I get the money now?" Clemens asked, looking across at the impressive looking Bode Panzer safe standing against the end wall.

"No, not today", said the dealer, I need to go to the bank. Unfortunately, I do not have that much money in French Francs. Come back tomorrow at midday, and I will have it for you then."

"Okay", replied Clemens, "until then I´ll hang onto the diamonds."

"They will be perfectly safe with me."

"No offense, Monsieur Van Der Broeck but I think I´ll hang onto them for now."

"As you wish", Van Der Broeck replied, turning away as Clemens scooped up the diamonds, and returned them to the pouch. "Tomorrow at twelve then."

Filled with excitement, tinged by a little disappointment, Clemens made his way back to the hotel. Should he try someone else, he wondered, get a second opinion perhaps? No there wasn´t time really, and where was he going to find an alternative buyer anyway. No, they would just have to accept that what Van Der Broeck was offering them was all they were going to get and just be grateful. Besides, much as he wanted the farm if what they had was not enough to buy it, then they would just have to find somewhere else. It shouldn´t be too hard. No, count your blessings, Albert lad, not so long ago you had nothing now you´re about to get your hands on six hundred thousand Francs. Which even to someone more used to the good old English pound, still sounded like a hell of a lot of money.

"Well?" cried Joliane excitedly, rushing across the room towards him as Clemens opened the door.

"A kiss first", said Clemens, taking her in his arms.

She allowed him his kiss but only a lingering one. "Tell, me! Tell me!" Joliane pleaded and pushed him away.

Seeing that he was fighting a losing battle, taking her by the hand Clemens led her across to the bed.

"Now sit and be quiet and I´ll explain everything." Said Clemens, ignoring the pout as Joliane sat down beside him.

"Right", said Clemens, "the good news is I´ve sold the diamonds. The not-so-good news is he will only pay us six hundred thousand francs for them. She tried to hide it, but the look of disappointment still manifested itself.

"It´s still a lot of money Joliane and who knows, if nobody else wants the farm, then maybe the old woman might accept what we have."

He was right of course. Yes, she must be positive, and reaching out Joliane pulled him towards her. With the rest of the day to themselves, and with nobody to disturb them now was the perfect time to reward him as only she knew how.

The next day, at precisely fourteen minutes past twelve, a brown paper parcel containing six hundred thousand French Francs tucked under his arm, Clemens stepped out onto Van Leriusstraat. Crossing the road onto Lange Herentalsestraat, with a spring in his step he set off for the hotel and with any luck a train back to Paris.

He couldn´t understand how he came to get lost, after all, it was a simple enough route; up Lange Herentalsestraat, then right into Schuptstraat and the hotel was halfway along on his left. Thankfully for Clemens, it turned out to be something of a blessing. As he retraced his steps, he suddenly caught sight of Van Der Broeck´s doorman come, bodyguard, reflected in the shop window on the opposite corner. With alarm bells ringing in his head, forcing himself to maintain a normal stride, Clemens made his way back towards Lange Herentalsestraat. With so few people about it didn´t take him long to spot the man´s accomplice, shadowing him on the opposite side of the road. He was quite a bit younger than the doorman, and although he was doing his best to avoid suspicion, he stood out like a sore thumb. So, not satisfied with the diamonds, it seemed Monsieur van Der Broeck also wanted his money back.

Entering the hotel, working on the assumption that they had not been sent to escort him safely home, Clemens quickly formed a plan of sorts. Pretty confident that the hotel owner would not hesitate to provide the two men with their room number, especially as one of them was carrying a gun, his only hope was the element of surprise.

Praying that Joliane had already gone to the café for lunch, taking the stairs two at a time Clemens raced up to the second floor. Flinging opening the door to their room, he saw that his prayer hadn´t been answered.

"Quick, get in." And thrusting the parcel into her hands he pulled open the closet door. "Don´t open it to anyone, understand?" and before she could argue, he pushed her inside. After closing the door, with nowhere suitable to hide, Clemens made his way to the bathroom at the end of the hall.

He didn´t have to wait long before the sound of footsteps on the stairs warned him of their approach. Peering through a gap in the door, Clemens watched as the two men made their way towards the room, he and Joliane were staying in. Pausing outside the door, reaching inside his jacket, the dealer´s bodyguard pulled the gun out of its holster. Then, with a nod to his accomplice, slamming his shoulder against the door, he forced it open, and the two men burst into the room.

Waiting until both the men had disappeared inside, pulling the dagger from the sheath strapped to his ankle, Clemens made his way along the hall. Before leaving, he had thought about bringing the Thompson with them. Without its butt, it would have just fitted in the suitcase, but he had decided it was too much of a risk. Thankfully, he hadn´t left the paratrooper´s dagger behind though. Just as well given their present position.

Although he had entered the room behind the gunman, it was the younger man who made his way towards the closet. Taking hold of the door handle, just as he was about to open it, he found himself distracted by a noise he certainly wasn´t expecting to hear; the sound of something heavy dropping onto the wooden floorboards.

If that was unexpected, when he turned around, what he saw next was even more of a surprise. Something quite shocking really, especially when you have never seen a man whose throat had just been cut before.

Lowering the dead man´s body onto the floor, Clemens watched as the colour drained away from the younger man´s face as he stood motionless, like a rabbit caught in the headlights of an oncoming car. Knowing he had no other option but to kill him, Clemens decided not to rush things. Unlikely as it seemed there was always the chance that the would-be thief might make it easier by putting up a fight and to ease his conscience a little.

The young man on the other hand was having other thoughts. Realising his predicament, hoping that his legs which felt like they had turned to jelly would respond when he needed them to, his eyes flitted nervously from the blood-stained dagger in Clemens´ hand to the welcoming sight of the open door. Carefully weighing up his chances of making it past one, and out through the other. One part of his brain telling him to go for it, and the other part, the more rational part, telling him it was hopeless to even try. Sadly, even as a youth, he had always made bad decisions, it was one of the reasons he now found himself in this situation. Having chosen a life of crime instead of a career in the merchant navy, the decision had well and truly come back to haunt him.

As expected, the go-for-it-for-it part of him won in the end, and like a sprinter leaving his blocks, the young henchman ran towards the open door. Sadly, although his legs did him proud, the odds were always stacked against him and halfway across the room, his progress was brought to an abrupt halt. His forward momentum driving the blade of the dagger deep into his chest. Standing inches apart, killer and victim looked into each other's eyes, pity mirrored in one, bewilderment in the other. Taking the dying man in his arms, Clemens gently lowered him onto the floor and wiping the blade on the man's coat, he walked across to the closet and opened the door.

"It´s alright, we´re safe," and taking Joliane in his arms, he hugged her to him.

"Who are they?" asked Joliane catching sight of the two bodies.

"They worked for the diamond dealer", replied Clemens, "it seems he wanted his money back."

"Our money. The money is ours, Albert", said Joliane angrily, I am pleased they are dead, bad people like them deserve to be punished."

"Well, these two won´t be doing any more robbing", Clemens replied, and grabbing hold of each man in turn, he dragged both of the bodies into the closet.

"Right", said Clemens, closing the closet door, now I want you to pack everything into the suitcase, and wait up here until I call for you, okay?"

"What will you do Albert?"

"I´m just going to make sure nobody sees us leave. Now wait here, I won´t be long." And picking up the bodyguard's gun Clemens left the room…

The lump of lard was still sitting in his armchair when Clemens reached the lobby. No newspaper this time, he was far too concerned about what was happening in one of his rooms to think about reading. He was even more concerned when he saw the gun in Clemens´s hand, especially as it was pointing right at him.

"Get up, you piece of shit."

Like someone who had just sat down on a sharp object, the man jumped up from the chair.

"Please, monsieur don´t shoot me, I … They … "

"Shut up!" said Clemens angrily, "which is your room?"

"Here," the proprietor replied, pointing to a door behind him.

"Open it."

Obediently, the man did as he was told, pushing the door wide open so that Clemens could see inside.

"Get in!"

Following the hotel owner into the room, Clemens closed the door behind him. Not so much a room, more a bedsit really with a sink, and kitchen area over by the window, a large unmade bed pushed up against one wall, and a small dining table covered in pieces of crockery and a couple of chairs. The only other door presumably led to a bathroom but Clemens didn´t bother to check. The place had a distinctive smell which Clemens couldn´t quite place but whatever it was it wasn´t something you could put in a bottle and sell.

Gesturing for him to sit on one of the chairs, tucking the pistol in his waistband, Clemens crossed to the bed. Removing the top sheet, he sliced along it with the dagger, cutting off two long strips of material. Forcing the man´s podgy hands behind his back, he tied them tightly together. Using the second strip to secure him to the chair.

"I should kill you, you bastard", said Clemens, pressing the muzzle of the gun against the man´s forehead. "And if you do anything to put us in danger again, that´s just what I´ll do, understand?"

Too traumatised to speak, the hotel owner nodded his head vigorously up and down. Stuffing a smaller piece of the sheet into the man´s mouth, satisfied that he wouldn´t be going anywhere, Clemens left the room. Given how spotless their room had been, the man must employ cleaners, thought Clemens so somebody will find him eventually. Not that he cared anyway, if he starved to death, it was his own fault. Mind you given the amount of fat on him that could take quite some time.

"You can come down, Joliane" Clemens shouted, standing at the foot of the stairs. Smiling as she stepped into the lobby.

"Now listen and I don´t want any arguments, okay? Go straight to the station and get on the first train going to Paris."

"But what about you?"

"I won´t be long. I just have something to do first."

"No, Albert, please, you must come with me."

"Trust me I´ll be back in time for the train," said Clemens, smiling reassuringly.

"But..."

"No buts, just do as I say, please."

"Okay, but you promise?"

"I promise. Now go!"

A part of him had wanted to go with her. To forget what has happened and get the hell out of Antwerp with what they had. But that was not Albert Clemens´s way. No, someone had tried to steal from him, even have him killed if necessary, and like the story said there was a price to pay for that. And on this occasion, he was going to play the part of the piper.

Having helped himself to the man´s gun, after rummaging through his pockets, Clemens relieved him of his key; he was never going to need them again anyway, so gaining entry to Van Leriusstraat 43 was going to be a piece of cake. Quite what he was going to do when he got there, he wasn´t too sure but whatever it was, Monsieur Van Der Broeck was not going to enjoy it one little bit.

Looking up as the door to his office opened, to say that Van Der Broeck was surprised by who he saw standing in the doorway would be something of an understatement. Judging by the half-eaten herring pate baguette on his desk, he had been enjoying a light lunch while awaiting the return of his two associates from their little errand. Except it wasn´t them who entered the room, it was Clemens, and he certainly hadn´t come to return the diamond dealers six hundred thousand French francs. No, he was there for quite a different reason, and it was this that was causing the palpitations the Belgian was suddenly experiencing. That and the thought that he might just have eaten his last meal.

"Get up", said Clemens.

Slowly, the diamond dealer climbed to his feet, his right hand nervously brushing the crumbs off the front of his grey houndstooth patterned jacket.

"Please, let me explain, it has all been a terrible misunderstanding, I can … "

"Sit in the chair", said Clemens, pointing with the barrel of the Walther P38 to one of the chairs in front of the desk. The same one he had occupied less than an hour ago as Van Der Broeck counted out the payment for the diamonds.

Recognising the pistol, the dealer knew instantly that the men he had sent to rob the Englishman were probably dead. How else would the man have obtained the gun? Strangely, rather than adding to the sense of fear, he was now experiencing, the realisation only served to focus his mind. The instinct for survival sending his brain into overdrive as he searched for a way to extricate himself from the terrible dilemma, he found himself in.

Forcing his legs into motion, Van Der Broeck slowly walked out from behind the desk and seated himself in the chair, he gripped the wooden arms with his sweaty palms.

"So, Mr Smith what is it you want? Or have you just come seeking retribution?" Van Der Broeck asked, struggling to quell the sense of fear from afflicting his voice.

"Call it what you like", said Clemens, but what I want you to do right now is to open that safe."

"And if I refuse?"

"I wouldn´t if I were you, because I´m not in a very good mood."

"Can we not come to some compromise? What if I were to give you back your diamonds?"

Ignoring the man´s proposal, pushing the pistol into the waistband of his trousers, Clemens reached down and pulled out the dagger. With the blade pointing downwards, he crossed to where the man was sitting. Leaning down, with his face inches from the diamond dealers, Clemens repeated the request. "I´ll ask you once more to open the safe."

"Never!" said Van Der Broeck, his voice an octave higher than normal.

It was then, as the blade of the dagger buried itself into his left thigh that it became clear to Van Der Broeck why Clemens had made him change chairs.

Waiting until the man´s agonizing scream had died away to a low moaning sound, pulling out the dagger, Clemens removed his hand from the dealer´s mouth.

"One last chance or I´ll do the same to your other leg."

Shocked by the man´s threat, gripping the arms of the chair like someone on a white-knuckle ride at the fairground, Van Der Broeck gazed up at his attacker. Fighting back the excruciating pain burning through his leg, with perspiration running down into his eyes, he muttered something.

"I didn´t hear you?" said Clemens.

With one hand pressing down on the wound in his thigh, wiping away the saliva dribbling out of the corner of his mouth with his other hand, the dealer repeated what he had said. "The keys are in the desk drawer."

After wiping the blade clean on the man´s trousers, Clemens walked around to the back of the desk and began pulling open the drawers. He found what he was looking for in the third one. Attached to a brass ring the two antique keys were quite recognisable; one even had the maker´s name inscribed on it; Bode & Troue Hannover.

"You will never get away with this, Englishman," said Van Der Broeck through gritted teeth, as Clemens inserted the first of the two keys into the lock.

Ignoring the man's idle threat, slipping the other key into the second lock, Clemens turned it anticlockwise until he felt resistance. Taking hold of the ornate brass handle, embossed with the manufacturer's name, twisting it sideways he pulled open the heavy safe door.

The diamond dealer was screaming at him now, his face contorted with rage, and although he was speaking in Dutch, Clemens had a pretty good idea most of the words were expletives.

Perhaps if he had been a little more contrite, a little more cooperative Clemens might well have treated him the same way he had the hotelier. Tying him to the chair and leaving with what he came for. But unlike the owner of the Hotel van Eyck, this one had pushed Clemens too far. Sending people to rob them was bad enough, but one of them had been carrying a gun which he was probably prepared to use. Not just on him, but also on Joliane, and this made Clemens very, very angry.

Incensed, picking up one of the cushions from the sofa Clemens walked over to Van Der Broeck, and pushing it into his face, with the muzzle of the pistol pressed against the cushion, he shot him in the head. Droplets of blood and fragments of scull splattering like raindrops onto the leather surface of the desk behind him.

Stepping back, Clemens looked down at the body of the dead man slumped in the chair a neat round hole in the centre of his forehead. Although killing people was nothing new to him, contrary to what his old pal Nobby used to think, murdering someone in cold blood did trouble him. More so now that he wasn't a soldier with a license to kill as part of the job description. Anyway, what was done was done, the bastard had deserved to die, and pushing the thought from his mind, sticking the Walther into his waistband, Clemens walked across to the safe. Regardless of what had brought him here, he certainly didn't intend to leave empty-handed.

At the top of the safe were two identical drawers, both without locks. Below them, the space was dissected by a metal shelf. Tucked into the lower half, was a brown leather bag, not unlike a Gladstone Bag named after the four-time Prime Minister, William Gladstone. On the shelf above it were two metal trays; rows of neatly stacked gold coins in one, and oblong gold bars stamped 500g in the other. Delighted by his initial discovery, filled with anticipation, Clemens pulled open one of the top drawers.

Whatever he was expecting to find it certainly wasn't wads of Belgium francs and American dollars. High denomination too, according to the values printed on the wrappers. It was in the second drawer that he discovered the diamonds. Hundreds of them. The majority were cut and polished like those you would see on display in a jeweller's window. Others looked like pieces of frosted glass. Nestled in amongst them was the small pouch which had brought them to Antwerp in the first place.

With the contents transferred to the bag, although there was no need to lock it, returning to the drawer in which he had found the keys to the safe, he quickly located the key to the bag. After all, the last thing he wanted was for it to suddenly spring open at some inopportune moment. Before leaving the room, acting on a whim Clemens decided to lock the safe. Not knowing that it was empty might just confuse the investigation once the dealer's body was discovered. And for Clemens confusion meant more time for them to get the hell out of Antwerp.

Steeling himself against breaking into a run, walking at a pace which he hoped wouldn't attract attention, Clemens made his way up Lange Herentalsestraat. Halfway along, spotting a rainwater drain, he stopped beside it, and on the pretext of doing up a shoelace, he dropped the Walther and the keys to the safe through a slot in the grill. Although it was unlikely, that he would be stopped and searched by the police, if he were, they were the last things he wanted to be found in his possession.

The only time he slackened his pace was when he was passing the Hotel van Eyck in Schuptstraat. The urge to go inside and eliminate the only witness to what had happened drawing him towards the entrance. But in the end, he decided against it. Common sense perhaps, or was it compassion? Whatever it was, praying the decision wouldn't come back to haunt him, he continued towards the station. One thing that was for certain, when the bodies of the two men were discovered the owner of the hotel was going to have quite a lot of explaining to do.

Emerging from the narrow side street into the vast expanse of Koningin Astridplein Square Clemens was surprised at how quiet it was. There was not an army vehicle to be seen, and hardly any people exiting the train station. He noticed that the row of stalls was still there, including the young boys. Acting on impulse Clemens hurried across the square towards it.

"Hello, do you want my help?" asked the boy, recognising him immediately.

Ignoring the boy´s question, placing the bag on the ground, he unlocked the two locks and reaching into the bag, Clemens pulled out a bundle of Belgium banknotes.

"Give some to the old man, okay?" said Clemens, glancing across at the pie stall. And handing the banknotes to the boy, he turned and walked away.

Stunned, the boy looked down at the wad of notes in his hand. He had never seen so much money in his life before.

"I will, I promise", the young boy shouted… Thank you, Monsieur."

Hurrying through the arched doorway into the vast station hall, Clemens began looking around for somebody in a railway uniform. Spotting a likely candidate, an elderly man in a long black coat and wearing a peaked cap, he went over to him.

"The train to Paris, which platform, please?"

The puzzled look on the man´s face was a disappointment, clearly, he didn´t understand English.

The booking hall, thought Clemens, I´ll try there. But just as he was about to turn away, the old railway official spoke to him.

"Paris, perron vijf, Paris, platform five", replied the man, pointing with his hand.

"Pardon", said Clemens, shrugging his shoulders. "I don´t understand."

"Vijf", repeated the station official, holding up his left hand, his fingers and thumb extended. "Vijf."

"Merci, Monsieur," Clemens replied, and praying he was in time, moving in the direction the man had indicated, Clemens hurried away in search of platform five.

Thankfully, when he reached the gate with the number five displayed over its entrance Clemens was relieved to see that passengers were still making their way through the barrier. Beyond them, others, laden down with suitcases and cardboard boxes were already making their way towards the waiting carriages. Taking his place in the queue, straining to see if Joliane was among them it was then that he realised that she had their tickets.

"Albert. Albert."

Alerted by the sound of Jolian´s voice, turning his head, Clemens saw her hurrying towards him, the suitcase clutched in her hand.

"Oh, Albert, I was so afraid you would not come", Joliane sobbed, tears streaming down her cheeks.

Dropping the heavy bag, Clemens took her into his arms.

"I told you to get on the train", but there was no anger in his voice, only relief that she was there.

"I could not leave without you, Albert, you are my life", she sobbed, burying her head in his chest.

Gently wiping away her tears, Clemens kissed her tenderly on the lips. Her words kindling a desire to live and to love in a way he had never experienced before.

With their reunion interrupted by the blast of a station master´s whistle, picking up the bag and the abandoned suitcase, with Joliane holding onto his arm, Clemens hurried across to the barrier.

Surprisingly, the carriage they found themselves in was half empty. The only other occupants were a group of families with very young children crowded together down at the far end surrounded by their luggage. Given how packed the train had been on their outward journey, it seemed that more people were keen to get to Antwerp than to leave it. After taking their seats at the other end of the compartment, it was then that Joliane noticed the bag Clemens was carrying.

"What is in the bag, Albert?"

"It´s a surprise", Clemens replied, putting the bag on the seat beside him.

"Show me", Joliane demanded excitedly.

"Then it wouldn´t be a surprise, would it? Wait until we get to Paris, and then I´ll let you see."

"Non! I wish to see now", said Joiane, sticking out her lower lip in an all too familiar pout.

"Alright", said Clemens, well aware that he wasn´t going to get any peace unless he did. "Close your eyes then."

"I am not a little girl, Albert."

"Close your eyes."

Knowing from his tone of voice that he was not going to be moved, puffing out her cheeks, Joliane did as she was told.

Placing the bag on his lap, flicking open the two locks, Clemens pulled open the bag.

"Okay, now you can look." said Clemens, smiling at the look of astonishment on Joliane´s face as she peered into the open bag.

"Happy now?"

"Oh, Albert it is magnifique."

"Enough to buy a farm, probably two."

Joliane didn´t know what to say. The sight of so much gold and money was overwhelming. And then there were the diamonds, hundreds of them all of different shapes and sizes. So much wealth in such a small bag, and it was all theirs.

Their moment of indulgence was suddenly interrupted by a second blast on the whistle followed by a sudden jolt as the train began to move off, slowly pulling the half-a-dozen or so carriages along its designated track. Standing on the empty platform the uniformed station master and a few porters, their work done, watched as it made its way out from under the domed glass canopy, and into the daylight.

With clouds of smoke billowing from its chimney, the locomotive quickly picked up speed, and within a matter of minutes, the train was chugging through Antwerp's sprawling suburbs, and out into the flat Belgium countryside beyond. Exhausted by the day's events, with her head resting on Clemens' shoulder, lulled by the clickety-clack of the train wheels, it wasn't long before Joliane drifted off into a deep sleep.

Clemens had decided not to show her the diamond dealer's ring until they got back to the farm. She had had quite enough excitement already.

It was still light when the train pulled into the Gard Du Nord. Its platforms, those still in operation thronged with people, pushing and shoving their way onto and off the stationary carriages. After battling through the tide of people flooding into the station, hand in hand Clemens and Joliane made their way through the booking hall and out onto the station concourse.

Wearing the same suit, and a tie which was so loud it could be heard a mile away, the man running the taxi service was instantly recognisable. Striding up and down the line of cars, his fedora clutched in his hand, gesturing them towards the queue of waiting customers with his hand. "Vite! Vite!"

Pausing to light the Gauloises pressed between his lips, as he exhaled a mouthful of smoke, he spotted Clemens and Joliane walking towards him.

"Ah, Bonsoir mes amis, so you have returned?"

"Bonsoir", replied Clemens.

"So, you have come for your Citroen, avez-vous?"

"Yes, and a cigarette too if you can spare one?"

"Ah, but of course," the man replied, offering Clemens the packet. "And for you, Mademoiselle?"

"Merci", said Joliane, taking one of the cigarettes.

After lighting their cigarettes, the taxi proprietor got down to business.

"Are you sure you don't want to sell it to me, Monsieur?"

"Sorry, but we need it."

"I can give you a very good price."

Clemens shook his head. "No thanks, but you can sell me some petrol though."

"It is an expensive commodity, mes amis", the man replied, shrugging his shoulders. If the Englishman wasn't willing to sell the car, who knows perhaps he could make a little extra money selling him some petrol.

"How much for a full tank and the Jerry can?"

"Three thousand francs."

With a feeling that he was paying over the odds, reaching into his pocket Clemens took out two one-hundred-dollar bills. "Will this cover it?"

"Oui, Monsieur, dollars are always acceptable."

"And you can leave the plates on, okay?"

"Okay," said the man, taking the two bills from Clemens' outstretched hand.

"Listen, as we won't need the car until tomorrow morning, can you recommend somewhere we can stay for the night?"

"Oui, of course, there is a small hotel just around the corner in Boulevard de Denain, very clean and they also serve good food."

"Does it have a name?"

"Hotel Bonaparte. Tell them Maurice sent you and you will be well looked after."

"Merci", said Clemens, we'll come for the car at eight o'clock tomorrow morning if that's okay?"

"It will be here waiting for you," replied the proprietor, slipping the two, dollar bills into an inside pocket. Not only had he made a killing on the petrol, but he also had the use of the car for another twelve hours. Feeling quite pleased with himself, he made his way back to the taxi rank. Whatever the two strangers had been up to, making their acquaintance had certainly proved to be his lucky day. Not only had the use of the car proved very lucrative but he had also made a nice profit on the sale of the petrol too. Yes, Maurice Paquet was a very happy man indeed.

Whether the mention of his name made any difference, but the hotel certainly lived up to expectations. The meal, a kind of rabbit stew with dumplings, complimented by a bottle of the establishment's most expensive wine was very enjoyable. The room with its private bathroom and a bed you needed a ladder to get into was perfect. Although with Joliane insisting that they inspect every stone and count every banknote it was quite late by the time they eventually climbed into it.

At eight o'clock the next morning, as promised the car was waiting for them. With the taxi owner having insisted on it being cleaned and valeted it looked like it had just left the showroom. There were a few minor blemishes to the paintwork where the temporary taxi sign had been attached but they were hardly noticeable. After stowing the suitcase and bag in the boot along with the full jerry can of petrol, after saying their goodbyes to the proprietor, Clemens and Joliane began their homeward journey. Back to a place which would soon belong to them. A place where they could begin their new life together.

Chapter Eight

Internment camp south of Saint-Malo

Initially, Brohl had been extremely angry but being a pragmatic man, the feeling hadn't lasted long. What had happened couldn't have been foreseen so he had to be thankful for how things had turned out, even though they were not what he had had in mind.

As a member of the SS Schutzstaffel, Brohl had embraced the Nazi ideology wholeheartedly. The promise of a new and powerful Germany under their Fuehrer fuelling his desire to serve the new order. Even when he was transferred to the Gestapo, not a move he was totally happy with, his belief never faltered, his desire to serve the Fatherland was always uppermost in his thoughts and actions. His desire to punish and suppress those who threatened it was unquenchable. But for all that Brohl was also a rather selfish man. Someone who, despite his outward show of commitment to the party always considered his own needs first. After all who better to entrust your welfare to but yourself? Based on this principle as well as taking steps to ensure his survival should things go wrong; he had also made provisions to provide himself with everything he needed to lead an enjoyable life regardless of which side ended up winning the war.

Of course, he would much prefer it if Germany won. After all a victorious Germany would give him all the rewards he could ever wanted. Power, status, and wealth. But on the other hand, if Germany were to be defeated, as a member of the hated Gestapo not only would he forfeit the aforementioned but quite possibly his own life. So, on that basis alone Brohl always liked to keep his finger on the pulse. Take a view of the bigger picture if you like. He was not a man who liked surprises.

A student of history, in Brohl's opinion Hitler made his first blunder on the 22nd June 1941 when he invaded Russia. Yes, it was true that initially, things had gone well, very well in fact. But so had they for Napoleon Bonaparte in 1812 only for him to suffer a disastrous defeat and the loss of 300,000 soldiers. The Führer's second blunder came on the 11th of December 1941 when he declared war on the United States of America, one of the world's most powerful countries, with endless resources of both men and materials. But for Brohl what finally shattered the myth of Hitler's invincibility was the defeat at Stalingrad in February 1943 and the loss of the 6th Army. In hindsight thought Brohl instead of writing Mein Kampf when he was a prisoner in Landsberg prison, he should have studied his history books instead. As his father had told him on many occasions, "A wise man learns from the mistakes of others, that way he doesn't make the same mistakes himself" and it was something Brohl had never forgotten.

However, despite all his planning things first began to go wrong for Brohl when he was posted to Normandy shortly before the Allied invasion. An invasion which once again exposed Hitler's unwillingness to listen to the advice of his generals. Even that of Field Marshal Rommel whose desperate plea for him to release the Panzer units held in reserve had fallen on deaf ears. A decision which just like Dunkirk would prove to be yet another nail in Germany's coffin. Another missed opportunity, another mistake to add to the catalogue of failings. Whether from stupidity or his own sense of infallibility for someone with the well-being of a nation resting on his shoulders, not heeding the advice of those who knew better than him in Brohl's opinion was tantamount to a betrayal.

Putting this aside, although things had not worked out as he had planned, all was not lost. For one thing unlike many others, he was still alive. He also had Fengler his faithful bloodhound with him. Or should that be Rottweiler, given the man's penchant for violence?

Ironically, their salvation had come in the form of a telephone call from an old friend, a Hauptmann the Captain in the SS who he had known before his secondment to the Gestapo. A drinking pal from their days in Berlin together, they had always kept in touch despite their different roles. Although short, the call from Hauptmann Werner Albrecht of the 2nd SS Panzer Corps in Le Hom was quite specific. "Caen is lost, you must get out of Normandy, Otto, get out of France!" Then, the line went dead. Another of Hitler's costly errors, ignoring the evidence presented to him, and relying instead on his own convictions that the expected invasion would be in the Pas-De-Calais.

Trusting his friend implicitly, Brohl immediately acted on his advice and sending Fengler to bring the car around to the rear of the building, he began removing the contents of the small filing cabinet. Fortunately, having only moved to their new offices in Soulevre en Bocage a few weeks ago there were not too many case files, certainly none worth keeping, so crossing to the stove, he began feeding them into the flames. With the files incinerated, and nothing of value worth taking, abandoning his beloved "tools" Brohl headed for the back door.

As well as being pragmatic and selfish, one of Brohl's other attributes was a strong sense of loyalty, especially to those who served him well. Which as it turned out was a blessing for Fengler. For with his ability to converse in perfect French and armed with the identity papers of a

Frenchman; Henri Vieillard sadly deceased, having the man along was something of a liability. But uncharacteristically, over the past two years he had become fond of the brutish Berliner. A man whose limited intelligence was amply compensated for by his ability to bludgeon a person to death with his fists. Man or woman, it made little difference. His selfless devotion to his boss also contributed of course. After all who doesn´t like to be placed on a pedestal by one´s subordinate, certainly not Otto Brohl.

"Where to?", asked Fengler, as Brohl climbed in beside him.

"West", replied Brohl, "as far away from Caen as possible."

Their second stroke of luck came later that day when they chanced upon a company of German soldiers on the roadside just outside the village of Saint Vigor-des-Monts. Bad luck as it happened because, after a quick inspection, it turned out that they were all dead. Never one to turn down an opportunity when it presented itself, Brohl decided to turn the soldier´s demise to their advantage. As two civilians journeying towards Brest, everything might appear quite normal. But if they were stopped, and someone decided to question Fengler, given his elementary knowledge of the French language then they would have a problem. No, thought Brohl if they were to stay together then the civilian clothes would have to go.

Although several uniform jackets were too bloodstained to be of any use, they did find two that they could use. They fitted both men quite well. The only slight concern, although Brohl didn´t see why it should create a problem, was that the jacket Fengler was wearing had belonged to a Gefreiter a Lance Corporal, meaning he would out-rank him. With their civilian clothes discarded, including their shoes, dressed in their German uniforms, as a precaution Brohl decided upon a little subterfuge.

It took a lot longer than he expected but at last the bodies of the two soldiers whose uniforms Brohl and Fengler had appropriated, were now dressed in their civilian clothes, complete with shoes, shirts, and ties. The next step was to get them into the car, which Fengler achieved with apparent ease. With their Doppelgangers in place, Brohl turned his attention to the Kubelwagon (the German equivalent of a Jeep) he had noticed earlier, up ahead of where they had found the dead soldiers. Without the use of a car, the lack of transportation could prove to be a serious setback. Hopefully, if it were undamaged this could solve the problem.

"See if it can be driven, Fengler", said Brohl, pointing towards the Kubelwagon. Helping himself to a well-earned cigarette as Fengler went off to inspect the abandoned vehicle.

Returning a few minutes later, Fengler made his report.

"It appears the engine is undamaged, Herr Brohl but one of the back tyres is punctured."

"Is there a spare?"

"Ja, there is one strapped to the bonnet."

"Excellent."

Following Fengler back to the stranded vehicle, leaving his henchman to change the damaged tyre, after removing the Jerry can strapped to one of its wheel arches, Brohl made his way back to the car. Stubbing out his cigarette, he unclipped the fuel cap and taking care not to spill any of the fuel on his clothes, he began dousing the car and the bodies of the two dead soldiers in petrol.

Satisfied, he returned to the Kubelwagon and replacing the half-empty can Brohl surveyed the abandoned vehicle. With the damaged tyre replaced, although it was tilting to one side, the vehicle looked salvageable. They just needed to get the front wheels back onto the road.

Sliding in behind the steering wheel, relieved to see that the key was in the ignition, with Fengler braced to push from the front of the vehicle, Brohl pressed the starter button. It took two attempts but eventually, the engine fired into life.

"Are you ready, Fengler?"

"Jawohl", replied Fengler, leaning his back against the bonnet, both his hands gripping the bumper bar.

Slipping the gear lever into reverse, Brohl slowly depressed the accelerator pedal. Steadily increasing the revs, with the rear wheels gripping the rough surface, and Fengler pushing for all he was worth, the vehicle inched its way onto the road.

"Good work, Fengler," shouted Brohl putting the gear lever into neutral, and applying the handbrake. "So now we don´t have to walk." And followed by Fengler he made his way over to the car.

"From now on we shall adopt our new identities", said Brohl, removing his lighter from a pocket. "So, you are no longer to address me as Herr Brohl, understood?"

"Ja", replied Fengler, a little uncertainly, having already forgotten his superior´s new name. Which given he had only just been told it a few minutes ago was not surprising.

"Instead, you are to call me Denke, Wilhelm Denke, understood?"

"Ja", Fengler replied, finding the whole thing quite strange.

"And you are Karl Bachmeier, Gefreiter Bachmeier, memorise it, it is very important. Do you have his identity tag and paybook?"

"Ja, Denke", Fengler replied, feeling quite pleased with himself.

"Good." said Brohl, before adding in a lighter tone of voice. "Just don't think you can give me orders though, Gefreiter Bachmeier, always remember that I am still your superior."

Detecting a hint of humour in what Brohl had just said, Fengler smiled. Regardless of the circumstances that was something he would never question anyway.

Setting alight to the late Henri Vieillard's identity card, Brohl tossed it into the lap of the dead soldier propped up behind the steering wheel, stepping back quickly as the petrol ignited with a whoosh. With the flick of a lighter it was done, and to all intents and purposes, Otto Brohl and Gottfried Fengler ceased to exist.

With Fengler at the wheel, the Kubelwagon pulled away, the image of the blazing car reflected in the driver's wing mirror and trusting in Herr Brohl's ingenious plan to save their skins, he pushed his foot down on the accelerator pedal.

Given his limited options, on the face of it, Brohl's plan to travel to the port of Roscoff or Brest on the Brittany coast and secure a passage to Bilbao made perfect sense. What he lacked however was up-to-date information on how the Allied invasion was progressing. Certainly, in the direction they were now heading. The only crumb of comfort was knowing that the main thrust of the invasion appeared to be centred around Caen to the north. What he wasn't to know, was that due to the need for a deep-water port, further to the west, the port of Cherbourg had also been included in the Allied invasion plans. Resulting in the fact that to succeed in his bid for freedom would mean entering an area now under the control of the American army.

On first appearances and given that the vehicle he was looking at was only designed to take four passengers Lieutenant Grassetti wasn't too concerned about the potential strength of the enemy, he, and the men from the 83rd Infantry Division had just come across. Plus, they also had the element of surprise in their favour. However, having promised his wife Maria and their four children back in Brooklyn that he would return home safely there was no way he was going to take any undue risks. That and the fact that just like the good guys in the Westerns, he was a great believer in shooting first and asking questions later. Two perfectly valid reasons why he gave the order for Private Elway to open fire.

While the doors to the barn Brohl and Fengler (alias Denke and Bachmeier) had chosen to spend the night in had survived for the past one hundred years, there was no way that they could withstand the concentrated fire from a Browning M191A4 machinegun. The .30 Caliber rounds boring holes in the oak planks like a plague of giant woodworms who hadn´t eaten for a long time.

Thankfully, the bales of straw the two Germans had chosen as their bed for the night were at the far end of the barn. Just as well really given what little remained of the doors after Private Elkhorne had relaxed his trigger finger.

"Komm raus, Haende hoch, come out, hands up!", shouted Private Beckenbaum a third-generation German from Montana who could still remember a little of his ancestral language.

Surprisingly, it was Fengler not Brohl who reacted first. Pulling the Luger from the waistband of his trousers, with the efficiency of a front-line soldier, removing the side plate he began stripping it down into its five component parts, side plate, barrel, breach-block, magazine, and grip. Handing the barrel and breach block to Brohl, he stuffed the remaining parts down the front of his trousers, watching as his superior did the same.

"Wir kommen, schiessen Sie nicht, we come, don´t shoot", Brohl shouted, pushing the parts from the dismantled luger down the front of his trousers, and opening what remained of the doors, with their arms raised above their heads, Brohl and Fengler emerged from the barn.

"Kameraden?" enquired Beckenbaum, pointing towards the barn with his carbine.

"Nein, keine Kameraden, no, comrades", Brohl replied. Thinking that as one of the soldiers knew a little German it was better to keep the fact that he spoke English to himself, at least for now anyway.

Two days later, and thankfully without being searched, Brohl and Fengler found themselves in an internment camp on the outskirts of Saint-Malo along with several hundred fellow Germans. Herded together in a large compound with a marque serving as both a dining hall and a place to sleep. Their only possessions were a mess tin, a spoon, and a straw palliasse.

Gradually, as the weeks passed into months things improved, or at least became more tolerable. Constructed by the prisoners from anything they could lay their hands on the compound now boasted four rows of makeshift huts. Half sunken into the ground with timber walls and doors, their V-shaped rooves were covered in strips of canvas or a discarded tarpaulin, with a piece of metal pipe scavenged from the ruins they were taken to each day acting as a chimney. Thankfully, the person or persons responsible for the camp´s layout had located the latrines and kitchen well away from each other at each end of the site. Thus, avoiding the smell of human excrement from coming into contact with the more pleasing aromas emanating from the kitchen.

The hut Brohl and Fengler shared with two other soldiers measured seven and a half feet wide by sixteen feet long with just enough headroom to accommodate Fengler's six-foot-two-inch stature. By mutual consent, the room had been divided into two halves, Brohl and Fengler's section, with a bed on either side farthest away from the door, and nearest to the stove. Apart from the fire, there were few creature comforts; an oil lamp, a few stunted candles, and a picture of a scantily clad woman, torn from a magazine which Brohl found quite offensive. Covering most of the boarded floor was the remnants of an old carpet one of the soldiers had found in the rubble. A place which was stifling in the heat of the day and cold at night when there was no fuel for the stove.

The camp's routine, which never altered began with an early breakfast, a kind of porridge, its consistency depending on what remained of the daily allowance of grain after the camp guards, and rats had helped themselves. With a slice of bread and a lump of cheese for their midday meal, usually eaten during a short break in the eight hours spent clearing away the rubble which clogged the streets of Saint-Malo. Homes and buildings which had been flattened by the constant bombardment from land, sea, and air. A city unrecognisable even by people who had lived there all their lives. On their return, they were treated to an evening meal, usually a watery, vegetable stew with the odd scrap of meat if you were lucky and a crust of bread to mop up anything left in the bottom of the mess tin.

For Brohl and Fengler the one consolation was that at least they were safe. Their new identities had not been questioned, and thankfully Fengler had remembered his lines. So, now it was just a case of waiting for the war to end, and then, God willing, they could both go home to Germany. That was until Brohl picked up a piece of gossip from one of the French soldiers guarding them. Having discovered that he spoke their language one or two of them would pass the time of day with him. A pastime Brohl found quite rewarding, as it helped him keep abreast of things that were going on beyond the confines of the compound. Titbits of information that helped to relieve the boredom of their day-to-day existence. On this occasion, however, the news was more worrying than rewarding.

It wasn't definite of course, things seldom were these days, it was just a rumour. But for Brohl, it was certainly a cause for concern, especially, if it turned out to be true. From what the French soldier had told him, with suspicions growing that to save their skins, members of the SS and the Gestapo were masquerading as ordinary German soldiers, a team of American and British intelligence officers were due to visit the camp.

To leave or to remain, for days the question haunted Brohl. He knew Fengler would never knowingly betray him, that went without saying. But under interrogation, he would be easy pickings for any intelligence officer worth his salt. Then, with their true identities exposed all they could expect was to be shot; the allies had become less squeamish in their dealings with members of the SS and the Gestapo. So, in the end, with the prospect of ending his life in front of a firing squad, the choice was a relatively easy one, they had to leave.

Although surrounded by a fence, escaping from the compound didn't pose too much of a problem. Supplies would be needed, of course, just enough food until they were far enough away for them not to be worth bothering about. A few inmates had already escaped and none had been caught. The Allies had more important things to do than go chasing after a few runaway German soldiers. No, let the French partisans deal with them was their way of thinking.

In the end, after bribing one of the guards with a silver cigarette case Fengler had found among the ruins to turn a blind eye, they made their escape while the remainder of the work detail were eating their lunch. Not towards Brest though. Brohl had learned some time ago from one of the guards of its capture or liberation depending on which side you were on. No, this time they would go south, following in the wake of the conquering allied armies. Given the distance involved, and the hazards they were likely to encounter, their prospects of reaching Spain were daunting, to say the least. But for two men with nothing to lose but their lives, it was the only option left open to them.

On the third day of their escape, at about the same time as Captain Peacock and Lieutenant Jemison of the British Military Intelligence Service were arriving at the internment camp on the outskirts of Saint-Malo, to begin their search for members of the SS, Fengler spotted a Jeep driving towards them, the late afternoon sunlight reflecting off the white helmets worn by its two occupants.

Chapter Nine

La Chenaie – Pays De La Loire

"It could be nothing", said Major Mireles handing the telex to the Military Policeman standing in front of his desk, "but you better go and check it out."

"Yes, Sir", the MP replied, having the feeling that he was being sent on a wild goose chase.

As it turned out it was more of a mystery than anything else. I mean what the hell was a Jeep doing in a goddam pond in the first place? At least that was Corporal Danny Pew´s first thought. His second thought, as he watched the young lad wading out towards the partly submerged vehicle clutching a length of rope, was whether the horse waiting patiently beside the pond would be able to pull it out.

As it turned out, the MP standing beside him, a tall, lanky Texan called Jones was thinking the same thing.

"You reckon that their horse can pull that thing out?", asked Jones in a languid drawl.

"Well", Pew replied, watching as the young French boy attached the end of the rope to the tow bar of the half-submerged Jeep, "I guess we´ll find out soon enough."

It was the man standing beside the horse who had reported the find. Although the farm it was on had been abandoned for years, from time to time he used the track to get one of his fields. On this occasion, due to the heat, and the lack of rain, with the water level in the pond reduced, it was then that he had noticed the upper part of the vehicle sticking out above the surface of the water.

"Maybe we should have just sent for a tow truck", said Jones, conscious that he was five dollars, and a packet of Marlboro down; the amount the farmer had agreed to for extricating the Jeep.

"Quit moaning will yah. You´ll get your five bucks back." Christ these damn Texans are mean bastards, thought Pew. The next thing you know he´ll be bellyaching over his packet of cigarettes.

With the rope secured the young lad, began wading back towards the shore, each stride stirring up the sediment at the bottom of the pond, turning the water a dark, muddy brown.

After a quick conversation between the man and the boy, the man´s youngest son, taking hold of the horse´s bridle the man walked the horse away from the pond. After taking up the slack, urged on by his words of encouragement the horse took the strain, the rope tightening like a bowstring.

Jacque could tell that the two American policemen had their doubts, but he knew his old Breton stallion would soon wipe the smiles off their faces. In all the time he had had him, the horse had never let him down. Pulling heavy loads was what he was bred for, and despite his age, years of pulling a heavy plough had kept him strong.

Inexorably the Jeep began to move, revealing itself little by little as it was slowly dragged closer to the shore, water pouring out through every exposed opening. With a final effort, its iron-shod hooves digging into the hard ground, its powerful shoulders straining against its leather harness the horse pulled the vehicle clear of the water and up onto the grassy bank.

With the absence of a five-pointed white star painted on the bonnet, it was immediately obvious to both MPs that this was not an American Jeep. The prefix on the side was also wrong. No, this was certainly not one of theirs. With the capital letter M followed by seven figures stencilled on the side of the hood this particular Jeep had "British Army" written all over it.

"Just like you said, Corporal, they gone and sent us on a goddam wild goose chase."

But Corporal Pew wasn´t listening. The fact that it was a British vehicle only served to pique his interest. If it had been an American Jeep, then things might have made sense. The fact that it wasn´t, coupled with the fact that there should never have been a British Jeep, or any British vehicle come to that in this area at all, only added to the mystery.

As a serving detective with the Illinois Police Department in Springfield, conscripted to the Military Police for the duration of the war, Pew had always enjoyed a good mystery.

"So, what do we do know, Corp?" said Jones, watching as the young boy untied the rope.

"I´m not sure," replied Pew. "Something here just doesn´t make sense."

"Well, if it ain´t one of ours, I don´t see how it´s any of our business."

"Somebody drives a Jeep into a pond and you ain´t in the least bit curious as to why?"

"Hell, damn right I ain´t. It´s a Limey Jeep, let them deal with it."

Pew, smiled, it seemed the one he had got himself partnered with was only good for traffic duty after all. But he wasn´t going to let something like that discourage him. No sir, the only reason that it was a mystery was because nobody had solved it yet. And finding himself at the scene of the crime, so to speak, as a detective, the least he could do was investigate.

A thorough inspection of the Jeep drew a blank. Nothing had been left behind that might give them a clue as to why it had been abandoned. The only thing that did seem a little odd, was that the Jerry can from the rear of the vehicle was missing.

After expressing his thanks to the farmer, taking out his wallet, Pew handed the young boy a five-dollar bill, the broad smile on the youngster's face reminding him of the look on his own son's face when he had been given his first bike. With a wave to the departing father and son, after making a note of the serial number on the side of the British Jeep's bonnet, Pew climbed in beside Jones.

"We heading back now?" Jones enquired, praying the answer would be, yes.

"No, not just yet", Pew replied. "Pass me that map."

"Looks like there's a small town called Mouzeil not far away from here", said Pew, consulting the map. "How about we mossy on down, partner, and take us a look around." His impersonation of a Texan cowboy not going down too well with his partner.

Goddam Yankee, thought Jones, scowling. The guys back at camp had warned him that this one fancied himself as a bit of a Sherlock Holmes.

As usually happens it was then that fate decided to intervene, and spotting Clemens working in the field alongside the house, Pew suddenly initiated a change of plan.

"Turn in here", said Pew, pointing to the sign by the side of the road, the words La Chenaie carved into the wood. Obediently, pulling on the steering wheel, Jones turned onto the track, the wheels of the Jeep kicking up clouds of dust as they drove towards the farmhouse.

Of all the things Clemens never expected to see, it was two MPs driving down the dirt road towards the farm. He didn't panic though, there was bound to be some simple explanation for their visit.

"Howdy", said Jones, bringing the Jeep to a stop beside where Clemens was working. He didn't go in for all this foreign bullshit. If they didn't understand what he was saying then that was their bad luck, he sure as hell was not gonna try speaking in French.

"Bonsoir", replied Clemens, leaning his scythe against a fence post.

"You speak any English?" Pew asked.

Non-committal, Clemens just shrugged his shoulders.

"Hello, can I help?" Joliane called out, hurrying along the track towards the stationary vehicle. She had seen the Jeep carrying the two MPs turn onto the track from the kitchen window.

"Bonsoir, Madame," Pew replied. "Parles-vous anglaise?"

"Oui", Joliane replied, ignoring the fact that he had addressed her as madame. "A little."

"A little is fine", commented Pew, relieved that she spoke any English at all. "Only we´ve just found a vehicle on a farm not far from you, an English Jeep. Would you know anything about it? Maybe you might have seen some soldiers?"

"Non, Monsieur, we have seen nobody."

"How about your man here?" said Pew looking towards Clemens.

"He is my brother, Albert", said Joliane by way of an introduction. "We have seen no soldiers, Monsieur."

Something was not quite right, Pew thought. Okay, maybe two American soldiers arriving out of the blue was enough to make her a little nervous, that was understandable. No, there was something else. He couldn´t put his finger on it but it was there, alright. After fifteen years in homicide, you get a nose for these things, and as a policeman, Pew always followed his instincts. Yeah, this little French lady was hiding something. He was sure of it, and he intended to find out what it was.

"Thank you for your time, Madame", said Pew, deciding to leave things for now. He could always come back another day and do a little more digging. Something he was looking forward to doing. This little mystery had more to it, he was sure of that.

Having identified a potential witness, come suspect, much to Jones´ delight, Pew decided against going into Mouzeil. So, it was home James and do not spare the horses. Hell, if they were lucky, thought Jones they might even make it back in time to enjoy a nice cold beer before the canteen closes for the night.

A mile to the north, a nice cold beer would have also been most acceptable to the two escaped prisoners making their way south along the quiet country road. A nice, ice-cold Berliner Buergerbraeu.

But at that particular moment, the attention of one of them was focused on something quite different.

"What is it, Fengler?" asked Brohl.

"A Jeep", Fengler replied, confident in what he had seen.

"Excellent, then we should see if they can be persuaded to give us a ride, yes?" said Brohl, removing the luger from the waistband of his trousers.

"Jawohl, Herr Brohl", replied Fengler, as he followed his superior officer towards the ditch running alongside the road.

"What the fuck!" Jones exclaimed as the figure of a man suddenly appeared in the middle of the road ahead, his right foot instinctively hitting the brake pedal.

After scrambling out of the shallow ditch, and up onto the road, raising both hands in the air Brohl began walking towards the Jeep.

"Kameraden! Kameraden!", shouted Brohl, slowly advancing towards the stationary vehicle.

"Stay put", said Pew, climbing out of the Jeep, and unbuttoning his holster, he walked around to the front of the vehicle. First a British Jeep in a pond, and now a German soldier, who it appeared wanted to surrender, this was turning out to be quite a day.

Brohl had always considered himself a good shot, especially with a Luger, and having closed the gap to less than ten yards, with the policeman´s hand gravitating towards the flap of his holster, he thought it was now time to prove it.

As the German lowered his right hand, Pew knew immediately that he should have taken the Colt 45 out of its holster sooner. Maybe then he might have stood a chance. As it was, hampered by its flap, this was one gunfight he was never going to win.

Reaching inside his Jacket, Brohl pulled the Luger from his waistband and aiming for the MP"s head he, squeezed the trigger. Watching with satisfaction as the 9mm calibre bullet struck the American policeman in the centre of his forehead, killing him instantly.

With his hands gripping the steering wheel, transfixed, Jones stared in horror as Corporal Pew´s lifeless body pitched backwards onto the bonnet of the Jeep before slowly sliding to the ground. Shocked into life by the terrible realisation that he was about to suffer the same fate, with the voice of self-preservation screaming out at him, he reached for his holster.

What was it they used to say, nice try but no cigar? Well, maybe that should be Private Jones´ epitaph because he did come pretty close to drawing his Colt. It was just that Fengler, who had emerged from the ditch alongside the Jeep was just that bit quicker. Stabbing the Shiv, he had fashioned from a scrap of metal back at the camp deep into the base of Jones´s neck.

"A fine shot, Herr Brohl", commented Fengler, looking down at the body of the dead Corporal.

"Danke, Willie," Brohl replied, delighted by the man´s compliment.

His words bringing an uncharacteristic smile to Fengler´s face. It was not often that his superior called him by his first name.

Unlike before, on this occasion, they stripped both bodies of every scrap of clothing, including underpants and socks. Although an affront to Brohl's sensitivity, given the state of his own underwear it was more a case of necessity than anything else. The same applied to both men's socks, which were in an even worse condition. Pew's jacket fitted Brohl well, and thankfully, due to the nature of the wound, there were very few blood-stains on the jacket. Even the MP's boots which had looked a little on the small size had turned out to be a good fit.

Fengler was not quite so fortunate. Although he and Jones were similar in height, being broader in the chest, the buttons on both the Texan's shirt and uniform jacket proved difficult to do up. Apart from that, the transformation from a German prisoner of war to an American MP was quite successful.

Delighted by their good fortune, with every chance that their new identities might get them as far as Toulouse or even the Pyrenees perhaps, after a successful three-point turn, Brohl and Fengler headed south once more. Behind them, well hidden by the dense vegetation growing up alongside the road, although the disappearance of the two MPs would not go unnoticed, hopefully, their naked bodies would remain hidden for quite some time.

After a short drive, conscious that they hadn't eaten for the past two days, the sight of the farm proved too tempting, and turning onto the track, for the second time that day, the Jeep made its way towards La Chenaie.

"They are returning, Albert," cried Joliane, spotting the Jeep carrying the same two MPs who had called earlier, driving towards the farmhouse.

"Bugger!" said Clemens. "Like a dog with a bone, those two." Dashing across the kitchen, he disappeared upstairs.

Entering the bedroom, Clemens dragged the large suitcase down from the top of the wardrobe, and removing the machine gun, with no time left to go out through the kitchen door, he crossed to the bedroom window. Pushing it open, he climbed out onto the roof, and with his back pressed against the pantiles, sliding down until his feet came into contact with the guttering, Clemens launched himself into the air.

This parachuting lark is getting a bit too regular, thought Clemens as he climbed to his feet, and ignoring the pain in his ankle, hidden by the barn, he made his way around to the side of the house.

The moment she opened the kitchen door Joliane recognised him instantly, the man's brutish features forever embedded in her mind.

Horrified, raising her hand to her mouth she instinctively stepped back into the room, her free hand reaching for the door.

But it was all too late. Having spotted the woman, leaping out of the stationary Jeep, Fengler raced across to the open door and bursting into the kitchen, he grabbed Joliane by her hair. Never someone who forgot a pretty face, it was then that he recognised her. She was that young French woman he had roughed up a little at their office in Cahagnes. He had wanted to do more to her of course. To see how much punishment, she could take before begging him to stop. But in the end, he followed his superior´s instructions. It was never wise to provoke Herr Brohl´s anger. Perhaps this time it might be different, and he would get his chance.

"Albert!" She screamed out. "They are Ges.... ", the final word cut short as Fengler clamped his hand over her mouth.

It was then that Brohl entered the kitchen. "Es scheint sie, hat Gesellschaft. Geh und kuemmere dich um ihn. It seems she has company, go and deal with him." Pulling the Luger from his belt, he aimed it at Joliane. "Tais-toi ou je te tire dessus. Be quiet or I will shoot you."

Releasing his grip on Joliane´s hair, Fengler removed the Colt 45 from its holster. Gun in hand he walked towards the open door.

As soon as the man emerged from the kitchen, Clemens knew instantly that he was not one of the two MPs who less than half an hour ago had turned up at the farm. It was the same Jeep, he had remembered part of the series number painted on the side of the bonnet, and the uniform and the helmet were the same but not the man wearing them. No matter how implausible, the only conclusion Clemens could come to was; that if he was not an American, then he had to be a Kraut. Why else would Joliane have called out if not to warn him?

Not being someone who went in for formal introductions, Clemens decided to keep this one short by letting the twelve rounds from the machine gun do the talking for him. Watching as the short burst from the Thompson slammed into the chest of the man dressed in an ill-fitting GI uniform chest, his body shuddering under the impact of the bullets. For a brief moment, it looked like he might just have enough life left in him to raise the MPs revolver but then his knees gave way, and Fengler slumped to the ground, his dream of one day returning to his beloved Berlin seeping into the soil together with his life blood.

The silence that followed went on for several minutes and with no response coming from the other man in the house, Clemens thought he would move things along a little. If the man holding Joliane captive was desperate enough to kill two American MPs taking another life would mean nothing to him.

"Sprechen Sie Englisch?"

"Ah! So, you have seen through our little disguise, English?"

"Just send out the girl and I´ll let you go."

"And why should I trust you?"

"Because I´m a man of my word."

"I think perhaps you are a man who is also quick to pull the trigger, no?"

"If you are talking about your friend, it was either him or me", replied Clemens, "and I didn´t want it to be me."

"Natuerlich, I would have done the same, English."

"So, what´s it to be?"

"I think before I allow the mademoiselle to go free, you must first throw away your weapon."

"Why, so you can kill us both?"

"I wish to kill no one. I only want to leave here with my life." Brohl replied, the strain beginning to tell. "For me, the war is over, my only wish is to go home."

"Do you give me your word?", asked Clemens, knowing that if he wanted to bring this Mexican Standoff to an end, at some point he was going to have to trust the man.

"Yes, you have my word as a German officer."

"If you go back on it", Clemens replied, "you had better make sure you kill me, because if you harm her, I´ll find you, and I´ll kill you. Do you understand?"

"Very gallant, English", replied Brohl "but quite unnecessary. I think perhaps you and I are a little alike, aren´t we? We have both had enough of this stupid war, and it is time for a new and better life, ja?"

With the time for talking over, removing the dagger from its sheath, Clemens stepped out from behind the tree. It was no match for the Luger the German had in his possession, but if the bastard did renegue on his promise at least it was something. Praying that it wouldn´t come to that, gripping the barrel of the machine gun, he tossed it out onto the ground a few yards ahead of him.

Having observed Clemens´ actions through the kitchen window, gripping Joliane by the arm, Brohl moved towards the open door.

"I am coming out, English", Brohl shouted and stepping through the open door, with the Luger pointed at Joliane´s head, he made his way towards the Jeep. Passing the prostrate body of his late lamented henchman, stooping down, Brohl retrieved the Cold 45 from his lifeless hand; one can never be too careful. Climbing into the driver's seat, with the Luger still aimed at her head, he turned on the ignition and fired up the engine. Slipping the Jeep into gear, Brohl called out. "Enjoy your new life English", and with the rear wheels kicking up clouds of dust the jeep roared away.

Overcome with relief, running towards each other, Clemens and Joliane threw themselves into each other arms.

"Oh, Albert I was so afraid", admitted Joliane, her body trembling.

"It's okay, we're safe now, he won't be coming back."

"How can you be sure?"

"Because he is on the run."

"Are we still, how you say, on the run, Albert?"

"No, not anymore", replied Clemens reassuringly. "Now go and cook your man some supper while I bury this one." Watching as she made her way back to the house, retrieving the machine gun, Clemens walked across to the body of the dead German.

Not that it was any reflection on the man he was burying but the site Clemens had in mind for his grave was one of the obsolete pig styes. On their return from Antwerp, with the purchase of the farm agreed, among the improvements he wanted to make to the farm, one of them was a new home for the pigs. A free-range enclosure which could accommodate them all. To accomplish this, with the help of a couple of local men, keen to earn a little money, he had converted one of the open-fronted barns into a communal pigsty. The sows seemed to like it, and so too did Rene's boar when he arrived to do his business. Three ladies in one bed, why wouldn't he?

Even using a pick and shovel it took him almost half an hour to make a hole large enough to accommodate Fengler's body. He didn't bother digging down to the mandatory depth of four feet, as the dead German was also going to be cremated, three feet was quite deep enough. Dragging the body into the improvised grave, after dousing it with petrol, setting light to a piece of rag Clemens tossed it into the grave. Satisfied, turning his back on the conflagration, he made his way towards the house. Tomorrow he would fill in the hole and then put a couple of the sows in there for a few days just to trample the earth down.

Chapter Ten

The La Seullette River -Normandy

While never a very deep river at the best of times, even during the winter, just like the pond La Seullette too had suffered from the lack of rainfall. The reduction in the amount of water feeding in from its network of streams reducing the wild rushing current to a gentle flow. This, together with the resolute nature of the two fishermen who were determined to find a place deep enough to fish in, resulting in the discovery of the two men´s bodies.

Submerged just below the surface of the water, weighted down by the rocks Clemens and Joliane had placed over them, had it not been for the man´s fishing lines snagging on one of the dead men´s jackets the bodies might have gone undiscovered. Thanks to the eels, and rats feeding on the decaying flesh, hopes of facial recognition were impossible. The only clue to their identities coming from the presence of a rifle and a German Luger stuck in one of the men´s belts.

With the disappearance of the two members of the local Maquis still fresh in people´s minds, being the son of one of the missing men, Jean-Paul Fourneau was taken to the spot where the bodies had been found. Although rats had chewed off most of the finger, the man´s wedding ring still remained attached to the stump. This and the luger, a gun that had been liberated from the body of a German officer, were enough proof for Jean-Paul to identify one of the men as his father, Francois Fourneau.

As was expected, the funeral of the two men was attended by hundreds of people. Men, women, and children all gathered to pay their respects to the two dead patriots. Standing alongside his mother, her frail body clothed in a black dress, her tear-stained face hidden behind a lace veil, Jean-Paul gazed out at the sea of faces. A head taller than his father, he had his features, a distinctive nose, and small dark brown eyes. He also possessed his father´s temperament, dogged, and short-tempered, someone who never forgot or forgave a misdemeanour no matter how small. A person who it was better to have as a friend than an enemy. This was probably why, although saddened by the passing of his father he was also angered by it.

Not just angered but also puzzled. Who, other than the Germans would want to kill them? And then to hide their bodies like that, it just didn´t make any sense. It was then that he noticed someone he recognised standing beside her husband in the crowd. The vision of her face stirring up such a flood of emotions that he thought he was going to be sick. She was quite a few years younger than her sister, but facially they could almost be twins. Her sister. Yes, where was her sister? And then things began to slot into place; it was her sister his father had been looking for. But why? Think, damn you, think? Yes, that was it, he remembered now, she was suspected of betraying some of her comrades to the Gestapo. The same four men who had been lined up against a wall in the village and shot.

And then it all began unravelling like a ball of wool; she had taken sanctuary in the convent near Saint-Jean-des-Essartiers, and his father had gone there looking for her. Could she still be there? No, much as his father respected the sanctuary of the church, he would never have let a few old nuns stand in his way. She must have escaped; it was the only possible explanation. But what happened after that? His father would never have given up. And, then the penny dropped, perhaps he hadn´t given up and that´s the reason why he was dead.

It was at that moment, as his father´s coffin together with that of his fellow compatriot Claude Soulier were lowered into the ground that he swore to find Joliane Cabouret and solve the mystery surrounding their deaths once and for all.

He began by watching her sister Elodine, and her husband. Their house was not far from his own, so observing their comings and goings was not difficult. Initially, his surveillance produced nothing of interest. Just a normal family going about their daily lives. Frustrating though this was, it did little to dampen his resolve, and after three weeks, his persistence was rewarded.

They were just small things to begin with but when you put them together, they all pointed to one thing, a sudden, and quite unexplained improvement in the family´s lifestyle. The trip to Paris, which was surely unaffordable on the wages of an office clerk at the local stone quarry, and Elodine showing off her new hairstyle when they returned. Although Jean-Paul was no aficionado when it came to women´s fashions, he was pretty sure that having your hair done at a Parisienne salon would not have been cheap. Finally, there was the news he had picked up from a local builder that the couple were planning to have their house extended by adding an extra room at the back. None of it made any sense. Where was the money coming from to fund this new lifestyle? No, there was something strange going on, and it was time for him to find out where this newfound wealth was coming from.

It took another week before the chance presented itself, and although he had never burgled a house before, Jean-Paul was not going to miss the opportunity. With the news that Elodine and her husband would be staying away overnight, he decided the best time to carry out his attempted burglary would be during the day. And with the towns' inhabitants at home enjoying their lunch, now was the perfect time to do it.

Conveniently, a ground-floor window at the back of the house had been left open, so the large screwdriver Jean-Paul had brought along proved redundant. Once inside the question was, where to look first? After discounting the kitchen and bathroom, he began his search in the living room. Sparsely furnished, it didn't take him long to go through the table drawers and the antique bureau, both of which yielded nothing of interest; a brochure on Paris which they had no doubt got on their visit there, an estimate from the builder for the proposed extension which made eyewatering reading, and that was all.

Nothing in the smallest of the two bedrooms looked very interesting. It wasn't even being used as a bedroom, for although there was a bed, all it had on it was a mattress, and the drawers in the kidney-shaped dressing table were all empty. Feeling a little despondent, Jean-Paul made his way into the main bedroom, and it was there that he struck gold. Not literally but certainly worth the risk he had taken in becoming a burglar for the day.

Hidden away in the top drawer of the chest of drawers, under a layer of very expensive looking lingerie, purchased in Paris no doubt, the envelope still contained a few thousand-franc notes. But that was not what interested him. No, what brought a smile to Jean-Paul's face was the folded sheet of paper tucked in with the money, and more importantly, what was written on it.

My Dearest Elodine,

As you can see from this letter to you, I am safe and well. I hope you and Henri are, too. I could not write sooner because of circumstances but I am settled now, and I hope that soon you will be able to visit me. I have sent you some money as I know things will be hard for you but spend it wisely. Please do not believe the things that have been said about me, I will explain everything to you when we meet. Because of this, you must also keep this letter from me a secret. Take care little one.

Your loving sister Joliane.

So, the bitch was still alive. Slipping the letter back in with the thousand-franc banknotes, Jean-Paul turned his attention to the envelope and the postmark in the top right-hand corner. Now all he had to do was to find out where the hell Mouzeil was. But first, there was something else he had to attend to, especially as he now had a use for it.

Retrieving the Luger from its hiding place under his bed, armed with a piece of rag and a can of bicycle oil Jean-Paul set to work. Sliding out the magazine he applied a few drops of oil to the spring, working it into the tube holding the eight 9mm bullets. Then, slipping the magazine back into the pistol grip, after pouring a little of the oil onto the rag, he began rubbing it over the pistol's metal casing. It was hard to tell exactly how long it had been in the river, certainly several months but despite that, it appeared to be in perfect working order. Although he hadn't attempted to fire it, he was confident that when he came to use it, the gun would not let him down.

Following a visit to the local school, after the children had gone home, discovering that the detailed map of France was still pinned to the wall in the classroom where he had been taught geography, it only took Jean-Paul a few minutes to locate Mouzeil. Now, all that was left to do, was to find some way of getting there which didn't involve him having to walk the one hundred and fifty or so miles between it and his home in La Cabosse.

On the day he left, he decided against telling his mother where he was going. She would only have tried to dissuade him if he had; what was done was done she would have said, and nothing he did was going to bring his father back. So, instead, he lied, telling her that he was going to look for work in Saint-Lo. Several men from the village had already gone there so it was a plausible enough reason.

After a day's walking, he reached Vile-Normandie eighteen miles to the south. Not only was it in the direction he was going anyway but hopefully, given its size there was a better chance of finding some form of transportation. At least that's what he hoped, because if he did end up having to walk all the way, even if he managed the same distance as he had today, it was still going to take him over eight days to get to Mouzeil.

Thankfully, a chance meeting with an old lorry driver in a local cafe got things off to a good start. It turned out he was on his way to Rennes with a consignment of scaffolding planks needed during the repairs to the Cathedral Saint-Pierre, which had been damaged by Allied bombs. Not a long drive in his old Renault OSB flatbed truck but a bit of company was welcome all the same.

It was never his intention to steal the bike but after being dropped off by the old lorry driver on the outskirts of Rennes, with a further sixty miles to go before he reached Mouzeil the temptation proved too great. His only excuse was that finding it lying beside the road, it did look like it could have been abandoned. Anyway, that was enough to ease his conscience. It might also teach whoever the bike belonged to a lesson as well.

A name, a plausible story (an aunt who had written to him but forgot to include her full address) and a beguiling smile were all it took for the middle-aged woman sitting behind the receptionist's desk at the Mairie in Mouzeil, a widow since losing her husband in the Great War, to provide Jean-Paul with all the information he needed. So delighted was she by his pleasing manner that she even gave him directions on how to find the farm, earning herself another one of his smiles.

Even though he couldn't make out what was being said, the sound of voices coming from the house was enough of a concern for Clemens to put down the fork he was using to spread out fresh bedding in the enlarged pig stye and make his way to the house.

Drawing nearer the first voice, he heard was Joliane's. Not loud but firm. The next voice which he didn't recognise sounded angry, very angry. Lengthening his stride, with a glance towards the bicycle propped up against the wall, pushing open the kitchen door, Clemens burst inside.

Instinctively, the heads of the two people facing each other in the middle of the room turned towards him. Although the young man was pointing a gun at her, Joliane looked quite calm. The young man, on the other hand, someone he had never seen before appeared to be quite agitated. Strangely nobody spoke, the three people just stared at one another. Standing stock-still like life models posing for an artist or a photographer.

Knowing that the impasse wouldn't last, with the gun still pointing at Joliane, Clemens knew he had to do something before the nervous-looking young man ended up pulling the trigger. Fortunately, as his eyes focused on the weapon in the youth's hand, he saw the answer to his dilemma and one which didn't involve getting himself shot in the process. Having found that it came in handy on occasions, Clemen had got into the habit of carrying the young Canadian paratrooper's dagger in his belt. Right now, he was very pleased that he had, because it meant that if anyone was going to die, it was the young man holding the gun.

To his credit, the moment Clemen's hand reached for the knife the young man reacted quickly. Swiftly diverting the muzzle of the Luger towards the chest of his potential assailant. And as Clemens lunged towards him, he wasn't slow in squeezing the trigger either. The only problem was that nothing happened. Which for Jean-Paul was quite worrying, especially when in the blink of an eye, a man had just plunged a dagger into his chest.

As Clemens gently lowered him onto the floor, Jean-Paul looked up at his killer, a thin trickle of blood dribbling out of the corner of his mouth. Although he knew he was dying, all he could think about was how stupid he had been not to try out the weapon first. After all, it had been lying at the bottom of a river for a long time. Sadly, even if he had lived a little longer the truth would only have made him feel much worse. Because although it´s easily done, especially for somebody who wasn´t used to firearms, forgetting to remove the Luger´s safety catch would only have made him feel very foolish.

Dropping to her knees beside him, with an anguished cry Joliane gazed down into Jean-Paul´s lifeless eyes.

"Oh, Albert, why did you have to kill him?"

"Because he was going to kill you", replied Clemens, stunned by the question.

"He would never have harmed me; he was just angry."

"How was I supposed to know that?"

Joliane didn´t reply, her gaze returning to the young man´s face.

What did she mean by "he was just angry" and who was he? None, of this made any sense, well not to Clemens anyway who was beginning to feel a little angry himself. What the hell was going on here? Then the proverbial penny dropped.

"You knew him." It wasn´t a question.

"Oui, his name is Jean Paul Fourneau. He is the son of the man you killed. One of the men whose bodies we hid in the river."

Although he had heard what she had said, to Clemens, it still didn´t make sense. What was the son of a man whose body was at the bottom of a river doing here anyway?

"Perhaps you had better tell me what is going on."

"Can we not bury him first?"

"Okay", said Clemens seeing how upset she was. "But then I want you to tell me what he was doing here."

"Can you make the coffin for him, Albert? Please, for my sake."

Clemens nodded. "Alright, but then I want some answers, okay?" And having made his point made, picking up the body of the young man, he made his way outside.

With the pigs now transferred to their new enclosure initially he had thought about transforming the obsolete pig styes into a hen house; the one that Madame Lacagne had housed her chickens was in a sorry state, and clearly beyond repair, but now, with the addition of another corpse it was turning into a graveyard instead.

As there was to be no cremation this time, Clemens dug down a further two feet, enlarging the hole by an extra six inches on both sides to accommodate the coffin he had constructed from some wood lying around in one of the barns. It was more like an oblong box really as woodwork was not something he was good at, but it suited its purpose. Considering that they were meant for something quite different, the lengths of wooden plank had fitted together pretty well. Getting it into the grave had proved quite difficult, and by the time he had finished filling in the hole, it was getting quite late. Satisfied; after tramping down the earth, Clemens made his way to the house and hopefully some answers to the questions swirling around inside his head.

It didn´t take Joliane long to confess to what she had done and to beg his forgiveness. Which he gave of course. He couldn´t punish her any more than she was punishing herself. She knew the blame for the young Frenchman´s death was because of her stupidity. Before Clemens had burst in on them, Jean-Paul had told her how he had found the money she had sent to Elodine and the letter she had written to her. Yes of course, Elodine and her husband had been foolish in being so reckless but that did not excuse her. No, the blame was hers alone.

What saddened her most was that although she had explained what had happened, Jean-Paul hadn´t believed in her innocence. His father would never have made such a mistake he said. And even though she swore in God´s name that she was telling him the truth nothing would sway him. The final irony was that the only person who could exonerate her was now lying in a hole under a pig stye just a few yards away from where they were standing.

Things were never quite the same between them after that. The spectre of the young man´s death cast a dark shadow over everything. The joy of their new life together, the new beginning each had craved for had somehow turned to ash. Clemens tried his best to dispel the gloom; toiling away on the farm, engaging with her on every improvement he wanted to make, desperately trying to infuse her with hopes of a bright future but it made little difference. Little by little, he was losing her.

Following on the heels of the melancholy came the condemnations, and the accusations.

"How many more people will you kill? Who else will you murder to keep us safe?" Bitter, venomous words.

"As many as it takes", Clemens had shouted back, appalled by her words. Shocked by her insinuations. All he had done, the risks he had taken, the killings, everything had been done to keep her safe. To protect her from harm. Yes, there were mitigating circumstances she wasn´t aware of. Things which had a bearing on what he had done. But she had been the catalyst for all that had happened between them. The driving force behind all that he had done, all he wanted to do. Yet now, because of the death of this vengeful young man she had turned on him like a cornered animal.

It was rare for him to be the last one to wake up but on this occasion, it would appear that he had overslept. Throwing off the duvet Clemens climbed out of bed, and pulling back the curtains, he gazed out at the farm buildings. With his plans for the day already made, pulling on his clothes, he made his way downstairs.

The first thing he noticed, was instead of the usual heart-warming breakfast of scrambled eggs and toast, he was expected to see on the table, there was a suitcase. The one Joliane had found in Madame Lacagne´s wardrobe. Standing beside it folding one of her dresses, Joliane looked across at him.

At first, Clemens didn´t know what to say. Surely, she wasn´t leaving him, was she?

"What´s all this then?" asked Clemens, finding his voice.

"I must leave, Albert, I cannot stay here with you." Joliane replied, closing the lid of the case.

"Come on", said Clemens, "things aren´t that bad, are they?"

"Please, you must let me go."

This can´t be happening, thought Clemens, his heart racing. She can´t mean it, not after all they have been through together.

"Why? Why do you have to leave?"

"Because there is too much sadness here, Albert, Joliane replied. "Everywhere there is death, I think perhaps death and killing will always follow you."

She was right of course, this new beginning they both wanted so desperately had left a bloody trail in its wake. But to give up now, to throw it all away surely, they couldn´t let that happen.

"Look, all that is behind us now. We are safe here. This is our home now."

Joliane smiled, but it was a lifeless thing. The light in her eyes whenever she looked at him had died. He had tried so hard after the death of Jean-Paul to rescue her from the grief she felt. The despair which was robbing her of the joy this new life with her knight in shining armour should have given her. But the battle was already lost.

Clemens had seen it, too, of course. Not just in the lack of affection but in other ways too. The happy, vibrant person he had come to love fading away before his eyes, and no matter what he said or did, it seemed that nothing could rescue her from this sadness that was consuming her.

"Where will you go? What will you do?" It was all he could think of to say.

"I shall go back to La Cabosse."

"And if they still want to kill you, what then?"

"Perhaps, now that my accusers are dead, I must hope that others will believe in my innocence."

"Let me come with you." The desire to protect her blinding him to the absurdity of what he had just asked. Clutching at straws which didn´t exist.

"Non, Albert, c´est impossible."

Now it was his turn to smile, but it was the smile of a defeated man. She was right of course.

"Okay, but take the money with you," said Clemens, "I won´t need it."

"Always you are so kind, Albert, but I do not want it."

With nothing left to say, Clemens just stood and stared at her.

"Au revoir, Albert", said Joliane, stepping towards him, her pale lips brushing against his stubbled cheek.

"Goodbye, my darling", Clemens whispered, pulling her towards him with his left arm while surreptitiously removing the dagger from its sheath. After a moment´s hesitation, placing the tip against her chest, he slowly pushed the steel blade deep into her heart. With her life ebbing away, cradling Joliane in his arms, Clemens sank to his knees, and for only the second time in his life, he began to cry.

But mixed in with the tears there was also anger, simmering below the surface like molten lava. How could she have driven him to this? To forget everything he had done for her and all because of some boy´s life. Given time she would have overcome her guilt, he was sure of it. Locked it away in a dark corner of her mind just as he had done. Banished it from her thoughts. But instead, she had allowed it to consume her. Though he hated to admit it, lurking in the shadows like an uninvited guest, self-preservation had also played its part in her murder. The thought that by letting her go, he might have put his life in danger. The very real possibility that to assuage her guilt and seek retribution for what he had done, she might expose his whereabouts to the authorities. The constant fear of always looking over his shoulder for some imagined danger. No, if he was honest with himself, she had, simply had to die.

Slowly, the seconds trickled by each passing moment serving to strengthen his resolve. His mind made up, dropping the dagger onto the tiled floor, Clemens climbed to his feet and cradling Joliane´s lifeless body in his arms, he climbed the stairs to their bedroom. Crossing to the bed, he lowered her body onto the freshly laundered sheet and gently smoothed out the folds of her dress. Considering the violent way in which she had died her face was a picture of serenity. It was as though death had freed her from her torment. Had she expected to die he wondered? Had she known that he would never let her leave him? That death would be her only escape. Questions that he would have to live with for the rest of his life. Questions which would never be answered. Pushing his thoughts aside, lowering his head Clemens kissed her lifeless lips.

After taking a moment to compose himself, he made his way across to the wardrobe, and reaching up he took down the large suitcase, the one Joliane had found in the house in Avranches. Putting in a few items of his clothing together with the bag containing the contents of the diamond dealer´s safe, he made his way downstairs.

Placing the suitcase down on the table, crossing to a small corner cupboard, Clemens pulled out the rolled-up towel with the Colt 45 he had retrieved from the dead German, and the young man´s Luger concealed in its folds. Next, he turned his attention to the question of food and drink. Despite what he had done, although it seemed quite a callous act, a man still had to eat.

Fifteen minutes later, having eaten as much as he wanted of the cheese and the leftover cuts of bacon from last night´s supper, wrapping what was left in a tea towel, together with a bottle of wine, and the rolled-up towel, Clemens added them to the contents of the suitcase.

Thankfully, even though it never got used much, the Citroen started up at the first time of asking, and after stowing the heavy suitcase on the rear seat, he climbed in behind the wheel. He backed the car out from under the open-fronted barn, Clemens pulled up alongside the kitchen door. Leaving the engine running, he opened the boot and removed the Jerry can of petrol. Thankfully, even after the return trip from Paris, it was still half full.

Re-entering the kitchen, pulling open the connecting door Clemens made his way into what turned out to be the living room. A room judging by the cobwebs and the layer of dust covering the furniture which Madame Lacagnes hadn't spent much time in. Surprisingly, it was also a room, he and Joliane had never used. Standing in it now, he was amazed that they hadn't. With a thorough cleaning and a lick of paint, it would have made a pleasant change from the kitchen. Ah well, it was too late now, and flipping open the cap, being careful not to get any on his clothes, Clemens began sloshing petrol over the furniture and carpet. Without bothering to shut the door he turned his attention to the kitchen.

It was as he was backing towards the kitchen door, that he noticed the blood-stained dagger lying on the floor. Picking it up his thoughts turned to the young Canadian paratrooper. His dagger had come a long way from that Normandy field. It had also taken quite a few lives, with the last of its victims lying in the bedroom above. Quite a different journey no doubt from the one it would have taken had the young soldier lived.

Returning the empty can to the boot, acting on impulse, Clemens turned towards the corpse of young oak trees and pulling back his arm, he hurled the dagger towards it. Watching as it tumbled end over end through the air before falling to the ground, its killing days were finally over.

Turning his back on the trees, setting alight to a piece of petrol-soaked rag with his lighter, Clemens tossed it in through the open kitchen door. Watching as the fuel ignited with a great whoosh. Sending tongues of flame leaping into the air like fiery genies escaping from a bottle.

Climbing in behind the wheel, shifting the Citroen into gear Clemens pulled away. At the junction with the road, bringing the car to a stop, he looked back at the farmhouse. Flames were already licking hungrily at the downstairs windows, tell-tale whisps of smoke drifting upwards into the morning sky. With no particular destination in mind, turning onto the road, Clemens gunned the engine. Another new beginning but this time he had no one to share it with.

Chapter Eleven

Springfield Road, Acklam – May 1947

What's that old saying, you wait for ages for a bus then two come along at once? Well, in Nobby Clark's case, it was a letter and a lorry that chose to arrive at the same time. It was his youngest daughter Ena who discovered the coincidence. And that was only because she wanted to catch a glimpse of the new postman. A good-looking young lad called Ronnie who had taken over from their regular postie on account of his arthritic knee was playing up again. Unfortunately, despite the record-breaking dash from her bedroom and down the flight of stairs to the front door, she was too late. She did find the letter though, the one he had just pushed through the letterbox. She also spotted the lorry pulling up outside the house. Something that doesn't happen very often, otherwise she wouldn't have paid it much attention.

"Any post, love?"

"Just a letter for Dad," Ena replied still a little disappointed at missing a chance to see Ronnie. "And a lorry has just pulled up outside."

The lorry Mabel was expecting but not the letter. Her Arthur never got letters. But before she had a chance to investigate further somebody was banging on the back door.

"Hello Mabel, not too early, am I?"

"No", replied Mabel, opening the door, "perfect timing, and you're just in time for some breakfast."

"Have you told him I was coming?" asked Jerry pulling up a chair at the kitchen table.

"No," said Mabel smiling, "I wanted it to be a surprise."

Judging by the look on Nobby's face it was a surprise. The last thing he expected to see on a Saturday morning, well any morning really, was Jerry Uttley sitting at his kitchen table tucking into a plate of eggs, bacon, and black pudding.

"What's all this then? Come to eat me out of house, and home, have you?"

With his mouth full of food, Jerry didn't answer right away, which gave Mabel a chance to have her say.

"For goodness' sake, Arthur, sit yourself down and have some breakfast.

Giving Jerry a wink, Nobby pulled out a chair.

"What's taken you so long anyway?"

"It's this damn leg," Nobby replied, I can't get used to the damn thing."

Being struck in the leg by a fragment of shell casing the day after the battalion had crossed the river Rhine was not at all what Nobby had planned. Despite Redman´s best efforts when the surgeon at the field hospital removed the dressing, he had known immediately that with a wound that bad, the only option was to amputate the leg just below the knee.

Arthur had only had the new prosthetic leg for a few weeks, and although it was a big improvement on the last leg, they had supplied him with, it was taking him some time to get used to it.

It was then, just as Nobby was about to begin questioning Uttley that the kitchen door opened and in walked his brother Herbert.

"What´s all this then, is it me birthday or something?" said Nobby, totally perplexed by the sudden onrush of unexpected visitors.

It wasn´t that people never called in on them. Jean from next door was always popping around for a cup of tea and a chat. And his eldest brother Charlie always called in on his way to the match when the Boro were playing at home. Herbert he hardly ever saw these days. But then that was down to his snooty wife, who didn´t approve of him mixing with disabled servicemen, and the like, even if one of them was his brother. As for Uttley, well he lived on the other side of the Pennines over near Rochdale so a visit from him was very unusual, to say the least. That´s when it dawned on Nobby that something was going on that he hadn´t been told about.

"Hush up Arthur and eat your breakfast", said Mabel, keen to get all the menfolk fed before revealing what she and Jerry had been keeping a secret for the past week. "I suppose you´ll be wanting a bacon butty will you Herbert? Knowing how fond he was of them, a treat he was never likely to get at home.

"Thanks, Pet", said Herbert, taking a seat at the kitchen table.

Unlike the two up and two down houses in Lumley Street where Arthurs´ parents had lived, the houses in Springfield Road were of a more modern design, and having a large kitchen there was plenty of room for them all to sit. Some families used it as a dining room, even though the sitting room could quite easily accommodate a dining table and chairs. There were also three good-sized bedrooms and a bathroom, and at the rear of the kitchen under a covered area was a coal shed and outside lavvy, the WC. The houses with even numbers also had large gardens backing onto wasteland.

"Come on then", said Jerry, pushing aside his empty plate, "I suppose we had better put you out of your misery."

"Use the front door", said Mabel, knowing it would be easier for Arthur, and with Uttley leading the way, they all trooped outside.

"Well?" said Arthur looking at what appeared to be a random collection of planks of wood loaded on the back of Uttley´s lorry, an Albion Chieftain with J. Uttley Haulier painted on the door in red letters, "what is it I´m supposed to be looking at then?"

"It´s a loft", replied Jerry, "a pigeon loft."

Now, if he had said it was a do-it-yourself model of the Taj Mahal Arthur might just have laughed it off but a pigeon loft! It was then, out the corner of his eye that he saw the smile appearing on Mabel´s face.

"Alright, what have the pair of you been getting up to?", said Arthur, glaring accusingly at Uttley and Mabel.

"Well", said Mabel, struggling to stop herself from laughing, "I thought it was time you had something to keep you occupied. Though what she really meant was to keep you from getting under my feet all day, "and you have always liked pigeons."

This was true of course. When he was a lad there hadn´t been many Saturdays when he wasn´t out in the garden with his dad waiting to clock in his racers when they arrived back at the loft. Or taking the basket of birds down to the club the day before a race when his dad was too sick to get out of bed. Not to mention putting a half-a-crown bet on his little Dordin hen for him which his mam would have played hell about if she had found out. Mind you, when he came home with his, Dad´s winnings she might not have been so cross then. But it was always their little secret.

"I don´t know what to say", said Arthur, clearly moved by what they had done.

"Well, a thank you wouldn´t go amiss", replied Mabel.

Now in the movies, to show his gratitude, the leading man would have swept her up in his manly arms and kissed her passionately on the lips. But this was Yorkshire, so all Mabel got was a peck on the cheek and a "Thank you Pet." Still, it was more than Uttley got but then Nobby didn´t need to say anything, Jerry had seen the look he gave him many times before, and words quite unnecessary.

"Better get started then", said Herbert, conscious of the fact that if he wasn´t back in time for tea, he would be treated to a withering look from his wife followed by one of her prolonged periods of silence. Something akin to Chinese water torture only without the water.

By a stroke of luck, Arthur just happened to have a dozen or so paving slabs stacked up at the end of the garden. He had intended to use them to make a path from the house to the air raid shelter but had never got around to it. Anyway, as it turned out they made a perfect base for the loft.

To give them credit whoever designed the loft had done a grand job. Constructed in sections, with each part, including the roof joined together by nuts and bolts. The only screws they needed were for the door hinges which had somehow got lost, and within three hours it was up. The last job of all, fitting the row of nest boxes to the back wall would have to wait until later, as Ena had just returned from the fish and chip shop with their lunch wrapped up in yesterday's newspaper.

After allowing a suitable period to elapse before resuming work, with the danger of them each getting in each other's way Herbert was allowed to leave. Having thoroughly enjoyed himself, been treated to a bacon butty and fish and chips, luxuries he very rarely experienced had been the icing on the cake.

With the work completed, although there was plenty of time for him to get home before it was dark, Jerry was persuaded to stay the night. They had a spare room, so it was no trouble. Besides, as he didn't have to pick up his next load until Monday so there was no reason for him to dash back. So, after popping round next door and using Jean's telephone to call his wife Barbara, with his lorry parked on a patch of waste ground opposite the house, both men walked up to the Roseberry pub at the top of the road for a well-earned pint.

Mabel had cooked tripe and onions for supper, and although it was a first for Jerry, much to her delight he wolfed it down. Retiring to the sitting room, their tongues sufficiently lubricated by the visit to the Rosebury, egged on by an inquisitive Ena, the two old soldiers didn't take much persuading to recount some of their wartime tales. But only the more humorous ones, the others were not for a young girl's ears, or wives come to that.

The one which captivated Ena the most, and the one she couldn't wait to tell her friends at school about was when her, Dad told her how Mademoiselle Cabouret had removed a bullet from Private Redman's chest with just her fingers. I mean, how cool was that?

After refusing Nobby's offer to pay him for the loft on the basis that it had been given to him by a retired pigeon fancier. An old chap living just down the road from him in Smallbridge who just wanted to get rid of it (actually it had cost Uttley five pounds but he wasn't going to let on). And a further offer to at least pay for his fuel, Uttley left early the next morning. Arthur hadn't said much afterwards. He didn't have to, Mabel could tell just how much Jerry's kindness had meant to him. Her Arthur was never one for showing his emotions, but she had witnessed the tears welling up in his eyes as Jerry´s lorry pulled away.

If Nobby thought the previous day had been his birthday, then today, even though it was the middle of May had to be Christmas. How else could he explain the arrival later that morning of Bob Ayles carrying a pigeon basket filled with pigeons? Along with a few of the older members of the Redcar Racing Club, he remembered Arthur´s Dad, so when Mabel contacted him and told him her plan, Bob had been only too pleased to help out.

"The two pairs of Dordins are mine", said Bob, pointing to the four pigeons with blue bars on their wings, "the other four are Beuchat´s. All young birds but they are from good stock."

"I don´t know what to say", said Arthur, "except that I´m grateful of course, that goes without saying."

"You´ll be joining the club then?"

"Aye, if you´ll have us."

"Don´t be daft man, we´re always looking for new members. Besides, it´ll give us old un´s a chance to win back some of that money your, Dad had off us." said Bob smiling, as the two men made their way back to the house.

"Are you sure you won´t stay for a cuppa?" said Mabel.

"No thanks very much Mrs Clark but I´d best be getting back home. I´ll just fetch that bag of corn in from the car. Oh, and if you have trouble getting down t´club Arthur one of our members lives just round corner in Mattison Avenue and he´ll always give you a lift."

"I might take him up on that", replied Arthur, "the bus conductor might not take kindly to having a basket full of pigeons on his bus."

"I´ll let him have your address then. I doubt you´ll be racing your birds this season but you´re always welcome to pop in for a chat."

"How much do I owe you for the feed?"

"All taken care of," said Bob, glancing over at Mabel.

Watching Arthur through the kitchen window while she was doing the washing up, Mabel knew she had done the right thing. Not that he had been difficult to live with since coming back from the war. Yes, the loss of his leg had changed him outwardly but inside he was the same man he had always been. "Better a leg than a life" he would say to anyone insensitive enough to comment on his missing limb. Wallowing in self-pity was not for Arthur. No, it had been his choice to be a soldier, so you take what happens to you on the chin was his motto. He had witnessed what war can do. He had seen enough to know that. He was one of the lucky ones. Unlike many others, he had made it home.

It was just getting dark when Arthur left the loft, he had been so engrossed with the birds, that he hadn´t realised how late it was. He had been following his late Dad´s advice, "Handle your young birds as much as you can" was what he used to say, "that way when they come back from a race it makes them easier to catch. Quite a few fanciers have lost a race because of a skittish bird." Smiling to himself at the memory of his father´s words.

Although the letter had arrived on Saturday, it wasn´t until Monday morning that it finally got opened. With all that had gone on, Mabel had tucked it behind the clock on the mantelpiece and forgotten all about it. As it turned out it was from a firm of local solicitors; Ligertwood & Forrest Attorneys at Law their logo was stamped on the left-hand corner of the envelope in blue ink.

"And what are you doing getting a letter from a solicitor," said Mabel, waving the envelope in the air. "That´s what I want to know."

"Ahh looks like me wicked past has caught up with me at last", Arthur replied, adopting a melancholy expression. "I knew it was only a matter of time, Pet."

Normally, Mabel would have taken the bait but not on this occasion."

"Just open it", she said, thrusting the letter into Nobby´s hand.

"Hand me, my glasses then, said Arthur, pointing to where he had left them on the kitchen table. With this damn leg, by the time he got up and fetched them, Mabel would have blown a gasket.

With his glasses perched on the bridge of his nose, slipping the blade of the knife into the gap at the end of the flap Arthur sliced open the envelope. Putting the knife aside, he removed the folded sheet of paper.

"Well?", Mabel asked, "what does it say?"

"Give me a chance woman", Arthur replied, running his eyes over the typewritten letter.

Concise and to the point, reading it didn´t take long, about five seconds, if that.

"Well?" said Mabel, quickly running out of patience.

"It says", said Arthur, reading the letter out loud.

"Dear Mr Clark,

We would be most grateful if you would attend our offices at number one Exchange Square Middlesbrough at ten o´clock on Tuesday morning on a matter of some importance. We would ask you to bring with you a form of identification; an identity card, a rent book or as a member of the armed forces serving or otherwise a paybook.

Yours sincerely etc, etc signed by Mr J. C. Forrest.

"Don't they say what they want to see you about?"

"No. No mention at all. Bit of a mystery eh, Pet?"

Mystery or not after catching the K bus at the top of Springfield Road, at precisely ten o'clock the next morning Arthur was standing in front of the receptionist's desk in the office of Messrs Ligertwood & Forrest. With his arrival duly noted by the receptionist, an elderly woman with a pinched face and dressed in a grey Paisley patterned two-piece suit, relieving him of his proof of identity, in Arthur's case his army paybook, she disappeared through the door behind her desk, returning moments later empty handed.

"If you will just wait over there Mr Clark", pointing with her small, ringless hand towards the row of chairs lined up against the wall. "Mr Forrest will see you shortly."

Obediently, Arthur lowered himself onto one of the chairs, although not exactly built for comfort at least it got him off his feet. His leg had been playing him up this morning, and the walk from the bus stop hadn't helped. A few minutes passed, and then the door the receptionist had disappeared through earlier opened, and a youngish man in a pin-striped suit appeared.

"Mr Clark?"

"Yes, that's me", Arthur replied.

"Sorry to keep you waiting", and with a sweeping gesture with his arm, Mr Forrest ushered Arthur into his office. "Please take a seat", pointing to the chair in front of a large antique desk, while at the same time easing himself into a leather-bound swivel chair.

"Well, Mr Clark, everything seems to be in order", and leaning forward, he handed Arthur his paybook. "We have to be doubly sure in these matters, you understand," said the solicitor, and pulling open a desk drawer, he removed an envelope. "This I believe is for you." He pushed the envelope across the highly polished surface of the desk.

Staring down at the envelope Arthur wasn't quite sure what he should do. It was definitely for him all right; it had his name written on it in capital letters.

"Is that it then?", asked Arthur, just wanting to be sure that there wasn't anything else he had to do.

"Yes, that´s all Mr Clark, our client´s instructions have been carried out." The solicitor replied, climbing up out of his chair. "Enjoy the rest of your day", and with a parting handshake, he escorted Arthur towards the door.

With his paybook and the envelope tucked inside his jacket pocket, it was only when he was halfway down the stairs that Arthur suddenly recalled what the solicitor had said, "Our client´s instructions have been carried out." That was what he had said. What client? And why hadn´t he thought to ask? Ah well, it was too late now, and there was no way he was going to tackle those stairs again. No, not to worry, thought Arthur, I´ll find out when I open the damn envelope anyway.

Although there was housework she could be getting on with, Mabel couldn´t settle. Ever since Arthur had walked out the front door she had been on edge. And if she had looked at the clock once, she had looked at it a dozen times. Where can he have got to? The appointment was for ten o´clock and here it was gone twelve. It was then as she was pacing up and down in front of the sitting room window that she saw him coming down the path to the front door.

Judging by the number of attempts it took him to fit the key into the lock, she could tell he had been drinking even before he opened the door. Further proof was provided by the struggle he had trying to remove the key once he was inside.

"Arthur Clark you´ve been drinking."

"Just a couple of whiskies, Pet, only me leg´s been playing me up something terrible."

She didn´t believe him of course. She knew his drinking had nothing to do with his leg. They had been married too long for him to get away with a story like that.

"Well, what did the solicitor have to say" asked Mabel, totally ignoring his feeble excuse.

"I need to sit down", Arthur replied, swaying unsteadily from side to side. "And you need to sit down, too, Pet."

Taking Arther by the arm, Mabel guided him across to one of the armchairs. Sitting down opposite him. "Well?" she asked, beside herself with curiosity.

With agonising slowness, Arthur pushed a hand into the inside pocket of his jacket and withdrew the envelope. Despite the mystery surrounding it, to begin with, Arthur had never intended to open the envelope. He wasn´t a curious person by nature, quite the opposite in fact but on this occasion the thing that killed the cat had got the better of him. It also cost him the price of two double whiskies which he had downed in quick succession.

Carefully opening the serrated flap, reaching inside Arthur pulled out an oblong piece of paper, and with a foolish grin on his face, he handed it to Mabel. The grin quickly turning into a full-blown smile when he saw the look on her face as she stared in disbelief at what she was holding in her hand; a cheque for five thousand pounds.

Although receiving such a huge amount of money was enough to make anyone smile, apart from his wife´s obvious delight, the real reason for the one which had transformed Arthur´s face was because of what was written on the back of the cheque; And don´t go spending it all on bloody pigeons! And the initials AC.

It was also a relief to know that whatever had happened to his old pal, at least he was alive and well; very well judging by the cheque he had sent, and that he hadn´t forgotten him, or his love of pigeons. Something which meant more to Nobby than the money. Money can buy you a lot but what it can´t buy you is friendship. God bless you Albert, Nobby thought, slumping back in the chair, no matter what he had done it was good to know that they remained good pals. And while he might use a little of the five thousand pounds on a few good birds, apart from paying off the loan on Jerry´s lorry, he would be sure to spend the rest wisely. Mabel would see to that anyway.

Chapter Twelve

New Beginnings all round

Apart from Nobby Clark's leg which would forever remain a part of Germany all the men of C Company made it safely home to Blighty at the end of the war. Although they had all been changed in some way by what they had been through and what they had experienced thankfully, they were all in good shape both physically and mentally. They had also pledged to keep in touch with each other, and by and large they had managed it; a saucy postcard from Blackpool or a less risqué one from Bognor Regis, the occasional letter with a photograph enclosed, and always a card at Christmas. They had even discussed the possibility of having a reunion but as some of them had moved away to far-flung places it was proving difficult to arrange. The consensus being that maybe one day they might manage it but for now, they would have to put it on hold.

Each of them had their own thoughts regarding Sergeant Clemens. He hadn't been mentioned much since his desertion. They had all been questioned by the SIB, the Special Intelligence Branch following news of his absence but there wasn't much they could tell the two policemen, and the matter was soon dropped. After all was said and done, winning the war was a lot more important than worrying about a missing NCO. None of them had mentioned the Frenchwoman, let alone the fact that Clemens had gone off with her. No, her identity would always remain a closely guarded secret. To them, especially Redman and Yates she would always be their Florence Nightingale, and none of them would ever forget her. The same went for Clemens, and even though they knew nothing about the death of his wife and son, secretly they all wished him well. He had been a good Company Sergeant. Some of them wouldn't be alive now if it hadn't been for him, so even though he was a deserter it was hard for them to think badly of him.

McCormack was the first to fly the nest. Moved by his experience at the convent and remembering the conversation he'd had with the Almighty concerning what he would and would not do if they all managed to get home safely, as soon as he was demobbed, he travelled to Ireland. At first, the Abbott at Mount St Joseph Abbey in Roscrea was reluctant to admit him. But after McCormack revealed his conversation with God at the convent in France to him, and as he fulfilled almost all the criteria required, male, single, and Roman Catholic. He wasn't too sure about having received the sacraments – his mother would have remembered but unfortunately, she was dead, but then the abbot relented. To his credit, he did give it a good try but after eighteen months, having at least attempted to fulfil his commitment to the Almighty, McCormack left. In his last letter to Uttley, he revealed that he had married a young French-Canadian girl called Colette and was now living in Quebec.

Hopkins was another member of C Company who decided on a new career path. Instead of returning to Messrs Dodds & Smiths engineering works to complete his apprenticeship, due to the fact that he had been a member of the Saint John Ambulance and with his medical experience in the army, he was accepted as a trainee nurse at the GWR Hospital. The irony is that if he had returned to the firm, given their different social standing, he and his future wife might never have even met. Fate up to its old tricks again, that and a nervous horse.

Trainee nurse or not, being a man, he wasn´t supposed to treat lady patients. But as he was the only qualified person available when the porter appeared pushing a young lady in a wheelchair what was he supposed to do?

"Young lady has come off her horse. No bones broken but she´s got a couple of nasty cuts." That was all he said, and then he was gone.

Wheeling the chair into the nearest treatment room, making sure that he had left the door ajar Hopkins finally got around to speaking to his patient, who as it turned out was a very pretty girl.

"I´m going to need you to sit on the bed please."

What followed next was uncharted waters for Hopkins. To begin with he had never been alone in a room with a girl before. Apart from his sister but that didn´t count. Certainly, not one when the girl in question was only wearing what looked like very expensive underwear. She had taken it all pretty well really, not at all embarrassed at having to strip down to her bra and nickers in front of him. He on the other hand had found it extremely difficult to stop himself from getting an erection. He could tell right away that the two cuts had been caused by barbed wire, he had treated similar wounds before in Germany. There were coils of the stuff everywhere. A last line of defence. The cut in her shoulder had required a few stitches but once he had cleaned up the one in her thigh it just needed a bandage. Thankfully, before her mother arrived to take her home, he had managed to find a dressing gown for her to wear.

They met again three months later when her father, Mr Dodds of Dodds & Smith his old employers brought her into the hospital. On this occasion, it was a dislocated shoulder. It seemed her horse had refused to take one of the jumps at the local gymkhana, deciding at the last minute to send her over it instead. Which is something horses do quite often apparently. Hopkins had been tempted to tell her that perhaps she should think about giving up horse riding altogether before she got herself killed but decided that would be rather rude of him under the circumstances. So, instead, stealing a line from an old film he´d seen recently, he just said "we must stop meeting like this."

It may have sounded corny, but it worked, and a year later, just after he had qualified, they were married; the bride arriving in a horse-drawn carriage, of course. Her father had bought them their new home, and while Hopkins had thought about objecting, in the end, he just accepted it. Although he was naïve Hopkins wasn´t stupid. No, let people think what they like, as an only child she was going to inherit her father´s wealth, so he might as well get used to the fact that this was the way things were going to be from now on. Pippa had called it a cottage but actually, it was a farmhouse which they shared with two dogs and a cat. She still had her three horses, each of which terrified him but thankfully no more accidents. Their daughter was born ten months later, and much to Hopkins´s delight Pippa agreed to her being called Joliane. He had told her the story of "Redman´s bullet" so how could she possibly refuse she said? The fact that as soon as the child was out of nappies people were going to call her Jo anyway probably had nothing to do with it. Either way, it didn´t bother Hopkins, he would always call her Joliane.

Redman wasn´t quite so fortunate. Like Hopkins, he now had a baby daughter but unlike Pippa, his wife had put her foot down when it came to having her christened Joliane. It is far too foreign sounding she said. Redman hadn´t argued, he had known what he was letting himself in for when he married her. Anyway, Charlotte was a nice enough name, and besides, he would always have his scar to remind him of the young Frenchwoman who had probably saved his life.

No, Redman´s trouble was that he liked pretty girls, and Natalie was a stunner. She was also ambitious, and he liked that too. Mac had been right of course she wasn´t marrying him for his looks, he knew that. No, the reason she had said yes when he proposed to her was because he had just inherited the family business. Love hadn´t entered into it. Still, he had got what he wanted and so had she. It was more of a business relationship really, with the occasional night of passion. He had his sights set on a chain of grocery shops, and she was the perfect driving force he needed.

Yates´s new life came about thanks to his late sister leaving him her house. This act of kindness had such a profound effect on him that returning to the house after the reading of the will at the solicitors, he took the full bottle of whisky he had bought the day before and poured the contents down the kitchen sink. He never drank another drop of alcohol after that. Nice as the house was, Hampshire wasn´t for him, and after agreeing to a cash sale with a local letting agency who were on the lookout for new properties to rent out, Yates headed back to Scotland.

More on a whim than anything, he settled on the town of Callander as his preferred destination and ended up buying a small croft on the banks of Loch Voil. The problem of what he was going to do with himself was solved by a visit to a second-hand shop in Callander High Street, and the purchase of a camera. "A very good one", the man in the shop assured him. "It´s all about the quality of the lens", he said; whether he was fishing for a sale or not but what he said was quite true. Yates bought the Praktiflex camera anyway, together with three rolls of 35mm film. He had assumed by the name that it was a German camera, but he had not let it bother him. Those days were over, it was time to move on.

Like the majority of amateur photographers, Yates employed the familiar point and click method. Landscapes mainly, and he was certainly spoilt for choice in that particular department. With the occasional snap of a red deer or an eagle if he was lucky. On one particular evening when the light was still good, he even managed to get a close-up of an otter enjoying a Loch Voil trout for supper.

Looking back over history, it´s strange how people have come together to form business partnerships, successful ones too; Proctor and Gamble, Marks, and Spencer, Rolls and Royce, and many more as well. In Yates´case, his partner turned out to be a man called Douglas, the owner of the shop where Yates had his films developed, and who also happened to be the owner of a local printing company. Impressed by Yates´ photographs being a cany Scot he saw an opportunity for a wee profit-making venture.

A week later, after putting his idea to Yates with the amount of investment required to cover the start-up costs deposited into the local bank, Callander Calendars Limited came into being. Quite a transformation for a man who not so long ago thought nothing of downing a bottle of whiskey in a day. And with their initial investment recouped from the sales of their 1948 calendar, the future was looking bright for Messrs Douglas & Yates. Very bright indeed.

Somebody else who had made it safely home was Otto Brohl. Not to his old house in Berlin, which had probably been reduced to a pile of rubble anyway. No, he had decided quite some time ago that his new place of residence would be Paris. More specifically, 13 Place Emile Goudeau off Rue Ravignan Montmartre. He had also assumed a new identity, one more in keeping with his new lifestyle. No longer was he Herr Otto Brohl, his new name was Monsieur Hugo Brun.

The MP´s jeep had taken him as far as the premises of an unscrupulous garage owner on the outskirts of Bordeaux who was willing to take it off his hands for the right price. With a fresh coat of paint to cover over the US Army markings who was going to know. With the money he had got for the jeep, after making a gift of the MP´s Colt 45 to the ship´s captain Brohl was able to obtain a one-way ticket on a tramp steamer to Lisbon.

Being a neutral country, he knew he would be safe in Portugal. Better still, as Lisbon had once been his old stamping ground it was also a place where Brohl had friends. Influential people who he could always count on for their help. People he had had dealings with when he was a member of the Abwehr, the German Counterintelligence stationed at the German Embassy in Lisbon. People, who he had helped to make a lot of money. People in high places whose unscrupulous dealings in supplying Germany with illegal shipments of Wolfram Tungsten were well known to him. Dealings which Brohl had kept a well-documented record of; in his line of work, it always paid to have a little insurance policy tucked away. You never know when it might come in useful. Like now for example.

As a member of the Portuguese Charges D´Affaires entourage on his visit to the French capital, Brohl; alias Hugo Brun arrived in Paris on the 30th of November 1945. A taxi dropped him off in the Rue Ravignan leaving him to walk the short distance to his new address. The property was just as he had left it. The shop window to the side of the front door remained boarded up, and the upstairs window appeared unbroken. Taking a small pen knife, Brohl prised open the cast iron ventilation grill in the wall and reaching inside the cavity, he retrieved the key to the front door.

The property had once belonged to a Jewish art dealer and his family, Brohl couldn´t remember his name, there had been so many of them. He hadn´t felt guilty about acquiring it the way he had. The French authorities were going to repatriate them anyway.

Not that they wanted to go. No being repatriated back to Germany was the last thing any Jewish family wanted. So, in exchange for his help, the man had eagerly accepted Brohl´s proposal; at times like this, any offer of help, especially from a Gestapo official no matter what it cost could mean the difference between life and death. Sadly, in the case of the art dealer and his family Brohl's offer to secure their safety was meaningless, for regardless of what he or anybody else said or did, their return to the Fatherland was inevitable. The man's only consolation was that at least the German he had given his home and business to in exchange for their freedom was an art lover.

The property wasn't large, with three floors with a cellar. The shop itself took up all of the ground floor. A rectangular room with a single plate glass window looking out onto the street, and a pair of French doors at the rear which opened out onto a small south-facing garden. On the first floor, there was a small kitchen and a living room with a bedroom, bathroom, and an attic room on the floor above.

For safekeeping, before leaving Paris Brohl had moved the dealer's art collection into the cellar. It was dry and well-ventilated and if the boarding over the window had been removed, at least the pictures would not have been on display for the whole world to see. None of the paintings were by leading artists, which suited Brohl. To suddenly appear on the scene and begin selling works by Rembrandt and Monet would have only attracted unwanted attention. No, the art dealers' collection of paintings by Pierre Bonnard, Maximilian Luce and Giovanni Fattori were perfect for launching his new business venture. The painting by Canaletto of the Grand Canal viewed from the Palazzo Balbi which he had surreptitiously appropriated from a shipment of art destined for Goering's private collection in Berlin, and which now hung in his living room was purely for his own viewing pleasure.

A week after his arrival, with the boarding removed and the walls of the gallery once more hung with paintings, seated in the fully furnished living room of his new home, a glass of brandy in his hand Brohl reflected on the events of the last few months. Strangely enough, if he had one regret, it was that Fengler wasn't here to share in his new life. Yes, the man had been an oaf, but he had also been a loyal and faithful companion, and he found that he missed his company.

Chapter Thirteen

Chateau-de-Neufvy – 11th November 1980

Tilting the cut-glass decanter, Clemens poured a generous amount of whiskey into his glass. He was not usually a morning drinker but today was special. Replacing the decanter, whiskey glass in hand, he made his way over to the French doors. Even at this time of year, he loved the view; the manicured lawn flanked by rows of recently pollarded London Planes running down to a kidney-shaped lake. Its reeded fringes shrouded in the mist rising off the mirrored surface of the water. The vista of tree-covered hills rolling away into the distance, a forest of naked branches awaiting the coming of spring.

Alerted by the sound of footsteps on the parquet floor, he turned away from the door and stepping back into the room, he placed his empty glass on top of the grand piano. Their youngest daughter Eloise was the pianist in the family but now that she had moved to Paris to study music at the Sorbonne it had become simply another piece of furniture. Its highly polished surface used to display a collection of ornate silver frames containing family photographs.

With his face creasing into a smile, Clemens watched as a woman carrying a man´s overcoat appeared in the open doorway and began walking towards him. Her slender figure was encased in a plain three-quarter-length dress with a diamond necklace made by Chaumet of Paris draped around her slender neck. She knew that he liked her to wear the black dress, especially on this particular day, and now it had become something of a tradition. Just like the exquisitely tailored charcoal grey suit he was wearing. She wore very little makeup, using it to good effect; the pale pink lipstick complimenting the porcelain whiteness of her skin. The carefully applied eyeliner accentuated her green almond-shaped eyes. He had been a little sceptical about the new pixie cut hairstyle to begin with, but it had quickly grown on him.

"It is time, Albert," she said, helping him on with the full-length, black cashmere overcoat. "Please, you must not be late", knowing that on occasions, he would have his chauffeur take him for a long drive. "Madelaine and Phillippe are coming for lunch, and you know how disappointed the children will be if their Grand-Pere is not here to play with them." Her slender fingers tightened the knot of his black tie as she spoke. He was always very particular about it fitting tightly in the V of the shirt collar.

Smiling, he gazed into her eyes. Despite the age difference their marriage had been and still was a happy one. It upset her that she had not been able to give him a son, but he had taken the blame; after all, it was the man who planted the seed. Besides with two beautiful daughters, what more could a man ask for? Although quite a few years younger than him she did have a tendency to mother him. Even in the bedroom, she was always the one who initiated proceedings. Not that he objected, sadly, lovemaking was not high on his list of priorities these days. A sign of old age just like his greying hair.

The car, a silver Citroen CX was already waiting on the driveway when he came out of the front entrance of the house. Standing beside it the chauffeur, a young man in a grey uniform opened the back door as his employer descended the flight of stone steps.

He always enjoyed the drive, especially at this time of year. Along quiet roads lined on both sides by long avenues of trees. The vast swathes of countryside covered in barren fields their northern slopes still tinged with frost.

When he had first seen it, all those years ago the chateau had been more visible from the road. Now, except for the winter months, it was hidden away behind swathes of mature trees. Driving through the front gates, he had known right away that the chateau was uninhabited. Intending to spend just the one night, he had ended up staying for much longer, three days in fact. Three long days spent wandering through its labyrinth of deserted rooms and acres of parkland, and by the end of it, he had made up his mind, that this would be his new home.

After driving to the nearby town of Chantonnay, having obtained the name of a local notaire, the French public officer from a friendly barman, Clemens found himself at the offices of Monsieur Saydoux and what he hoped would be the start of a new chapter in his life.

His first surprise was stepping into the notary´s office and being greeted by the sight of a beautiful young woman. It seemed the barman´s information had been somewhat out of date as Monsieur Saydoux had died several months ago and the person waiting to greet him was his daughter Veronique Saydoux who, as his only heir, was now in charge of the family business.

His second was that, yes, she knew all about the abandoned chateau. Her late father had represented the family who owned it for many years. Following her husband´s death ten years ago, due to ill health, his wife

Madame Filleux had given up living there and the chateau had stood empty ever since.

A month later with the legalities finalised Chateau de Neufvy, as it was named, had a new owner, a Monsieur Albert Cabouret. And a month after that, following a civil ceremony in Nantes, Monsieur Cabouret also had a new wife.

It had only taken a few days of being together to make them realise that they had each found their soulmate. A union of wealth and beauty. If Joliane had been his anchor, Veronique was to become his rock, the foundation stone on which he could build a new life. She had no interest in knowing how he had acquired his wealth, or how a mysterious Englishman with a bag of treasure, and a suitcase filled with guns and ill-fitting clothes had acquired a French name. All that concerned her was their future together and that suited Clemens perfectly.

Entering the town centre, the chauffeur parked the car in its usual spot; it had become an unwritten law among the townspeople that no one should park there on this particular day. And just like the black dress, and the charcoal grey suit it too had become a part of the tradition. Leaving his driver to enjoy a cigarette, turning his back on the car Clemens made his way towards the semi-circle of cypress trees at the end of the Place de Croisettes. His previous chauffeur, a man in his seventies, had always accompanied him on these occasions but not his young replacement. It had annoyed him at first, so much so in fact that he was on the point of dismissing him, but Veronique had talked him out of it.

Approaching the small crowd of people already gathered in front of the grey marble cenotaph, Clemens glanced down at his Breguet wristwatch; five minutes to eleven. In all the thirty-five years he had been coming here, he had not once been late. Something which couldn´t be said for the parades" organisers. But then as he was frequently having to remind himself, this was France, and they marched to the beat of a different drum. Thankfully, this year was to be one of those rare occasions when their drumbeat happened to coincide with the rest of the world.

Reaching into his overcoat Clemens removed a black beret and ensuring that the highly polished cap badge was perfectly in line with his left eye, he placed it on his head. Standing to attention, as the brassy notes of the trumpet died away, at precisely eleven o´clock he raised his right arm and saluted. And for those few minutes each year, Monsieur Albert Cabouret´s true identity was revealed.

Your Satisfaction Is Our Goal!

Dear Reader,
We hope you enjoyed this book. Do you have any comments, criticism or ideas for books you want to read in the future? Please do not hesitate to contact us. We read every Email personally and answer it as soon as possible. Your opinion is of great value for us.

Contact us: info@ek2-publishing.com

You can help us to keep history alive by taking a moment's time to review this book on Amazon. Many positive reviews lead to more visibility for our books. A few words or a simple star review help our authors and our publishing company to increase our quality with every book published. Thank you for your support!

PS: In rare case scenarios a book might get damaged during shipment. If that should be the case, please do not hesitate to contact us and we will replace the book at no charge.

Your EK-2 Publishing Team
The publisher close to its readers

Published by EK-2 Publishing GmbH

Friedensstraße 12
47228 Duisburg - Germany
Register court: Duisburg - Germany
Company registration number: HRB 30321
CEO: Monika Münstermann

E-Mail: info@ek2-publishing.com
Website: www.ek2-publishing.com

Cover art: Mario Heyer
Author: Barry Cole
Editing: Manuela Schneider
Layout: Eduard Krisan

1. edition, May 2025

Printed in Great Britain
by Amazon

62991066R00109